The Magnificents

The World's Longest Field Trip

By Barry McMahon

ISBN: **0-9960215-0-7**
ISBN 13: **978-0-9960215-0-0**
Library of Congress Control Number: **2014916091**
LCCN Imprint Name: **BFA Press United States**

Dedication

This book is dedicated to Violet McMahon, who not only listened to my stories nearly every night but also helped me keep the plot sorted out. She would often anticipate a direction in which the story must be headed, and even when she was in error, her ideas were creative, inspirational, and sometimes just too good to pass up. I will leave it to your imagination where I became a transcriber rather than an author.

Contents

~ CHAPTER 1: WORMHOLES ~...1

~CHAPTER 2: REFLECTING POOLS~ 19

~ CHAPTER 3: SUPERPOWERS ~...27

~ CHAPTER 4: THE BIG BIRD ~..41

~ CHAPTER 5: BOOTSY ~ 59

~ CHAPTER 6: DINOSAURS ~..75

~ CHAPTER 7: TOTALLY AWESOME DUDES ~.....................................85

~ CHAPTER 8: DRAGONLAND ~ 95

~ CHAPTER 9: THE FUNGEON ~ 111

~ CHAPTER 10: TUNNEL OF LOVE ~ 139

~ CHAPTER 11: RECORD BREAKING ~...151

~ CHAPTER 12: ICE CREAM ~ 165

~ CHAPTER 13: THE SHORT BUS ~...175

~ CHAPTER 14: BOMBI ~..187

~ CHAPTER 15: THE PEN & THE TOSSER ~ 197

~ CHAPTER 16: THE RESCUE ~..209

~ CHAPTER 17: THE TRIP BACK HOME ~..235

~ABOUT THE AUTHOR / ILLUSTRATOR~ 251

~ *Chapter 1: Wormholes* ~

A small man with wild hair stood at the front of a class of sixth graders at Stamford Middle School. He held a stack of three boxes.

"Good morning, class. You are going to want to stop talking to one another and to begin listening to me because this is the day that you get to learn about wormholes." He set the boxes on the large, teacher's desk. "My name is Mr. Fiddle. Just like the instrument, fiddle. But I'm not playing around." He picked up one of the boxes again and walked to his left, holding the box, which was roughly the size of a basketball, in front of him. He tapped it on the sides, triggering a switch that released a set of legs from the bottom of the box. "I'm here to astound. The truth matters, and matter is the truth," Mr. Fiddle continued as he worked his way to the other side of the desk. He took another box of the same size off of the desk, leaving a smaller box in the middle of it. Holding the second box in front of him, he triggered another set of legs. He raised his voice just a little for emphasis: "Or more specifically, exotic matter is the truth, and…hello."

"You lost me at hello," Mark Matheson joked to a group of his football buddies, who populated the back right corner of the classroom. Their obligatory laughing trailed off quickly as they realized that the joke had had no effect on the substitute teacher.

The small man with the wild hair continued. "I am your substitute teacher for science today. I have a short amount of time to inform you on the subject of wormholes, but I can assure you…nothing! Nothing can get you where you want to go faster." Mr. Fiddle straightened his tie.

He looked around the room. It seemed as though very few of the students were as intrigued as he thought they might be regarding the subject of wormholes, and then one girl, a very neat and tidy child with perfect hair and clothes, raised her hand triumphantly.

"Yes, Lisa?" Mr. Fiddle acknowledged the girl, who was so full of her own question that she failed to recognize that he had called her by name even though he had never met her. He wasn't even looking at a seating chart.

"Aren't you supposed to take attendance?" She beamed with pleasure as she looked around the room for acknowledgment that she understood proper procedure better than the substitute teacher did. Her best friend, Stephanie, crossed her arms over her chest and sat up straight, indicating that she too understood the rules and was wholly in support of Lisa's observation.

"I can see that you are all here, Ms. Johnson, and I have much to cover, but thank you for your concern," Mr. Fiddle responded. Lisa and Stephanie adopted expressions of complete consternation. "I am sorry if I have disappointed you as well, Ms. Stephanie Moore, but I see no reason to waste precious time." Fiddle paused, and, speaking to himself, mused, "Precious time, yes, indeed, so precious to so many, yet so fluid—well, that's the point now, isn't it, so..." Then, in a voice loud enough for all to hear, he continued, "On with wormholes! You may have heard of the theory of relativity." He scanned the room. Most of the class was still ignoring him, but a half dozen or so were actually looking at him, and one boy had his hand in the air. "Yes, Ralph. I take it you have heard of the theory, so can you tell us who proposed the theory of relativity?"

"Albert Einstein," Ralph responded. "But I had a question, Mr. Fiddle."

"Correct, and thank you; Albert Einstein it is. Go ahead, Ralph; what's your question?" Mr. Fiddle seemed quite pleased that there was interest expressed and was quite ready to handle any question.

"Are you going to collect our homework from last night?" Ralph asked with a tone that implied that he did not have his homework.

"No, Ralph, I am not going to collect your homework," Mr. Fiddle responded. "You can hang on to it until Ms. Norburton returns." Mr. Fiddle was quite disappointed in Ralph's question. He had hoped it would be about wormholes.

Ralph was very happy that he did not have to produce a finished homework assignment. He had a very good reason to be concerned about his homework but he didn't want to share it with Mr. Fiddle. Ralph was perceived as an odd kid by most of the other students. He was a bit short for his age with reddish hair that would go instantly curly if it wasn't cut short. Ralph kept his hair short.

Mr. Fiddle began to twirl some of his hair around his finger. His hair was very unusual, both in color and style. In general, when random people were asked to describe Mr. Fiddle's hair, they were unable to do it. The descriptions usually ran something like "He's got a lot of it in some places and quite a bit less in others." This observation came from the principal of Stamford Middle School, Dr. Arnold.

Mr. Cool, short for Cooligan, one of the full-time science teachers, attempted to describe its color by saying, "It's a bit like asking, what color is a gray rabbit? Well, it's gray, but it's a gray that is comprised of black, gray, and white hairs, whereas in the case of Mr. Fiddle, there are also brown and tan and silver and burnt sienna hairs. Well, there are more, but you get the idea."

Mr. Fiddle removed his finger from his hair, leaving a spiraled plume springing back and forth from the top right side of his head. "Does anyone have a question about wormholes?" he asked with very little hope of a response. Suddenly another hand was raised. The boy was slightly tall for his age; he too had hair of a color that defied description. Tommy was good looking, good natured and athletic. He actually craved education and actively took part in all of his classes. "Yes, Tommy, what can I tell you about wormholes?"

"Are wormholes really like they are in movies, like where spaceships go flying from galaxy to galaxy in an instant?" Tommy was genuinely curious about wormholes. "And if they are, why aren't we making any spaceships and going out and exploring things like other solar systems and stuff?"

"Excellent! Tommy, that is a very good question, and the answer will surprise you." Mr. Fiddle had two kinds of answers he could give: the one that he knew would be safe to teach and the other, which was far closer to the truth but was absolute suicide for his teaching career. He knew which answer he had to give, but he wanted to leave the door open to the truth.

"In 1935, two physicists, Albert Einstein and Nathan Rosen, proposed the existence of space-time bridges. These paths were called Einstein-Rosen bridges, or wormholes. They were said to connect two different points in space-time, creating a shortcut that, in theory, could reduce travel time and distance. However, humankind has not discovered any real wormholes as of yet, and even if they had been discovered, they would be useless for travel because they collapse too quickly. Since 1935 further research has found that a wormhole containing exotic matter could stay open and unchanging for longer periods of time. So, honestly, no, you're not going to see NASA taking off for a trip to another galaxy anytime soon." Mr. Fiddle could see that Tommy was feeling a little let down and that most of the class had already tuned him out, so he raised his voice and pointed a finger in the air triumphantly as he bellowed, "If we could get our hands on some exotic matter and were able to locate a wormhole, then we could send an object from one place to another in an instant, just like in the movies!"

"Excuse me, Mr. Fiddle," Stephanie interrupted in the same voice as her friend Lisa. "We are studying electricity, like making batteries and stuff like that. What do wormholes have to do with batteries, and is this going to be on a test?"

Mr. Fiddle was an extremely patient man, but he did not put a great deal of effort into lost causes, so he wasted no energy or time on a meaningful explanation or an attempt to spark the interest of those children, who at the age of eleven had already determined how they were going to live at the age of thirty.

"No, Miss Moore, there will be no test." With these words he was free to carry on as he liked for those in attendance who were interested in the subject purely out of curiosity and the desire to learn something new. There were about five of them. He had been thinking about starting out with a demonstration but had changed his mind the moment he saw the class. There was every type of kid in there, and they did not act as a single unit. He knew he had to identify the various factions to find a key audience. The time had come. The five would listen, and the rest would not. It was far easier to explain away five stories of "crazy" than thirty.

"Okay, everybody." Mr. Fiddle spoke in a very wise and inviting tone that was peppered with intelligence and levity. "I am going to show you something amazing. I brought along three boxes. You see two of them on either side of me and one in front of me." He motioned to each spot in succession, bringing his hands together in the end to rest upon either side of the center box. Lifting it ceremoniously, he walked it carefully over to the box to his right and laid it on the top, where it engaged magnetically and then instantly transformed the lower box into a swirling circle of stars in a sea of darkness while making the upper box transform into a tennis ball. He held the tennis ball in his right hand. Raising it over his head, he said, "I'm going to send this tennis ball through time and space to the other box, which is simply the other end of the wormhole. When it reaches the box, the box will disappear, and the other side of the wormhole will be open. Are you ready?"

Tommy said "yes" under his breath, and so did Ralph.

Josephine wasn't the shortest girl in her grade but she was close, even though she had grown considerably since the fifth grade. Her hair was a slightly brighter shade of strawberry blond. It was straight and long. She was naturally pretty and didn't go in for make-up like some of the girls in her grade. Josephine liked school and learning in general. She was a bright girl who didn't really see the allure of trying to be special, but she really, really wanted to see the wormhole.

Agnes, Josephine's best friend, was roughly the same height and weight as Josephine but carried herself completely differently. She was a bit more of a tomboy with metallic black hair and a bit of an attitude. She always listened to the substitute teachers more than the regular teachers because they knew something about the real world, the one that existed beyond the field of education. She was ready for wormholes, vampires, dragons—anything but normal school.

Billy, Tommy's best friend always felt lucky to have Tommy as a friend. Billy was short and a little on the plump side of stocky. He loved to crack jokes and make fun of anything he could that had to do with school. Billy wanted to do and see everything that Tommy wanted, including watching a weird demonstration about space-time performed by a strange little dude with a tennis ball.

No one responded to Mr. Fiddle's query about their readiness to observe his demonstration.

Taking their silence as commitment, Mr. Fiddle lobbed the tennis ball into the wormhole area. At the exact moment that the tennis ball entered the wormhole, the box disappeared, and the ball emerged at the opposite side of the room. It didn't speed up or shoot out; it simply continued its trajectory from the lob. The only difference was that it had traveled the entire width of the classroom in zero time, and it could not be seen between the starting wormhole and the box at the other end of the room, which had become a mirror image of the starting wormhole.

The five kids in the room who were actually watching gasped, "Whoa!"

The tennis ball bounced a bit when it landed on the floor and rolled under Lisa Johnson's desk. Irritated, she looked down.

Mr. Fiddle said, "Excuse me as I bend down to retrieve the ball."

Lisa's response was, "Whatever," said through a face that showed something entirely different. The face said, "You stupid old man, if that ball had hit me, I would have had my daddy down here in two minutes, and your job would be over."

Mr. Fiddle held the ball in his right hand and looked at the five kids who comprised his audience as he repeated, "Excuse me, I seem to have forgotten something." He walked back to his desk and put down the ball. He went around behind the desk, bent over, and pulled up on something that was exactly as wide as the span of his arms. It was a large chest with legs extending toward the floor as he raised it up. A snapping sound occurred as the chest locked into place at the perfect height for him to open, which he did. Mr. Fiddle reached in and pulled out something that seemed impossibly tall to have fit in the chest. It was a black board on a silver stand. He placed the stand to his left. He reached in again and pulled out another one, which he placed to his right, and then closed the chest. He picked up the stand with the board that he had placed to his left and moved it to a position on the floor roughly a foot and a half away from the wormhole on his left, being certain to line the board up so it was parallel to the wormhole opening. Then he repeated the procedure to the right. "Thank you for your patience, everyone." He smiled as he grabbed the tennis ball from his desktop. "Watch this." He beamed as he walked to his right. Gripping the tennis ball firmly in his right hand, he threw the ball with great force directly into the wormhole. Instantly it came out the other side and bounced off of the board on the left, back into the wormhole, and then returned just as quickly through the wormhole by which he stood. There it bounced off the board and rocketed back to the board across the room. The tennis ball continued to Ping-Pong back and forth as Mr. Fiddle stepped forward between the wormholes.

"Impressive, isn't it?" Mr. Fiddle asked rhetorically as the five students stared in amazement. They began to talk among one another, trading explanations ranging from holograms to magic tricks as Mr. Fiddle walked over to the board on the left. As he reached it, he snatched the ball from midair before it could bounce its way back into the wormhole. Then, tapping the top of the outer limits of the wormhole with the tennis ball, he grinned as the wormhole disappeared, replaced by the box from which it had erupted. Similarly, he crossed the room and returned the other wormhole to its box, and as he did so, the tennis ball transformed into its original boxlike form. While Tommy, Billy, Ralph, Josephine, and Agnes continued to discuss the merits of each other's explanations, Mr. Fiddle opened the chest once again, retrieved the boxes and the stands, and packed them into the chest. He then lowered the chest to the floor with a clicking sound. As he stood up again, he held a briefcase, the same color as the chest though considerably smaller, which he placed upon the desk.

All five hands shot up into the air as Josephine, Agnes, Ralph, Billy, and Tommy cried out, "Mr. Fiddle!" The other kids in the class snapped out of their groups of private conversations, gossip, and naps and looked at the other five with a reluctant realization that they may have missed something cool.

"Agnes, your hand was up first; what would you like to know?" Mr. Fiddle had a pretty good idea what sort of questions he would get and had answers for all of them.

"How did you do that?" Agnes asked. "I don't get it, and I'm pretty sure that it wasn't science."

"Science can answer a lot of questions, Agnes, but it must ask the right questions. The truth is I am only responsible for a small part of what you saw." He was about to give a more thorough explanation, but the other hands were still up, each one of them stretching as far from the shoulders that anchored it as physically possible, and class was almost over. "Yes, Billy?"

"Is it magic?" Billy asked. "You know, some kind of trick?"

"It's not magic, Billy," Mr. Fiddle responded kindly. "It's something far more powerful than magic and something much more meaningful than any trick." Mr. Fiddle knew that he only had a minute before the bell would ring, but Josephine had managed to stretch her hand a good six inches higher than Tommy's hand despite the fact that Tommy stood three inches taller than she did, unless she was wearing her leather boots, but those hurt her feet. "What is it, Josephine?"

"How did you know all of our names?" she asked quietly. "You've never even been here before."

"Actually, Josephine, I have been here before, many times," Mr. Fiddle explained. "You just haven't noticed me. But that's not how I know your names." The bell rang, and all of the kids jumped up from their seats and herded toward the door, except for the five who had listened for the entire class. They remained and continued to listen as Mr. Fiddle continued above the din, "I simply took attendance when I came in, and then I went back in time a few minutes to the beginning of class. You'd better get going; I don't want to make you late for your next class." Mr. Fiddle smiled, held his briefcase in one hand, and motioned to the door with the other.

Josephine looked at Tommy to see if he was just as puzzled as she was. His eyes answered yes. Each one of the five searched each other's faces for understanding as they shuffled in a group toward the door. As they reached the hallway, Mr. Fiddle slipped out behind them and walked away in the direction of the main office. As he walked backward down the hall, he called out to the five, "If you ever need to know about wormholes, just call out my name. Thanks for listening!"

The five just stared in the direction of the main office, into which Mr. Fiddle had just disappeared.

"It's gotta be magic." Billy said as he broke the silence. "Couldn't be anything else."

"He said it wasn't magic," Ralph responded, but he was thinking the same thing.

"Whatever it was," Agnes whispered, feeling as though they all shared a secret, "those wormhole things were awesome."

The five agreed that wormholes were awesome. They spent the next week talking about Mr. Fiddle and wormholes, music, books they were reading, and kids at school. Each of them saw Mr. Fiddle every day at the school even though they never had him as a substitute in any other class. Tommy mentioned that it was weird that Mr. Fiddle had only taught for one day but then was suddenly around all of the time.

"Maybe he's a stalker," Billy said right away.

"Who is he stalking, Billy, the whole school?" Ralph asked in his usual sarcastic, breath-conserving monotone.

Two weeks after Mr. Fiddle had told them about wormholes, as they were all leaving Ms. Norburton's class, Billy announced that he knew where they could see a wormhole. They were always ready for a joke from Billy, so it was no surprise.

"Hey, I know where there's one of those wormholes, you guys," Billy shouted. A bunch of people looked at him as they walked through the halls, but only the group of five stuck around to hear him finish. "Meet me outside after school, and I'll show ya!" This was most likely going to be the joke they expected, but they all agreed to meet him. They had a lot of fun messing with Billy. He spent a lot of time trying to impress everyone, mostly Tommy, but almost everything he did was either ridiculous or just plain sad.

Each of them headed to their separate classes, but they all looked forward to getting together after school. It was always the best part of the day. They could horse around for a while because their parents knew that they would be together.

They really liked each other even though they occasionally made fun of one another, and they were fairly good students. They would have been really good students, but Billy was one of them, so their overall average camped somewhere around fair. That wasn't totally because of Billy, but Agnes liked to make him think so.

The truth was that Agnes had a real disdain for homework, and she rarely did it, unlike Ralph, who always did his homework. His problem was bizarre. They all knew about it, but none of them could explain it. He would complete his homework and put it in his backpack, and when he got to school it would be missing from his homework folder. They had all seen it at one point or another, and each of them would testify on his behalf to any teacher at any time, but no one ever believed them, except for Ralph's father, Peter. But the teachers at Stamford stuck together, and they were convinced that Ralph was trying to pull a fast one on them, despite his absolutely perfect scores and eloquently written papers.

Josephine and Tommy were A students. They had been walking to school together since the beginning of the year, and they actually discussed the homework from the previous night while walking to school. Josephine loved those walks more than anything, but the only one who knew about it was Agnes. She couldn't bring herself to tell Tommy how she felt. Tommy liked Josephine, and he was pretty sure she knew it. He always asked her if she would like him to carry anything for her. His dad had told him that he had better make sure that the girl he liked knew that he would help her with anything she needed, and that was exactly what he did. The moment Tommy offered to carry Josephine's backpack it didn't seem as stupid as it really was. Upon further review, it was worse. The truth was that most backpacks at Stamford weighed more than any backpack should, and now he had to carry two of them. Tommy tried to explain the problem to his father, but his father came from a time when a person just didn't complain. If you had to carry two backpacks, then you carried two backpacks; if you had to wake up at 6:00 a.m. to deliver papers, you woke up and delivered the papers. So he complained to his mother. She asked him if this girl might be taking advantage of him and suggested that the next time they walk home, he might bring her around to the house. His mother knew Josephine's name but chose to refer to her as "that girl" or "this girl" whenever her mother bear instincts were triggered. Tommy decided that it was better to carry two backpacks than to have Josephine scrutinized by his mother. She tended to be a bit overprotective and was prone to crusading on Tommy's behalf, which was the last thing he wanted when it came to Josephine.

The final bell sounded, and the mad rush to leave school ensued. Billy found Tommy by his locker and reminded him about the wormhole he wanted to show everybody. Billy always found Tommy by his locker after school for two reasons. The first was that Mark Matheson liked to threaten Billy, and he never tried it when Tommy was around. He wasn't scared of Tommy, but he was intimidated by him. Tommy was naturally gifted at just about everything. He was smart, fast, and strong. Mark Matheson was mostly just strong, but he lumbered his way through life. If he could move it with brute strength or just crush it with his weight, he would dominate whatever it was. The two of them had a healthy respect for one another. Billy only respected Tommy and longed for the day that he would be the same size as Matheson so he could stand up to him. Matheson was only a little heavier than Billy, but he was taller, much taller, just like Tommy.

Matheson walked by the two of them and barely acknowledged their presence because Agnes was walking toward all of them. Matheson liked Agnes but showed it by saying stupid things like how much he hated red hair but when she put a streak of red in her hair it was all right. Agnes did not like Mark Matheson, so her response was always sarcastic, like, "I'm so happy to meet with your approval" or "then I'm glad I'm not a redhead." Matheson would spend days trying to sort out whether or not she meant it. Josephine was never far away from Agnes, and the two of them would laugh at Matheson's advances, which he usually mistook for a display of embarrassment. Billy wasn't too sure about the sarcasm or the embarrassment either, and it bugged him, but he couldn't quite explain why.

"Hey, Tommy," he asked. "Do you think she likes that Matheson guy at all?"

Tommy placed a calming hand on Billy's shoulder. "No way, man; she's all yours!" Billy slugged Tommy in the gut, and Tommy pretended to barf.

Ralph, who seemed to appear out of nowhere, slapped Billy on the back and said, "Attaboy, Billy; once again you have claimed the title of heavyweight champion of the world!" Ralph usually made some joke about Billy's weight because Billy constantly teased Ralph in one way or another. It was all good-natured fun, but each one of them felt like everyone else around them had it all worked out better in some way, like life was just a big, confusing mess of school, relationships, extracurricular activities, and peer pressure. That was why these five kids stuck together. They knew that none of them had it all figured out, and among themselves they were cool with that. Admitting it to each other was easy. In fact, Ralph had suggested that perhaps all kids their age might feel the same way, but they decided to keep their eyes open for signs that this may be true rather than holding a forum or making a school-wide announcement.

Billy led the group out of the school by way of the rear door, the one that faced the woods that led to the Mississippi River. They loved going down to the river with the Minnehaha Falls in walking distance, Minneapolis on one side and St. Paul on the other, it gave the feeling that you could travel anywhere. As they were leaving, Josephine held her backpack toward Tommy as she had become accustomed to on their private walks together. Tommy reached out to take it and paused.

"Josephine," he said rather quietly, "I know that I usually carry your backpack, but I think it would be really cool if you could carry it from now on." He was embarrassed to admit it but he did anyway. "These things are just too darn heavy, and it makes my shoulders all sore when I try to carry both." Josephine held on to her backpack and smiled. All she needed to hear was that Tommy thought it would be really cool if she carried her own backpack. As she threw it over her shoulder, she held out her clarinet case and tilted her head a bit, as if to ask Tommy for a hand with the case. He instinctively grabbed the case, which was remarkably lighter than the backpack, and started walking in the direction in which Billy was leading them.

Agnes bumped into Josephine and cupped her hands to Josephine's ears. "You have trained him well, my queen," she joked as both girls began to giggle a bit.

Josephine, with both of her hands free, responded in kind. She cupped her hands to Agnes's ears and whispered, "Do you think it's time to ask him about the dance yet?"

Both girls continued to giggle until Ralph came up behind them and, passing them, said, "Everybody knows you like Tommy, except maybe Tommy, so if you're plotting something, like a date to the dance, you may as well just ask him and spare the rest of us the soap opera antics."

"Very funny, Ralph," both girls responded, with faces that said that they did not appreciate his particular form of wit.

"We're almost there," Billy announced as he ran down a path between the trees. The group sped up to meet him as he stopped at the base of a large oak tree, just thirty feet from the river's edge. It was rooted into the hillside with half of its roots exposed by erosion; they were knotted and tangled in a gnarled mess. There was at least a ten-foot drop from the exposed roots to the sandy bank of the river below. "There it is," Billy shouted as he pointed to a hole in a very large root. "Look at that wormhole!" Billy laughed so hard he nearly fell off of the mass of roots. It was true though; the hole was full of worms all writhing around on one another.

"This is the wormhole?" Tommy asked in disbelief. "This is what you brought us all here to see?"

"Yeah, man," Billy jabbed back at Tommy. "Look at 'em; those worms are totally chillin' up in there."

"Why are there so many worms in one place?" Josephine asked rhetorically as she moved closer to the hole. As she worked her way around Billy, she looked him directly in the eyes and asked, "Did you put all of these worms into one place, Billy?"

Billy didn't respond as he stepped around her, off of the roots and onto safer ground. He was a little less than athletic but loved skateboarding, running, and swimming, even football. He just wasn't very good at any of them. So when he engaged in anything physical, like climbing around tangled roots, it took all of his concentration. When he had reached a safe spot on the hillside, he answered Josephine. "Of course not. I wouldn't bother with something weird like that. I just saw it here when I went looking for one of my gym shoes that Matheson threw down here, the stupid jerk."

Josephine was intrigued by the fact that there was a hole full of worms and they were looking at it just hours after a class about a completely different type of wormhole. She was explaining why she found that interesting as she climbed closer to the hole and peered into it. As she leaned to get a closer look, her backpack shifted and knocked her off-balance, and she fell.

"Josephine!" Tommy shouted; everyone looked in her direction. It was a ten-foot drop toward the riverbank. They all tried to reach out a hand for her as she fell, but no one could get a hold of her. They knew that she was going to land hard on her back, right on that stupid backpack.

She didn't.

Instead of landing on her back, on top of the world's heaviest backpack, a title shared by all Stamford Middle School backpacks, she simply disappeared.

"Josephine!" Tommy yelled even louder than before. Without a moment of hesitation, he dived off of the hillside at the exact spot in the sand where Josephine would have landed if she hadn't disappeared.

Tommy disappeared.

"Tommy!" the remaining three kids shouted as they quickly looked at one another, trying to figure it out. "What just happened?" they all said in unison.

"They both disappeared in the same spot," Billy said nervously as he inched toward the edge of the drop, trying to see exactly where they had disappeared.

Agnes moved alongside Billy and peered over the edge. "All I can see is the sand. I wish I could see where it actually happened, but I just can't remember exactly. I want to dive in and follow Josephine—well, both of them, but..." Agnes stopped talking.

Below them, roughly ten feet away, a circle of whirling gases and colors encircled a center point, an endless view of blackness, populated with stars, solar systems upon solar systems, galaxies upon galaxies.

"Wormhole," Ralph said. He had climbed upon the roots. "I don't know why, or how, but I got this." He looked into the hole and then cannonballed into it while announcing, "*Cannonball!*"

Billy and Agnes were left staring at one another. They climbed together until each of them stood inches from the edge of the roots, directly over the wormhole. They looked at one another longer than seemed comfortable than either of them would have liked to admit.

"Looks like fun," they said in unison, and just as similarly they leaped into the wormhole.

Just as similarly, they disappeared.

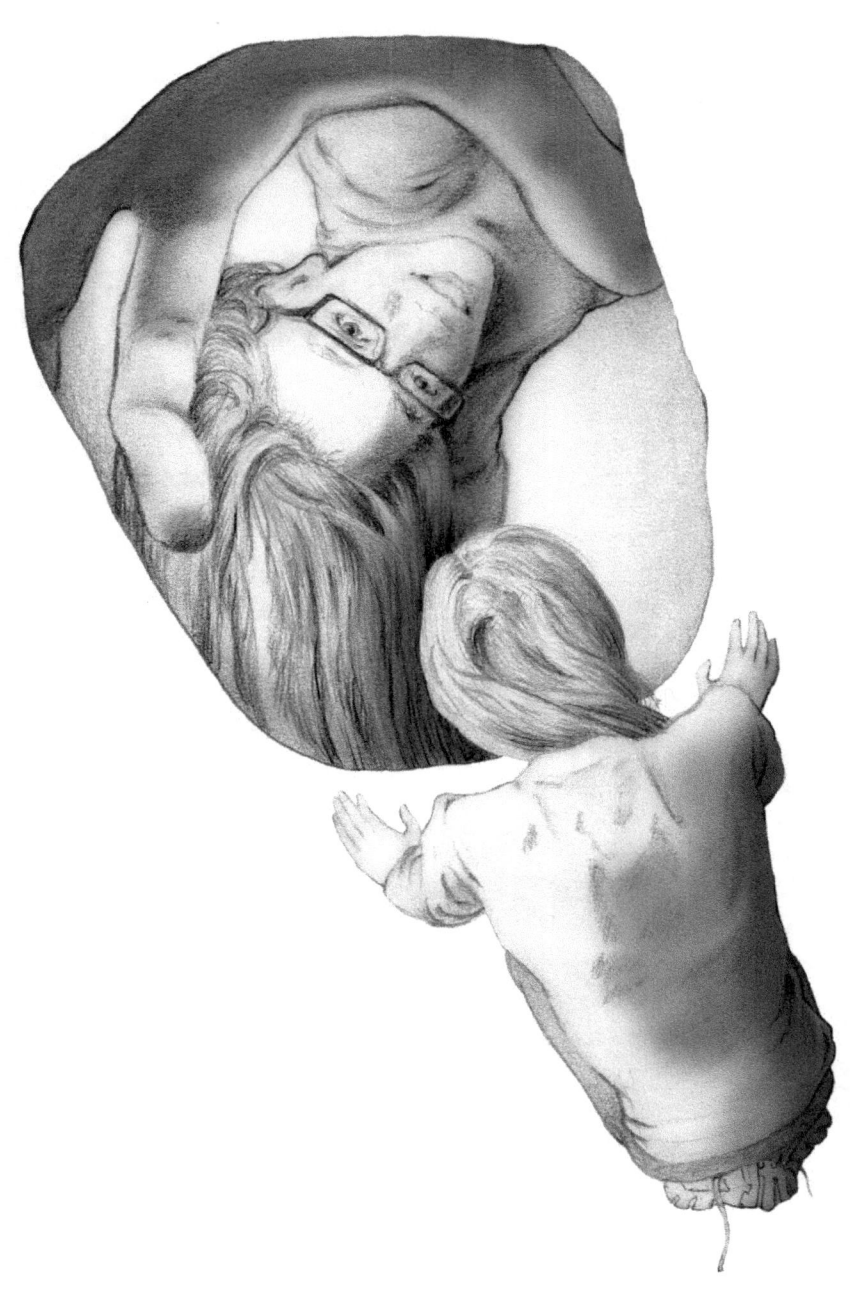

~Chapter 2: Reflecting Pools~

Billy and Agnes landed on their feet at first but rolled when the weights of their bodies really kicked in; just a slight somersault later they found themselves lying in the sand on a beach, not the bank of a river. Standing above them were Ralph, Tommy, and Josephine. Over their heads was a clear blue sky obscured only by palm leaves.

"Palm leaves?" Billy asked as he shielded his eyes from the bright, hot sun. "Where are we?"

"Not sure," said Tommy as he extended a hand to pull up Billy.

Josephine and Ralph helped Agnes, who quickly hugged Josephine and sighed, "Whew, am I glad you're okay!"

Billy smiled at Agnes. "That was fun," he said. "Quick, but fun!" Agnes smiled in agreement.

"How did we end up next to an ocean?" Ralph wondered. "This reminds me of a trip I went on with my parents, but that was to the West Coast. We couldn't be on the West Coast, could we?"

"Can't be," Billy said with great confidence. "We were just on the banks of the Mississippi, and I'm pretty sure that doesn't lead to the West Coast. Maybe we're in Duluth."

"With palm trees?" Ralph was just as puzzled as to their whereabouts as Billy, but he was pretty sure that Duluth wasn't it. "Lake Itasca, Billy; not Duluth. That's the source of the Mississippi. The other end has palm trees—you know, Louisiana, but this doesn't *feel* like Louisiana."

"Maybe we should all walk together and try to find a road," Josephine suggested, "or some people."

"And tell them what exactly?" Agnes snapped.

She was remembering a time when her mom and dad had first split up and neither one of them came to pick her up from day care.

Neither parent could be reached, and the day care place thought that she had just been abandoned.

It turned out that her aunt had forgotten to pick her up, but it took months to convince child services that her parents were indeed capable of raising her, despite the fact that neither one of them had ever been in the slightest trouble legally or in their respective careers. As a result, Agnes developed what she considered to be a healthy mistrust of anyone over her own age.

Agnes pretended to address a cop, "Hello, officer; we happen to be lost. What, California? No, officer; we're from Minnesota. How did we get here? Well, you see, there was this wormhole and..." Agnes looked at the other four to see if they could see how crazy that would sound to a cop in California.

"She has a point," Ralph chimed in. "Nobody will believe our story."

"Hey!" Tommy shouted. "We haven't tried going back the other way! Let's just figure out where we landed and jump back up into the wormhole."

Everyone agreed that this was the first, best plan.

The group argued about the exact landing spot for a couple of minutes until Tommy reminded them, "Mr. Fiddle said that these things collapse. We'd better just try a spot that we think is close. Everybody go to where you think we fell in and start jumping."

They began bouncing up and down like pogo sticks in an area roughly twenty feet in diameter. Billy tired out first, followed by Ralph, Agnes, and then Josephine. Tommy continued leaping into the sky until Josephine cried out, "Mr. Fiddle!"

Tommy stopped jumping, and everyone looked at Josephine. "Mr. Fiddle said that we should just call out his name if we had any questions about wormholes."

They all agreed that it was just as good a plan as any, so they got in a circle and at the same time cried out, "Mr. Fiddle!" They waited for a minute or two, but nothing happened. Then, individually, they started calling out his name at different times until one by one they gave up.

"This is all my fault, you guys," Billy said, his voice full of despair.

"No. It's my fault, Billy." Mr. Fiddle's voice came from what looked like a fairly old palm tree trunk. Mr. Fiddle stepped out from behind the trunk and said, "I led you all to that wormhole."

Billy stepped out in front of the group, "No, you didn't; I led them there."

Mr. Fiddle smiled. "It's very kind of you to assume responsibility, Billy, but how do you think so many worms ended up in that hole in the first place?"

"Mr. Fiddle, you came," Josephine sighed. "We called you, and you came."

At this point they had all gathered around Mr. Fiddle.

"How do we get out of here?" Agnes asked on behalf of the group.

"Well, that all depends on you," Mr. Fiddle answered, baiting their curiosity. "How much do you want to know?" They looked around at one another as Mr. Fiddle continued, "Do you know where we are right now, and maybe even more importantly do you know *when* we are?" This made the group even more confused. "What if I told you that you are in Minnesota, right where you started, only a few hundred years in the future?" This really blew their minds.

"We're in the future?" Billy asked.

"Do you want to find out?" Mr. Fiddle asked the entire group.

They stood before him, nodding yes in unison.

"Great, right, now where to start? Oh, I know," Mr. Fiddle began to explain. "First of all, we're not in Minnesota, although conceivably Minnesota might look like this place in three hundred years, maybe even sooner. Actually, where we are is not quite as important as *who* we are, or perhaps more appropriately, who do you want to be?"

"Maybe we should call you Mr. Riddle." Ralph couldn't help himself.

Mr. Fiddle was the first to laugh, and the group joined in, not only because it was a good joke but also because of the absurdity of the entire situation. As Mr. Fiddle turned his back to the group, they shot each other looks, trying to determine if any one of them had a clue as to what was going on. They hadn't.

"I know that none of you has a clue what is going on right now," Mr. Fiddle said as he led the group down a narrow path through a jungle of exotic plants, wonderful flowers and ferns, and magnificent fruit trees.

All five kids were thinking the exact same thing, *this is paradise.*

"It's a bit like paradise, isn't it?" Mr. Fiddle asked as he suddenly turned. "But do you know why you are here?" He looked at each one of them individually, scanning their eyes and expressions. "No, of course you don't." Mr. Fiddle was talking to them but also to himself. "And that is perfectly right and fine because if you did know why you are here, then it would mean that you brought yourselves here, which is entirely untrue because, in fact, it was me who did the bringing.

"But it's always good to ask, just in case there is someone doing the bringing that you may not have expected, and by that I mean the universal you, not you people specifically."

By this time Mr. Fiddle had completely lost the kids. They were still walking closely behind him, but they had no idea where he was going with any of this.

They emerged from the jungle path into an oasis of sand and water: a collection of five distinct pools surrounded by sand.

"Do you know the story of Narcissus?" Mr. Fiddle asked the group as he motioned for each of them to stand by a pool.

"That's the dude who fell in love with himself," Agnes replied as she looked into the pool and saw a reflection of herself that she did not expect. "What does that have to do with us..." her voice trailed off as she stared at her reflection.

One by one the members of the group looked into their own pools.

Ralph stared at a reflection of himself that he did not understand.

Billy looked into the pool and was as if glued, his fingers dug into the sand as if he could grasp at what he saw in the pool by clutching the sand.

Josephine looked into her pool and caught sight of something huge, and she quickly looked away. As she did she caught a glimpse of Tommy's pool. His eyes were glued to it. For a moment she thought that she saw herself in his pool. Her eyes scanned the group and fell into her own pool, where she was swallowed up by her own visions.

"You can be who and what you want to be. The pool reflects what you are thinking, what you are knowing." A voice resounded in each of their heads; it was Mr. Fiddle and someone else, millions upon millions of someone elses. "No one can tell you who you are meant to be but you. No one can be you better than you can."

These words and their own personal visions were all that they experienced before sleep.

~ *Chapter 3: Superpowers* ~

Tommy woke up late. He barely ate anything. Not because he wasn't hungry; he was ravenous. His mother managed to tell him in six different ways how time worked and that "you can't remain in bed for the entire morning and expect to have a leisurely breakfast, as if time will just stand still because you want it to." She was quite certain of that. "And you can't get to school on time if you try to eat your entire breakfast when your classes start in less than half an hour," she added as she took his bowl out from under his mouth after hoisting his backpack, which weighed more than his father's bowling ball, onto the table next to him. In a single motion, she dropped the bowl into the sink and spun Tommy's chair to face the door. "Go," she finished as she turned away, grabbing the laundry basket and a family-sized bottle of detergent on her way to the basement.

Tommy dashed to the sink, threw down another three mouthfuls of cereal, grabbed his backpack, and headed out the door.

Within a block, the sense of urgency had completely leaked out of his brain as a shower of thoughts, memories, and questions about wormholes washed over him. Yesterday they had traveled through a wormhole. Today he felt like he was watching life as much as he was actively participating in it. He stood in one place for a moment, feeling a little woozy, and slowly looked around. Something was different. Something he couldn't quite place.

Eventually the notion that he might be late for school if he just stood there broke through the wooziness, and he began to walk toward school, eyes straight forward, in an effort to still be on time. Suddenly, right in front of his nose, something sped by, so fast he could barely see it. If he had been there a half second earlier, whatever passed him would have hit him rather than pass.

Tommy stood there, frozen in his tracks, darn sure that whatever had just come by his nose would have crushed him if he had been there a half second earlier.

He thought about wormholes, and he thought, *That just happened, and there was no Mr. Fiddle around. I just saw that!* He realized that he was beginning to see where the wormholes were without Mr. Fiddle. He could detect the places where time held gateways, places that he hadn't even known existed the day before, places that sci-fi fans dreamed of stumbling upon and religious zealots feared to tread, places that everyone else in the world didn't know or care about. Not only could he detect them, but he also seemed to feel whether or not they were around.

Tommy had been raised to be quite aware of the fact that nobody saw wormholes and that everything in the world made perfect sense. When his dad bowled three strikes in a row but missed the fourth, it was surely due to the law of averages. And when Pops missed the seven-ten split, it was undoubtedly due to the new wax on the lane. These things made sense. Seeing wormholes landed squarely in the "What you talkin' 'bout, Willis?" column, as Pops referred to it. It came from *Diff'rent Strokes*, one of his father's favorite television shows. That column was reserved for anything that no one got. If it couldn't be explained, or there was no real evidence to support it, it ended up in the WYTBW column.

Unfortunately for Tommy, he now belonged in the WYTBW column.

He decided to keep it to himself. No one needed to know. No harm done.

He was definitely going to need to walk a little faster if he had a prayer of getting to school on time. This time he was definitely going to look around. He walked. He looked to his left. He looked to his right. He looked left again, and just to be sure, again to his right.

Just as he was crossing at the intersection, he saw Billy, on his skateboard, doing a handstand, in the middle of the street, closing in fast.

Tommy thought that he was being proactive. His brain sent a message to his feet and legs that went something like this: *Hey, feet and legs, get ready to jump because it looks like Billy is going to smash into us.*

Before that message actually reached his feet and legs, Billy was one inch away from Tommy. Billy had been, only a second earlier, a football field away. Now he was an inch away, on a skateboard traveling at one hundred yards per second, directly at Tommy. Tommy closed his eyes, unwilling to look at Billy as he was ripped apart upon impact, preferring to remember his friend from better times, unwilling to die with the added insult of knowing that his life was taken by this friend, traveling at supersonic speeds on a skateboard from Hades.

Nothing happened. Actually, something quite stupendous happened, which meant that whatever Tommy had thought was going to happen didn't, and what did happen could not be explained. Billy stopped on a dime. It was an old expression, meaning, his forward motion was arrested so completely that neither he nor his body moved a fraction of an inch in the direction he was headed. Great ice skaters could do this. Well-tuned athletes in a variety of sports could do this. Magicians could do this. Nature could not, and would not, do this.

Billy stopped so completely that it was as if he had not been moving at all, but it got weirder.

Billy had been skateboarding toward Tommy while doing a handstand, in the middle of the street, in the middle of the day. His board was moving faster than any car Tommy had seen or ever remembered seeing, and Billy was headed right for him. The moment his board stopped, less than a foot away, Billy's entire body flipped 180 degrees so he was standing upright, looking directly at Tommy. Physics would tell us that this just couldn't happen. With that kind of forward momentum, plus the flip, surely Billy would plow into Tommy.

That was not what happened. Billy just stopped moving completely.

He did not fall into Tommy propelled by the jarring motion of his mass being forced to arrest its momentum in a certain direction.

Billy's impetus had ceased.

He stood straight up and down on his board, like he was a pole attached to the skateboard and the skateboard weighed a ton and was attached to the ground. It was instant, it was sudden, and it did not break his bones or mar his flesh. Solid, unmoving, Billy grinned from ear to ear.

He stepped off his board and flipped it up into his hand without looking. Tommy knew that yesterday Billy couldn't do any of that.

"Not bad, eh Tommy?" Billy laughed, partly because it was fun to be able to do all of those tricks and partly because he didn't know what else to do. He had no idea why he was able to do those tricks; he just knew that he had to show Tommy. "This is insane, Tommy. I can do things I could never do before. I can do things that you could never do before." Billy was so excited that he just stammered, "I-I-I-I-I..."

Normally Tommy would be with Josephine by now and wouldn't see Billy until school. But today Billy had to show off what was happening with him. Billy had no idea that something was also happening with Tommy. Tommy put a hand on Billy's shoulder to calm him down.

"I can see wormholes," Tommy said quietly.

Billy stopped stammering as his jaw dropped open and hung there like an overripe apple, poised to fall from the tree. "Wormholes?" he asked in the same quiet voice that Tommy had used to calm him down.

Tommy smiled and repeated, "Wormholes."

"Awesome," Billy shouted as he jumped into the air. Apparently he hadn't tried jumping yet because he was about ten feet in the air, and his surprised expression told Tommy that he didn't have a landing plan. Billy sort of dropped onto the ground more than he landed. Tommy looked on with concern that Billy had broken something because he didn't move. Billy's face was pointed downward toward the ground, his upper body heaving like he was crying. Tommy took a step toward Billy, reaching his hand out to help.

Billy rolled over onto his back, tears rolling down his face, laughing. "Did you see that?" Billy sprang back up onto his feet and grabbed Tommy with both hands. With crazed enthusiasm he asked, "What happened to us, Tommy?"

"I have no..." Tommy stopped talking, his eyes looking past Billy, his mouth agape. Billy turned around to see what Tommy was looking at.

Billy shouted. "No way; you have got to be kidding me. It's..."

"Josephine." Tommy helped Billy finish his sentence.

She was about a mile away, but they could see her plain as day. She was nearly fifty feet tall, and she was walking through the town, taking entire city blocks in a single step, heading directly toward them. Josephine walked through town without touching a single car or a single person. She stepped through town with the greatest of ease; she smashed no trucks, police cars, vans, taxis, buses or light rail trains, though all of them were busy going about their everyday routines throughout the entire city. She was a giant who could walk on the earth without disturbing it at all.

Inside their heads, Billy and Tommy had the same exact thought floating around: *Is Josephine always going to be a giant now?* This was their shared first thought. The second was *is anyone else seeing this?* Before either one of them could tell the other either one of those thoughts, Josephine was standing directly next to them. She towered over them, to be more precise.

Simultaneously they arched their backs, craned their necks, and looked up at her with a mixture of awe, fear, and a slight unease that any normal boy of that age might feel when looking directly up at a girl from the perspective of her own big toe. They also shared another thought—namely, both were glad that she was wearing pants rather than a skirt.

"Hi ,Tommy; hi Billy," Josephine said with a voice that could fill a stadium, her smiling face about twenty feet above them as she bent down.

"Hello, Josephine," they responded quietly, in voices too afraid to leave their bodies. It was taking a little while to reconcile the fact that the giant who stood over them was the same vulnerable young girl they had rescued from the wormhole the day before.

"Look at me." Josephine laughed as she twirled around to show the boys, nearly stepping right on them as she spun.

"Yeah," Tommy said, forcing an uneasy laugh, "you sure are..." Tommy stalled to find the right word. He had heard his father tell his mother that she was a big presence in his life, to disastrous consequences. His father had spent two weeks convincing his mother that "big" was not at all a statement regarding her physical size or weight and most certainly had nothing to do with her being a burden in any way, psychological or emotional. "...tall. You are very tall, Josephine; very, very tall."

"I know, isn't this weird?" Josephine went on. "And what about the whole bit where I walked through town and nobody noticed and I could walk down the center of the street and not step on anybody? I mean this is great, and weird and strange and..." Her words trailed off as she seemed to become lost in thought, her excitement winding down to a sort of lonely dismay.

Tommy couldn't see her face now, but he knew that she needed to know that she wasn't the only one who had changed. He pounded on her big toe as hard as he could, and he wondered how her shoes had become bigger as she had. No response. He was clearly too small to do anything to her that might make her look down. As Josephine stared into the sky, wondering for how long she might be a giant, Tommy yelled up to her, trying to get her attention. Nothing.

"Billy, you try; punch her in the toe or something." Tommy was starting to feel a little desperate, almost responsible for Josephine. He didn't quite understand it.

"You want me to punch her toe?" Billy laughed until he saw the look in Tommy's eyes. "Okay, I'll punch her toe."

He stepped toward the giant. Clearly Billy hadn't tried punching anything since his transformation. Had he actually tried it earlier, he would have known what to expect. His fist cut right through her shoe like it was tissue paper, and his hand sunk into her toe like a syringe. He stopped and stepped back as quickly as he could, but it wasn't quickly enough.

She cried out, "Ouch!" in a voice that resonated off of the sky, leaped into the air, and came down directly on Billy with one foot, crushing him into the ground.

Her other foot landed directly on Tommy but did nothing to him. She looked down and remembered that Tommy and Billy were right beneath her. She took a step back. Tommy was unharmed, but Billy was sunk into the ground like he had been pounded in with a hammer. To everyone's amazement, he stood right up, dusted himself off, and shouted, "All I did was punch your stupid toe!"

"Billy! I thought I crushed you." Josephine said apologetically as she knelt down to get closer to the boys.

Tommy stepped forward and bowed to the fifty foot tall girl, cupped his hands to create a megaphone and in his best ringmaster's voice announced...

"Josephine, I would like to introduce you to SuperBilly," Tommy joked as he waved his hand toward Billy, who still looked a bit upset at being crushed. Tommy recognized this and quickly added, "You can't break him, and you can't beat him." It seemed to do the trick.

Billy stepped up next to Tommy, looked Josephine in the eyes, and said, "That's not all! You should see me skateboard!" Billy stepped back a few feet. "*And* you should see me flip!" He flipped. "*And* you should see me jump!" This time he jumped all the way up to Josephine's eye level, and on the way back down he actually thought about landing, which he did with no problem.

"Billy. You are amazing!" Josephine was so happy that something had happened to somebody else that she didn't care who it was—at least she wasn't alone.

"Thank you," Billy said as he bowed and stepped backward as if exiting the stage.

"I can see wormholes," Tommy said in a less than important way.

"Really?" Josephine laid her chin on the ground right next to Tommy.

He stared at her lips and mumbled, "Yeah, I mean...yes, I mean...lips."

"What?" Josephine couldn't tell where Tommy was looking or what exactly was going on.

Tommy snapped out of it, just in time. "*Yes!* Wormholes, the holes that go all over, everywhere; I can see them—yep!" This was actually quite impressive, but in the shadow of the giant and the indestructible kid, Tommy felt, in essence, less gifted.

He felt someone poke him in the back. He turned around quickly to catch Billy. Billy was ten feet away. Tommy thought, *Billy is superfast; he could easily tap me and move back.* The thought of Josephine's lips inexorably superseded concerns about the annoying poke.

"Maybe you can use wormholes like Mr. Fiddle can, Tommy," Josephine said in a soft voice with a warm wind, making Tommy forget everything except for Josephine. Suddenly he was poked from behind again. This time he turned even faster to find Billy, practicing his handstand, nearly thirty feet away. The poking continued. Tommy turned in circles until he was dizzy.

"I give up!" Tommy was nearly falling over. "What is going on? Do you see anybody, Josephine?" Tommy asked, pointing over his shoulder. "Billy? Anything?" All three looked around.

"Nothing," they all confirmed.

"Hey, guys." A strange cartoonish voice came from nowhere.

"Hello!" The odd voice continued.

"Hello?"

They did not respond. The three of them looked at one another, trying to determine where the voice might be coming from.

"Okay, it's me."

They looked at one another again.

"What, nobody else around here is feeling just a little invisible today? It's me, Ralph." He said in a voice they could recognize.

They looked at one another and then in the general vicinity of the voice.

"Where are you?" they asked in unison.

"Right here," Ralph said quietly. He was standing directly between Tommy and Billy.

"Ralph," they all shouted, "You are invisible!"

"Oh, really?" Ralph seemed a bit perturbed with the whole situation. "I'm invisible. That's just amazing; that is just...fascinating." The sarcasm was far more palpable at this point than Ralph himself was.

While there was a certain discomfort with waking to discover that you had a superpower, much of that discomfort could be avoided by waking with the understanding that you were actually in control of your superpower. Ralph did not feel in control. "You guys sound like you think it's cool that I'm invisible, but I don't know how to change back, and I do not want to be invisible forever!"

"I'm with Ralph." Josephine's hair brushed over Tommy as she raised her chin off the ground, turned her head, and rose to one knee. "We have to find a way to change back."

"I don't." Billy began running in small circles around the space between himself and Tommy at the moment Ralph identified his location. "I am quite happy to have these powers at all times." The dust he had stirred was now wrapping itself around the slowly appearing form of Ralph. Never fully materializing, the mummy-like wrapping of dust remained just long enough for Billy to place his finger on Ralph's nose. "I am going to help you, though."

The dust already disappearing, Ralph asked, "How you gonna do that?"

"The only way we can." Tommy stepped in Ralph's direction, his hand out to shake. He felt Ralph's hand in his and gripped it, and he looked down and saw his own fingers through Ralph's hand. "We're all going to call for Mr. Fiddle together. Hey, Josephine, mind giving us a lift?"

"All right, I guess." The thought of three boys climbing into her hand was a little unsettling, but she laid her hand out, palm up, on the ground next to the boys. "I wonder where Agnes is." She was getting sadder.

"Maybe Mr. Fiddle knows," Tommy hoped as he gently climbed onto Josephine's fingers. "He seems to know a lot of strange things, and it's my guess that it's all related."

"See, Ralphy boy, I told you we were going to help you out," Billy laughed, leaping, ridiculously gracefully, onto Josephine's palm. He landed so softly, she barely felt it. "Now what are we waitin' for? You on here yet, Ralph?"

"I'm on," Ralph said, a little more optimistically than he expected, so he decided to go with it. "Let's call Mr. Fiddle and get back to normal!"

"You were never normal, Ralph. I think miracles are off Mr. Fiddle's list." Billy liked to bug Ralph a little, but it never seemed to faze him.

"The great Billy Freud has spoken," Ralph countered.

"Can we call Mr. Fiddle now?" Josephine asked as she held the boys about forty feet off the ground. The visible boys nodded. Actually, the invisible one nodded too, but that wasn't going to do much for Josephine. However, she did notice that the nodding made the boys weight shift slightly, and she could feel them nodding in her palm, so the fact that Ralph did nod, while not seen, was in another sense sensed.

"Okay, when I count to three we call for Mr. Fiddle," Josephine instructed. "One, two, three..."

"Mr. Fiddle," they called in unison.

A fourth weight was added to Josephine's palm.

"Mr. Fiddle!" Josephine shrieked with joy, nearly knocking everyone in her hand over. They were lucky they didn't fall off.

"Would you mind very terribly if I asked you to set us down, Josephine? My, you have grown since the last time I saw you," Mr. Fiddle turned to the spot where Ralph was standing and said, "I haven't seen you looking like this before, Ralph," he chuckled as he climbed off of Josephine's hand, which now hovered inches above the ground. She did not have a pleasant expression on her face, but Mr. Fiddle ignored that. "Okay, young lady, what do you need from Mr. Fiddle?"

Josephine was shocked. She thought that it would be obvious what she needed. What else would anyone need who was fifty feet tall? To not be fifty feet tall, of course. Duh.

"What do you mean what do I need? Isn't it obvious? I need to not be fifty feet tall anymore. I can't go around being fifty feet tall. What would I eat? I couldn't even fit into my house! I couldn't even fit into my school. Really? I mean, can't you see that I don't want to be fifty feet tall? I want to be my regular size."

Mr. Fiddle looked up to Josephine with his arms spread out wide and yelled up to her, "Okay, well, then, just be your regular size."

Josephine replied, "I can't just be my regular size. I'm fifty feet tall."

"No, you're not getting it." Mr. Fiddle cupped his hands to make a megaphone. "Just be your regular size."

"I'm afraid I don't understand you," Josephine said. "My regular size is, um, well, I'm about four eleven, maybe eleven and a half. I don't know 'cause someone tells you to stand against the wall and then you gotta take your shoes off, and then someone, maybe your mom or your dad, draws a line, and your dad's line is always higher than your mom's line, but your mom is sure that hers is right..." Josephine realized as she continued that she had been so busy talking about her height that she failed to notice that she was changing. "And now I'm looking up at you, Mr. Fiddle. Mr. Fiddle! It worked, it worked; I'm my regular size!" Josephine bounced up and down and around in circles, singing, "I'm my regular size; I'm my regular size; what a glorious feeling; I'm happy again!" Then she hugged Tommy. Only for a second, till she felt weird, let go of him, and continued dancing while humming more quietly, sort of to herself, with another occasional verse of "I'm my regular size," sneaking in between the humming.

Meanwhile, Ralph asked Mr. Fiddle, "Can I do that same thing?"

"Why not, Ralph?" Mr. Fiddle urged. "What are you waiting for?"

"Well, I don't know, I guess I was just...freaked out, because..." Ralph searched for the words. "Y'know, it's not like every day you wake up and you can't see yourself in the mirror. I mean, I thought it was weird when I-I-I threw my legs out of bed and my sheets moved, but I didn't see anything like my knees or my feet. I guess I was movin' fast enough that I didn't notice or look down at my feet or whatever, but then I got to the bathroom, and you know what? It's ridiculous; you walk in—into the bathroom, and the door's moving, you can see it in the mirror, but you can't see you, and you know you're supposed to be there. Do you know what that feels like?"

They all said no, except for Josephine, who was still blissfully dancing around in her own size.

"It is really, really weird," Ralph continued. "I mean, like right now when you guys are looking at me, you must be thinking, that's really, really weird, it is so weird, I hear a voice but there is nobody ther—" He saw his own hand, gesturing in front of his face. He stopped talking.

"Good, now that we are all here," Mr. Fiddle pronounced, "it's time that you learned why I have brought you all together."

Josephine stopped dancing and singing, "What about Agnes?"

~ *Chapter 4: The Big Bird* ~

Mr. Fiddle didn't want to talk about Agnes. The fact was that he really couldn't answer their questions about her. He didn't know what to say, but he felt that he had better say something, and usually when you didn't know what to say, you had better just say the truth, or at least the truth as you knew it. So this was just what he did.

"Agnes isn't here. So I don't think she has any powers." Mr. Fiddle was truly upset. "I wish something happened to her, just like it did to you, but since it didn't, I can only assume the worst, which if you really think about it, isn't really altogether terrible. She's just a normal kid." Mr. Fiddle hung his head and shook it from side to side as if admitting defeat. Josephine sighed. "I know, Josephine. I understand your disappointment, but everything happens for a reason. The reason you are all here, with me right now, is that you all developed powers after our recent adventure. You called to me, I came, and I knew what to expect." Mr. Fiddle paused for a moment, as if listening for a whisper of something he had missed. His eyes rolled upward and a little off-center, as if he were listening to his own brain. "Hmm," he continued. "You are not the first of my pupils, and I imagine I have some time left, so you probably will not be the last. So we had better be going."

"Going where?" Tommy asked, more out of shock than curiosity. Everything was moving a bit quickly for him, the only relief being that they had Mr. Fiddle to explain what was going on.

"Well, Tommy, that's entirely up to you," Mr. Fiddle replied, his eyes smiling reassuringly.

"Whaddya mean it's up to me?" Tommy asked, not entirely sure that he was ready for the answer.

"Well, I think that you can tell where the wormholes are now," Mr. Fiddle prodded. "Right?"

"You mean I can always tell where the wormholes are? I-I thought that it just happened when I wasn't looking or didn't expect it or something." Tommy was confused.

"Well, it's a little like that, only you don't have to be spacing out or daydreaming or staring at the ground; you just have to look for the wormhole, but not too hard." Mr. Fiddle made it sound so simple, sort of. "You can always see the wormholes now, and you can bring anyone along with you."

Tommy looked all around him. "I can't see anything," he said as he looked up, down, forward, and backward. He went behind a nearby tree and looked there. He grabbed Billy by both arms and moved him just enough to look where his feet had been. "Nothing!" Tommy groaned a bit, scrunched his face up tight, and asked in a voice that sounded like it was being forced through a cheese grater, "How do I see them?"

"You just said it yourself, Tommy," Mr. Fiddle suggested. "Nothing; try to think of nothing."

"Oh, man, Tommy'll be good at that!" Billy said and laughed, and Tommy slugged him on the shoulder. Billy put up his fists like he was in a boxing ring, "C'mon, so you wanna littl'a this, eh, tough guy? Put 'em up." He lunged forward with a mock left jab just as Tommy turned. Tommy's eyes were focused on something over Billy's right shoulder. From where she stood, Josephine thought that Billy had actually hit Tommy.

She ran to him. "Tommy, are you all right?"

"It's there," he said almost imperceptibly. "It's right there," he said more perceptibly. "Right over there," he bellowed as he turned and held Josephine's arms. "The wormhole—I see it." He was smiling and looking right into Josephine's eyes. It took him a few seconds to realize he was still holding her. He let go almost robotically and raised one hand, index finger pointing straight up. "I must show everyone where it is." He turned self-consciously away from Josephine, in the direction of the others, and announced, "I see the wormhole, and I can take you to it." He started bouncing up and down like he was riding a pogo stick. He wasn't. And pointing—he was pointing a lot in one particular direction while he pogoed down the street until he stopped. He turned to the group and said, "Here I go," just before running headlong toward the giant sandbox. When he reached the sandbox, he dove, face first, into the sand, and disappeared.

"I'm comin' to join ya, Tommy Boy!" Billy ran, jumped, flipped, and belly flopped directly into the center of the sand and disappeared.

"Here goes nothing. Cannonball," Josephine cried out as she leaped into the air and tucked for the cannonball, disappearing like Tommy and Billy. Oddly enough, she actually created a sand splash that plumed out of the sandbox and landed on Ralph. He turned invisible just before it hit him. His invisibility instantly changed the visibility of the sand, which only meant that he ended up brushing invisible sand off of himself rather than visible sand. He had hoped it would have truly made the sand disappear. He should have known better after Billy's stunt earlier. He did. He just thought he'd give it a try. Suddenly he felt himself being pushed into the sandbox. "These wormholes don't stick around all day," he heard Mr. Fiddle say as they both hit the wormhole together.

"Unless you leave your foot in the door," was what Ralph didn't hear Mr. Fiddle say. That was because Fiddle had whispered it to himself, under his breath as he scrunched up his shoulders and rubbed his hands together like little gnomes did when they thought they were being exceptionally clever or devious.

They all arrived within seconds of one another. One by one they landed on a bed of clover—well, at least it looked like clover, and that was exactly what each of them thought as they landed there, whether on their feet, their faces, or their butts. They probably would have looked at the soft green stuff longer to determine whether it really was clover, if that was half as important as the very next question that came to everyone's mind: *Where am I?* Where had Tommy taken them? It was possibly the scariest, least desirable, and most bewildering spot they had ever been, Mr. Fiddle not included. He didn't seem the slightest bit ruffled.

"Definitely not clover," he said as he tasted the tiny little green leaf and lay back to stretch out his whole body on the soft green bed.

Meanwhile, the rest of them turned in circles, looking off into the distance in every direction.

Slowly they moved in a radius away from Mr. Fiddle, easing closer to the edge of the ground that held them up, a flat area of not clover that couldn't have been more than fifteen feet in diameter. As they neared the edge, it became apparent that there was no slope, no mountainside below them upon which to make a descent.

"I see something," Tommy shouted while pointing. "About a mile that way. Do you all see it? It's a butte, like in Montana, except a lot taller and thinner." Billy, Josephine, and Ralph drew closer to see where he was pointing. "I think we're on one of those!" He looked again at the other butte and tried to look over the side of the area upon which he and his friends stood. "We've got to be at least a mile up," he guessed. "And I can't see a way down."

They all started talking at once, mostly questions about "how" and thoughts of "maybe," all mixed with mounting fear and desperation, until they spoke as if with a single voice: "Mr. Fiddle, what do we do?"

He sat up and looked at them. "Maybe the question should be what *can* you do?"

"Tommy!" Billy barked. "A wormhole; find another wormhole."

"I've been looking," Tommy replied. "I can't see any other wormholes. I can't even see the one we came through. Why can't I see the one we came through?" he asked as he swung around to face Mr. Fiddle once again. Fiddle had risen to his feet and was walking calmly toward Tommy.

"There are different kinds of wormholes, Tommy," he continued. "You just happened to pick what we call a Slightly Half-Open Returnless Type, YES, or SHORTY for short."

Tommy looked as though he were going to flip out; his voice was low, and he was making it even lower, hoping that lowering it would help him to remain calm. "Mr. Fiddle, sir."

It started in low, "you knew that it was a SHORTY," and then it started to grow, "*and* you let me go ahead and *pick it?*"

He jumped up and down and stomped to punctuate his frustration.

Fiddle smiled the kind of smile that young people hated, the smile that said, "I knew all along what you were going to do and what would happen as a result, but I let you do it anyway, and now I am going to look super calm while you fume over something that I could have totally prevented." Everyone who had ever had the not so good fortune of having been taught anything in this manner knew exactly what happened next.

Fiddle said, "You were going to have to learn about SHORTYs eventually." It may have seemed cruel that Fiddle would allow such misfortune to happen on Tommy's very first try at wormholing, but it wasn't.

"Truthfully, Tommy, I wasn't so sure myself," Mr. Fiddle explained. "You saw that wormhole even before I did. I was quite frankly still looking around for Agnes. When you rallied everyone to the location and dove right in, I had very little choice but to follow."

"What's it matter, Tommy? We are stuck here, and we have no way down." Josephine was getting a bit freaked out, and it looked as though she might start crying.

"Maybe I can run down the sides. I'm pretty fast," Billy offered as he started toward an edge. His start was entirely too noncommittal to achieve anywhere near the required velocity to make a go of it, and he stopped himself, inches from going over. "Sorry; I just can't," he reluctantly admitted.

"Oh, no; we're never going to get out of here. I wish I was fifty feet tall again, and then this wouldn't seem so high, and maybe I could just jump or walk or I-I—what am I going to—"

Josephine's rant was interrupted by voices from far away yelling, "Stop growing." She looked down. Mr. Fiddle and the boys were holding on to her shoelaces and balancing on what was left of the top face of the butte, and her feet had grown to take up most of the area.

"Just calm down," Tommy called up. "It's going to be okay. Maybe you should shrink down again," he suggested.

"No, wait." Billy jumped into the conversation. "We can tie ourselves to your shoes, and you can slide down the side of the butte, on your butt."

"I am *not* going to try to slide down the side of this thing, Billy." Josephine was having a hard time just standing there at this point and being responsible for everyone else. No way. "And I am definitely not picking up passengers!"

Josephine wished that Agnes was there. Agnes understood her. Agnes too, would still get scared if she was fifty feet tall. Josephine was looking down at the guys who just plain didn't understand her, and she blurted out, "I just want to step on you little guys." She hadn't meant to articulate the way she was feeling, but the response made her feel good. Billy said he was sorry and admitted that he was a little scared too. Tommy confessed that he was maybe about half as scared as she was, at least, and Ralph was fully willing to let Josephine know that he was scared too.

"I'm scared right now," Ralph said. "There is something big and black and birdlike coming straight for your head! Look out!" He yelled to Josephine, pointing past her head, farther skyward.

Josephine turned her gaze quickly skyward, carefully spinning on the precarious perch, the little guys riding her sneakers like a catamaran. The bird was twice the size of Josephine and looked like a cross between an eagle, a falcon, and a sixth-grade girl, with a one-hundred-foot wingspan and the voice of Agnes, bird of prey, saying, "Duck, Josephine!" The moment Josephine recognized that the bird was Agnes, she calmed down and shrunk to her regular size, abating the requirement of ducking for survival.

Agnes banked around toward the group. "Sorry," she screeched. "Just getting used to the wings." She swung around again, this time with a controlled glide. "Hop on."

"I'll go first," Fiddle volunteered as Agnes banked for another pass.

"Wanna boost?" Billy was down on one knee with his hands cupped for Mr. Fiddle to put a foot in.

"Absolutely," Fiddle accepted, realizing Billy's plan, which worked like a charm.

The timing was perfect.

Fiddle leaned into the boost with enough momentum that Billy's boost launched him straight up.

He rose up into the air a good eighty feet before he began to fall, and within a second Agnes arrived. Fiddle leaned forward as he fell, clutching at whatever he could hold as he hit Agnes's back. Her feathers were easy to grasp, and the ride was comfortable, and Mr. Fiddle couldn't help but let out a holler.

"Woo-eee!"

The others were cheering and clapping and congratulating Billy on a fine launch when they began to look around at one another, wondering who would go next.

"What took you so long?" Mr. Fiddle asked Agnes as she soared.

She pulled a hard bank in reaction to his comment and shrieked, "I was a mouse for six hours, crawled around forever until a cat chased me into a sandbox, and I fell into this place. I tumbled through the sky for a whole minute until I thought about the fact that an eagle or a hawk would not mind falling through the sky without a parachute, and bam, I'm a giant bird girl. I'm not sure what kind of bird girl I am, but at least I'm flying."

"Yes, you are, Agnes; now let's go pick up the others." Mr. Fiddle suggested. "Billy should be ready to toss another one up here by now."

Tommy said that he would go next and reassured Josephine that he would be there to catch a hold of her when it was her turn to go.

"Okay, okay, enough already," Billy cried out. "They're turning our way; hurry up and get ready, Tommy."

Billy was right; Agnes and Fiddle were closing in fast, and Tommy needed to be above them when they crossed over. Tommy ran as fast as he could, planted his foot squarely in Billy's interlocked hands, and, with plenty of forward momentum, transitioned into the perfect ascent. He came down a little behind Fiddle but was able to get a good hold of Agnes, just between her outstretched wings. He worked his way forward to sit on Agnes's neck, next to Mr. Fiddle.

"Hey, Agnes; glad you could join us," he laughed. "Me too," Agnes screeched in a voice that none of them liked, especially Agnes.

Agnes turned back more quickly this time, and Josephine was ready. Her launch wasn't perfect and she seemed to sit through the air rather than slicing through like the rocket Tommy had been. Agnes adjusted quickly and dove closer to the butte, As Josephine descended she nearly caught Tommy's head with her feet, but he dodged sideways and extended his hand. Josephine reached out to him, and their arms locked, hand to forearm. Tommy was able to swing her into place, tucking her in behind himself, just like in the old western movies he loved to watch with his dad on Saturday afternoons. He felt as though years had passed since the last time they watched a western together, but it had only been five days.

"Nice one," he said to Josephine, who was only too happy to wrap her arms around his waist, relieved to be off of the butte. "Ralph is next, Agnes, so be ready for anything," Tommy warned. In a way he was right to caution Agnes. Ralph had a certain unpredictability about him. He either got the idea of something really well or not at all.

Unfortunately for Ralph, this seemed to be one of the "not at all" times. He ran up to Billy pretty well. He even landed his foot in just the right spot, but rather than projecting his arms forward like the others, he wrapped his arms over his head like a helmet. This seemed to turn him into a cannonball of sorts, rather than a rocket, which made judging for the landing difficult at best. Ralph hit Agnes's back just behind the wings and rolled off. He slid down the side of her leg, trying to get one last grasp before falling. Ralph managed to hold on to the tip of one of Agnes's talons and, dangling for dear life, yelled, "*Help!*"

Billy had already seen Ralph's poor landing and was as far across the face of the butte as he could get. With all of his speed, he took off, leaping with every ounce of his might as he reached the other edge.

His jump was outstanding; he landed directly in the center of Agnes's right foot, from which Ralph dangled precariously.

Billy quickly reached out a hand for Ralph just as Ralph's fingers lost the strength to hold on.

Billy caught him by the wrist and swung him up into Agnes's left foot. She felt both of the boys within her feet and gently closed her toes around them, forming a comfortable cage from which to survey the surroundings, which was precisely what Billy did. Ralph grasped one of the toes with all his strength, eyes glued shut.

"You're okay now, Ralph," Billy said. "You should open your eyes; it's a really cool view." Ralph eased his grip and peeked out from between two of Agnes's toes. Billy was right.

Billy and Ralph weren't the only ones with an awesome view; the rest of the group had some pretty spectacular topside seats for what could only be described as the ride of a lifetime. None of them could tell what they were flying over, so Agnes rocketed down to get a better view. The terrain was definitely unique, with rows of spire-like buttes scattered everywhere that the eye could see. Agnes couldn't resist the urge to fly faster, dodging and weaving her way through the spires. Billy forced his head out between Agnes's toes, like a dog sticking its head out of the window of a car. His mouth filled with the rush of air, making his cheeks flutter. He stuck his tongue out, and it flapped against the side of his face. Ralph laughed so hard he forgot he was hundreds of feet up in the air.

The landscape was uniform in all directions; even the spires seemed evenly distributed. There was nothing different: no towns, no people, no rivers, no cattle, no animals at all for as far as the eye could see, until "I see something up ahead," Agnes shrieked.

"I can't see it," Mr. Fiddle called out to her. "What are you seeing?"

Agnes tilted her head and said, "Green. I see a lot of green, a field or valley about five miles from here."

"Great," said Mr. Fiddle. "Land there."

Agnes increased her speed through the butte landscape and arrived at the field of green within a minute. They had arrived at the edge of the field of green, more not clover in every direction; rolling hills and a rich forest of trees encircled the valley.

Agnes slowed to almost a hover as she flew lower and lower, her feet nearly scraping the ground. She slowly opened her toes and said, "Billy and Ralph, jump when you're ready."

Billy and Ralph looked at each other and then surveyed the ground moving slowly beneath them like they were standing at the back of a slow-moving freight train.

"You ready?" Billy asked Ralph as he bent his knees for the jump, "I can go first and help you out."

Ralph bent his knees and shouted, "No, I got this," as he jumped from Agnes's foot and landed with a slight tumble.

Billy jumped off and landed like he had stepped from a staircase. Both of them began to run after Agnes.

Mr. Fiddle, Josephine, and Tommy worked their way to the back of Agnes's body, preparing for a tail-wing exit.

Before they knew it, Agnes said, "Get ready to jump," and shortly thereafter, "Jump." Had they known what to expect, the landing might have gone better, but most likely not. Jumping off of a giant bird as it was changing back into a sixth-grade girl wasn't exactly the type of thing they had any practice at.

Agnes landed quite well, as if she had been a giant bird a thousand times; she changed just as she was reaching the ground, nailing the landing like a gold medal gymnast. The others did not fare so well. They all sort of fell off of Agnes rather than jumping, tumbling when they hit the ground.

"Thanks for the warning, Agnes," Tommy said sarcastically as he brushed himself off.

Agnes replied, "I told you to jump!"

Josephine ran to her friend and hugged her, unfazed by the rough landing. "I am so glad you made it, Agnes." She bounced up and down as she clapped her hands.

Billy joined the rest as soon as Agnes landed. "Awesome flying there, Agnes; you make a pretty great big bird."

"Thanks, Billy." Agnes smiled. "It sure beats being a little mouse."

Ralph was still trying to catch up to the group.

"Wait a second, Agnes," Josephine said. "Did you say that you were a mouse?"

"Yep, that's why I was late to the wormhole; it's hard to get around quickly when you are mouse-sized." Agnes frowned.

"Although I got a lot faster when the cat showed up," she smiled.

Billy gasped, "You could have been eaten!" Billy turned to Mr. Fiddle, who was playing with a button that was dangling loosely from his shirt as a result of the landing. "Can we die? Could Agnes have been eaten?" Billy asked with concern.

Mr. Fiddle stopped playing with his button. He knew that the whole group wanted to know the answer, so he asked them all to sit around him. He looked at each one for a while before he spoke.

"You each have different powers, and not one of you has had time enough to understand all of the amazing things you are capable of, but escaping death may be out of your control. If Agnes had been caught by that cat, she may have been eaten, but if she thought and acted quickly enough, she could have become a dog or even a lion for that matter. The more accustomed you become to your powers, the more you can extend them."

Tommy had had a question burning in his mind since Agnes showed up. "How did Agnes get here? I thought the wormhole was a SHORTY!"

"It was," Mr. Fiddle answered, "but I left my foot in the door."

"What do you mean?" Tommy had his face all bunched up like it was hurting just to imagine what Mr. Fiddle meant.

"When you have been around wormholes for as long as I have, you pick up a few tricks along the way," Mr. Fiddle continued. "Things like extending wormholes, leaving one side open, changing where they begin and end, and creating them out of thin air are all within my abilities."

"What?" They all said in unison, each of them thinking exactly what Tommy said next.

"You can make wormholes out of thin air, whenever you want?" He raised his voice. "And you left us all stranded on top of the killer butte from H-E-double-hockey-sticks?"

Mr. Fiddle knew that they all had a right to be upset, so he apologized promptly. "I am very sorry if that experience frightened all of you, but I had two very good reasons for not creating a new wormhole to get us off of there the easy way.

"I had faith that Agnes would be showing up at some time and did not want her arriving here while we were elsewhere.

"Furthermore, I found it to be a perfect situation in which to test your abilities in working together as a team. I am very proud of all of you and I give you all an A plus. That brings me to my next point. I am not really a substitute teacher, technically. I mean, I was a schoolteacher a very long time ago. I really just came to your school to find you all. The school and the school board think I'm a teacher because I have all of the right papers, but I'm really a different kind of teacher. My official title is Headmaster of Higher Powers." The group looked at one another with impressed expressions.

"Oh, and also," Mr. Fiddle went on, "just call me Fiddle, without the mister, except at school; you get the idea, right?"

The group nodded their heads in unison.

"Hey, Fiddle," Billy said. "How do we figure out what we can do?"

"Well, Billy, you have to test yourselves. Think about something you'd like to try to do, or you wish you could do, and then try to do it. I have an idea for you." Fiddle pointed to an enormous tree, with a trunk as wide as the butte they were standing on earlier. "Run as fast as you can into that tree trunk over there."

Billy looked at Fiddle like he was insane and said, "I am not going to do that. I would kill myself."

"Then you would kill yourself," Fiddle responded.

"That's what I said." Billy laughed at Fiddle. "I just said that I would kill myself, and you said, 'then you would kill yourself,' like I didn't already know that!"

"So you knew it already then?" Fiddle asked with an amused expression that made Billy scratch his head.

"Is this a riddle, Fiddle? I am not getting where you are going with this. Does anybody else get where Fiddle is going with this?"

Billy was not alone. The rest of the group looked at each other, and while Tommy looked like he was going to venture a guess, he backed down and just looked at Fiddle.

"You see, Billy," Fiddle started, "and all of you," he continued, his hand pointing, sweeping from one to another with dramatic emphasis, "each of you knows within your very soul what you are capable of. Getting your soul to let your mind and heart know it may be more difficult for some than for others." His eyes came to rest on Billy.

"Hey," Billy shouted in protest, as if his integrity and ability had been severely tarnished.

"I got one! I know what I can do, and I'll prove it right now. Do you all see that big rock over there?" Billy pointed to a boulder the size of a large house, which was embedded into the side of hill, roughly a half-mile away from the group.

When he was certain that everyone was looking at his boulder, Billy became the ringmaster, announcing his own performance, "I, Billy the Awesome, will attempt what no man has done before. I ask that you all remain still, for your own safety, as I perform a stunt so breathtaking..."

"Just tell us what you're going to do," Ralph interjected, to the approval of all assembled.

"Okay." Billy dropped the ringmaster voice. "I am going to run from here over to the other side of that hill, turn around, run up that hill, jump from the top of that boulder, flip in the air a few times, and land right back here where I am standing now."

The group looked at one another with mixed expressions, ranging from impressed and curious to concerned.

"Wish me luck," Billy said as he darted away from the group.

He was already to the far side of the hill and making his turn by the time they finished saying those two little words: "Good luck."

They stood still there, not because Billy had told them to but because they were dazed by his amazing speed.

Before they could even process how amazed they were, Billy had hit the top of the boulder and was in the air, flipping in their direction. He landed in a three-point stance with so much force that they could feel it in their feet. Billy stayed crouched and looked at them with an expression that said, "Beat that." Everyone was so impressed they just stood there with their jaws open.

Tommy was so blown away that he had to crack a joke about it. "Billy, I think you missed your landing by a couple feet, and why are you still crouched like a football player? Are you stuck?" Everyone laughed, even Billy, and then he slowly picked up the hand that was on the ground, turning his fist to open his clutched fingers. In his palm he had a coin. "Nickel," Billy said, pausing for a moment, once again ensuring that all eyes were on the coin as he straightened to his full height. "Dropped it here so I'd know where to land." The applause, hooting, and whistling from the group was so loud that it could have been heard a mile away, if there had been anyone within a mile to hear it.

Agnes ran over to Billy and started dancing around him, singing, "Billy the Awesome, Billy the Awesome," repeatedly. She was joined by Josephine, who bowed to him while circling the place he had landed as if it were now some sort of holy ground. Tommy gave Billy a high five and howled like a wolf.

Ralph stepped up to give Billy a high five, but when their two hands smacked together, both of their hands glowed a fluorescent blue.

"Man, Ralph, this is so cool," Billy said, staring at his blue hand, which was fading back to normal. "Hey, Tommy, look at this," Billy continued as he held his hand up for Tommy to see. Tommy had been too busy howling to see it happen, and by the time he looked, Billy's hand had returned to normal.

"Aww, what happened to the glow?" Billy looked at Ralph, whose hand had also faded to normal. "You gotta do that again, Ralph; high-five Tommy, and this time make it last longer," Billy said as he grabbed Tommy and nudged him toward Ralph.

"All right, Tommy, high five," Ralph said as he raised his hand into the air.

Tommy stepped into the high five, and they connected with a loud smack. Their hands glowed fluorescent orange, even brighter than before.

"Incredible," Tommy said as he held his hand out to show everyone, turning it around to see it glowing from all sides.

"It's beautiful," Josephine said as she reached out to touch it. She ran her finger along the inside of Tommy's palm, his hand continuing to glow, not affecting her finger.

"Can I touch it?" Agnes asked Ralph as she stepped toward him. Ralph put out his hand to her. She ran a finger along his palm. Instantly the tip of her finger was infused with a red light, leaving a trail in Ralph's palm, a glowing red line. "Wow," Agnes said in a soft voice, and then she turned to Josephine and the rest and said in a louder one, "Hey, you guys, you have got to check this out!"

The group gathered around Ralph's still glowing hand as Agnes traced another line in his palm. Her whole finger started to glow this time as she drew the intersecting line.

"Awesome," everyone agreed with one voice.

"Why is her color red and Tommy's is orange and mine is blue?" Billy asked as he inspected Ralph's hand more closely.

"I'm not sure," Ralph replied. "Hey, Fiddle, do you know why there are different colors?" he asked as the colors began to fade.

"I have an idea as to why there are different colors for each of your friends, but I'd like you to search your heart for the answer."

"Is it because they match our favorite colors? 'Cause mine's blue," Billy interrupted.

"That's not it," Ralph said as he held his palm out toward Billy like a traffic cop stopping traffic, a look of intense concentration on his face. "They are your spirit guides. Well, the colors aren't your guides; your guides are the colors," Ralph said, confusing everyone. "I mean, I can see your spirit guides, and when I made you glow, I made you glow the color of the guide I see with you," he explained.

"What's a spirit guide and what do they look like?" Billy asked. "And what do they do?"

"I am not entirely sure," Ralph answered, rubbing his head like the answer was trapped inside and he just had to massage it out of his brain. "But I think it has to do with your destiny or purpose, like they are a part of you and help guide you through life. They look a little like ghost copies of you guys all dressed up in fancy clothes; I wish I could show you."

~ *Chapter 5: Bootsy* ~

At that moment each member of the group was surrounded by vaporous glowing spirits. There was a ghostly equivalent of each person. Josephine's was purple, but she was not alone; there was also a plant that seemed to grow all around Josephine. It grew quickly to the sky, raining seeds upon the ground as it grew, and then it shrunk down to the size of a sprout and did the whole thing all over again. While this was happening, a crystal ball floated around her head. As each of the group tried to look at the ball, they saw that everything vanished: the ghostly Josephine, the plant Josephine and all its seeds, the ball, and even Josephine herself. After a few seconds of purposely not looking at the ball, each member of the group was able to see Josephine again.

Tommy's ghostly counterpart was busy showing off for Josephine's other self, creating wormholes on either side of her and popping in and out of them, easy as pie. Everyone began to laugh as Billy said, "Looks like ghost Tommy has a little crush on Ghostaphine!"

"An orange crush," Ralph added, and the laughing grew louder.

Suddenly something flew through the group very quickly, fast enough to grab ghost Tommy from the alternating wormholes he was popping into and out of to impress Ghostaphine. The apparition deposited ghost Tommy, all wrapped up in ghostly shackles, unable to move from real Tommy's side. The apparition vanished. In addition to real Tommy and shackled Tommy there was a small orange gnome-like creature wearing a top hat. It seemed to be reading and exhibited no interest in the group at all.

Agnes was surrounded by red animals of every size, all engaged in activities ranging from good-natured play to battle and flesh-ripping feasting. A very red exact duplicate of Agnes stood next to her, patting her on the back, pointing and laughing at a giant red crow feasting on a rat.

As the eyes of the group settled on Agnes, she became slightly self-conscious. The red crow flew off with the rat in its beak; in its place stood the most adorable little red bunny any of them had ever seen.

"Aww," Billy sighed, looking from the bunny to Agnes, who returned a smile. Billy was standing in the center of a circle of intense blue light. Suddenly the circle was just a blur, and a blue ghost Billy was standing next to Billy, nudging him with an elbow and winking in the direction of Agnes. Shortly thereafter, several more ghost Billys appeared, each one performing an amazing stunt.

"It's like watching a village of Smurfs trying to impress a visiting angel of destruction," Ralph joked as the entire area was overrun with ghost Billys.

Everyone but Billy had a good laugh until Billy responded, "Hey, everybody, look at Ralph."

Ralph was standing alone, his own body glowing with all of the colors of the rainbow. Multiple balls of light circled him as if he were the center or nucleus of some cosmic molecule.

"Whoa," the group sighed in awe. Ralph looked at himself and then at Fiddle. All eyes followed his to Fiddle, in search of some explanation.

"What's happening, Mr. Fiddle?" Ralph asked, forgetting the whole "just call me Fiddle thing"; he needed an answer from someone older, wiser, and hopefully in possession of the right answer. "And why can't we see any of your spirit guides?"

Fiddle responded with a warm smile. "I am hiding my guides from all of you for now," he admitted. "I have seen and been many things in my time; I will share each of these with you as I deem it appropriate. As far as what is happening with you, Ralph; I believe it would be best if you discover that on your own, but I can assure you that you are very powerful indeed."

Ralph jumped in the air, yelling, "Awwright!" When he did all of the spirits disappeared.

Silence fell upon the group as they looked around at one another, thinking about what they had seen within themselves and each other.

After a good minute or two, Tommy said, "I don't get it, Fiddle. I mean, I get what you just said about intention; it's just that I didn't set my intention to see the very first wormhole that I saw."

"Good point, Tommy," Fiddle responded. "You see, everyone, Tommy is right. The very first time that your powers presented themselves, you didn't know you had them, but once you discovered your powers, you assumed control of them. In fact, you may still have unknown powers. These too may present themselves without your knowledge. They may come at a time of need or in response to a feeling you have, but once you recognize the power, it is yours to control. It is your responsibility."

The group again turned silent, all of them contemplating their own powers and what they wanted to do with them, how they might be controlled, and what could go wrong. Billy imagined himself just a splat on a tree trunk. Josephine saw herself standing above everyone around her, her foot the size of a football field, her house splintered across her shoelaces. Ralph saw himself disappearing from everyone. Tommy was doing everything he could to not think. From the beginning, his power had been certainly the most confusing; what he needed more than knowledge was understanding.

Agnes was silently mulling over a vision in her mind. It was as if she was seeing into the future, witnessing something a bit difficult to evaluate. The fact was that turning into a bear and demolishing your math teacher's home, boat, cabin, and ice fishing shack, and then swatting him around his living room, adorned with stuffed bear heads and other assorted heads of wildlife, was not only illegal but maybe also a bit judgmental. In the future she would revise her perspective. Telling herself that her math teacher was a terrible teacher and an even worse human being she would take the form of a grizzly and trounce her former math teacher, leaving him belly-up like a dead fish upon the collective mass of his stuffed head collection.

As Agnes sat in reflection, trying to determine if she would, one day, throttle her teacher or not, she felt a knock upon her temple.

The base of her neck and the root of her sinus reverberated as a result.

"He deserved a lot worse," the future voice inside her head, was speaking. "I'm surprised you even let him live," the voice continued. "You know he's just going to go out and kill twice as many bears, elephants, giraffes, and swordfish as he would have if you hadn't smacked him around, so you totally blew it, wasted a good beating," the voice of the future chastised her.

"Maybe I was too soft on him," her future self replied. "But the rest of them, guys just like him, may not be ready for a bear attack," future Agnes reassured herself. "Those guys, those goons," Agnes envisioned her future self watching a video on her smart phone. "They are going to pee in their pants when they find out that there is an intelligent bear that can use the web, and has friends who can shoot video."

Agnes knew that doing something like that was probably not cool with the whole Fiddle/superpower/hero group, but she decided that it was worth looking into.

"Hey, Fiddle." Agnes spoke like she was a server taking an order in a Midwestern diner and she had better things to do than wait for his order. "Can we mess with people? I mean, what if I knew a guy was a jerk, hung up on ego and power, and I turned into a bear and beat the livin' daylights out of him?"

To her surprise, Fiddle responded, "If you decide to beat the livin' daylights out of someone, I most certainly hope that it is not me, and you had better make sure that the jerk deserves it."

"I know what I want to do," Josephine said, as if she had been waiting for a million years to get a chance to talk. She sort of bubbled out and up a bit as she got excited. "I want you all to turn around the other way, close your eyes, and count to three." Josephine sounded remarkably confident. Everyone did as she said.

"Three."

They all turned around, and Josephine was gone.

"Hello," Josephine said.

No one responded or looked around.

"Hello," Josephine said.

No one responded or looked around. Josephine realized that no one could hear her.

"Hello," Josephine said, thinking that her voice should be as loud as always, which had the effect of actually making her voice as loud as she normally spoke despite the fact that she was now nearly microscopic.

The entire group jumped at the voice from nowhere. Even Ralph was taken by surprise. This was not to say that all invisible people looked the same. The truth was they didn't look the same. *Look* was actually a bad word; in the case of transparency it should probably be best referred to as *appear*. According to the "*Book of All Things Actual*", published by the University of Truth, Invisible people didn't look the same because they did, actually, look exactly alike; they simply couldn't be seen; they had no appearance.

"Where are you, Josephine?" Agnes asked as she looked all around.

"Right here," Josephine replied.

Everyone looked directly at Tommy. Even Tommy looked at himself because Josephine's voice seemed to be coming from him.

"She's invisible," Billy said. "Hey, Ralph, go invisible, and see if you can see her."

"I am pretty sure it doesn't work that way," Ralph replied.

"Just try it," Billy pleaded, half-suspecting that Ralph was right.

Ralph sighed and turned invisible and said, "I am now invisible, and I am looking around, and I can't see her."

"Maybe she left," Billy said.

"I didn't leave," Josephine's voice said from Tommy's head area. Tommy began feeling different parts of his face and head. Josephine was actually about the size of a flea and was sitting out on Tommy's shoulder.

"C'mon, Josephine," Tommy begged. "Show us where you are."

"Okay," she responded.

With that she transformed back to her own size moving from Tommy's shoulder to a position right behind his neck.

As she grew she held on to his head until she was full sized and sitting on his shoulders. The sudden weight of Josephine threw Tommy off-balance, but he managed to remain standing as he grabbed her knees and righted himself and Josephine, the towering twosome. He began laughing as he realized what she had done; everyone did. Tommy bent forward far enough for Josephine to jump off of his head like she was playing leapfrog.

"You can shrink too," he exclaimed. "That's awesome. So you can be any size?" Josephine was still laughing to the point of nearly crying. "I think so," she said as she brushed a tear from her eye. "You were like grab [she imitated Tommy's wild search of his own head] and rub, and grab, and your arms were moving all over, and I'm just sitting, parked out on your shoulder, watching the whole thing."

"Funny," Tommy replied sarcastically. He looked around and saw that everyone was still laughing a little at the whole scene. "All right, I guess it was pretty funny," he admitted.

If time travel defines anything at all, it defines the fact that people who can fathom it are not anything like those who can't. More importantly, it establishes the fact that people who understand it have a very hard time explaining it to people who are otherwise predisposed to disbelieving. Tommy stood quietly, mulling over the profound differences in people, imagining how they might react to his abilities.

Okay, Fiddle, what gives?" Tommy snapped as if Fiddle had been holding out on him. "Billy is Mr. Awesome, Ralph is the god of Glow, Agnes is Princess Any-mal, and Josephine is Queen Size-a-Lot, and all I get to do see wormholes?"

Fiddle laughed a deep but good-natured laugh, placed his hand on Tommy's shoulder, and said, "So, Tommy, do you really think that the only thing you can do is see wormholes?"

Tommy looked into Fiddles eyes, trying to see into his brain.

"C'mon, Tommy; you can do better than this," was what Fiddle said. *It's always the smart ones who have the most trouble*, was what Fiddle thought.

Fiddle went on to further think, *but this one has no excuse.*

Fiddle's mind burned like a calculator function tied to a word-search script, through all of the years of his existence, to create the perfect trigger: "If we are t'miss our ferry, we must not pass up our chance for love."

Tommy's eyes changed expression; his mouth changed; his ears, jaw, and hair changed. He had always been a good-looking young man, but, at that moment, he became something of legend. He became, perhaps, the most perfect young man one might envision.

This became immediately apparent by the reaction of the entire group.

Billy saw Tommy as the superhero he hoped he could become; Ralph saw the sensitive genius, no longer conflicted about exposing the weaknesses of those around him. For Agnes he was Billy with sideburns; for Fiddle he was someone familiar and long gone from his life; and for Josephine nothing had changed. What he felt about himself was the most profound change of all. He got it.

Billy looked at Tommy and said, "Hey, man, what got into you? Why are you looking at me like that? Is anybody else seeing this? Tommy looks like he's up to something."

Everyone looked at Tommy, who was definitely up to something. He walked toward Billy with a swagger that said, "I know something you don't know, and I'm about to drop it on you."

"Yeah, Billy, I am up to something, something totally awesome that you are going to love! Check this out," Tommy said as he pulled a phone from his pocket. Billy stepped up next to Tommy, shoulder to shoulder, and looked at the phone in Tommy's hand.

Only seconds passed before Billy hollered, "You have *got* to be kidding me! How did you get this? Where, er, when is this from?" Billy started looking all around him, and then he began to run, jump, and dig like an excited puppy until he returned to Tommy and said, "You have got to show everybody, but first you have got to tell me: how did you do this?"

Tommy said, "I'll show everybody, and *then* I'll tell you how I did it."

The group gathered around him, looking at his phone.

"Hang on, everybody," Fiddle interjected. "Tommy, come over here." Fiddle motioned to a spot next to him. "Let's try this," he continued, waving his hand over the phone while raising both hands to the sky. Immediately a large screen arose from thin air, displaying the contents of the video on Tommy's phone; as if the contents created the viewing area, his video projected from the phone to a slightly distant plane, the audio surrounded them as if they were actually there, within the video.

Even the imagery seemed more three-dimensional than any video capture could be. They were *in* it. Each one of them recognized themselves immediately within the video, and, in that moment, they were once again there. Billy was running away to the other side of a hill to come back and flip through the air in their direction and then land among them. Each one of them watched as the video continued, Tommy's phone hovering in midair, projecting the day's events. Everything that had happened that day had been recorded. They couldn't understand how that could be. Every single one of the members of the group, including Tommy, was in almost all of the shots. It was simply not possible that any of them had recorded the video. They watched as Josephine hid on Tommy's shoulder. They watched as Ralph revealed the spirit guides.

"Okay," Billy shouted. "I have *got* to know how this is possible." Everyone looked around. Tommy was standing near his phone, grinning.

"I'll take it from here." Fiddle spoke as he pulled Tommy's phone from midair and replaced it with his own. He tapped the device, and a slide show of images of Tommy, pointing his camera phone through a variety of wormholes, cycled across the screen.

"You knew I was there," Tommy said to Fiddle. "But how?"

"You develop a sense for these things over the years, Tommy," Fiddle responded.

"The hard part was getting the shots without letting you know I was on to you. Hang on; look at this one. It's my favorite of the bunch."

The next image was that of Tommy, transitioning from his doubtful self to the person he had become.

Fiddle had captured all of the different elements of each state in a single image, as if Tommy had been reconstructed in a collage from a stack of photographs.

"Enough!" Billy looked like his brain was going to explode. "A few minutes before Tommy showed me his phone, he asked you, Mr. Fiddle, why he was only able to see wormholes. So how did this happen?"

"I can make wormholes," Tommy answered. "Anywhere I want them, any time I want them. I was able to go back in time and see you guys do this amazing stuff all over again, leaving my doubting self exactly where I had been standing the whole time. I can't explain it; I just know I can do it."

Fiddle said, "That's right. Tommy can see wormholes, he can create wormholes, and he can even affect and manipulate time and space on a certain level. You've got to be very careful with this one, Tommy, because you could really screw things up."

"I know; I understand," Tommy acknowledged.

Fiddle went on to say, "You remember, like with Josephine's dog…"

Josephine interrupted, "Bootsy? What about Bootsy?" She immediately became fifty feet tall and looked down on them menacingly.

Tommy gasped, "Oh, no, Fiddle; you said we were never ever supposed to tell anybody about what we do when we go traveling through time—anybody!"

"Yeah, you're right, Tommy," Fiddle continued. "But these aren't just any anybodies. I mean, this is the fifty-foot girl we're talking to. Oh, and about that, do you think you could calm yourself and come down here so we can have this conversation face-to-face?"

Josephine restored herself to her normal size. "Okay, Tommy, what's this about Bootsy?" She was still intimidating despite her regular stature.

"Can I tell 'er?" Tommy asked Fiddle.

"Go ahead, Tommy," Fiddle said.

"Okay," Tommy started nervously.

"Uh, well, one day you didn't meet me on the corner. I heard you cry out 'Bootsy,' and then came the sound of tires screeching to a halt, and I ran to your house to see you holding Bootsy, dead in your arms. You were crying, and there was nothing I could do for you. You didn't even go to school that day."

Josephine cringed in disbelief. "What?"

"Yeah, yeah," Tommy explained. "Y'remember that day when you said that there was a car that came really fast down your street and if I hadn't called to tell you I'd be a little late then we would have left earlier and Bootsy might have been hit by that car?"

"Yeah?" Josephine whispered, as if speaking more quietly would help her understand the unbelievable story Tommy was telling her about her beloved pet.

"Well, I wasn't actually late. I was on time, and you did leave a minute earlier. Bootsy chased after you, and the car that came speeding down your street hit Bootsy and killed her."

Josephine continued to look at Tommy in disbelief.

"Well, that day at school I asked Mr. Fiddle if there was anything he could do with wormholes to fix it so Bootsy didn't die.

"He took me to a place that looked like a gallery or museum, but everything was floating in the air all around us, but it wasn't art. It appeared to be moments, frozen in time. There were millions upon millions of them, and I said to Fiddle, 'We'll never find Bootsy in this mess,' but he told me not to worry.

"He waved his hand, and the images parted, he said 'Bootsy,' and an image raced toward us through the parted images. It was an image of Bootsy in your arms, just after he had been struck.

"Fiddle twirled his fingers, and I saw time rewind, like you rewind a movie.

"Fiddle rewound time to just before I left my house, and then he said to me, 'call Josephine, and tell her you are going to be a little late.

Then he said, 'Oh, and not a word of this to anybody, ever, never ever, to anybody.'

"The next thing I knew, I was at my house, standing next to my backpack and cell phone, which were on my kitchen table. I called you and told you I was going to be a little late. I asked you if you'd wait for me, and then I said 'please.' You said you'd only do it for me, and you'd do it because I asked so nicely."

"I remember that day," Josephine said softly. Then she suddenly shouted, "No way!" She jumped into the air. "You guys traveled back in time to save my Bootsy? That is so *cool!*" Josephine reached out for Tommy with arms and hands twice their normal size and pulled him closer to her, and then she went up on her tiptoes and kissed his forehead. Tommy blushed as red as Agnes's spirit guides.

"Ooh-wee," said Billy. "Just look at Tommy blush."

Josephine released Tommy, and her arms returned to normal size as she stepped over to Fiddle.

"Thank You, Mr. Fiddle. I will always remember how you saved Bootsy and will be eternally grateful—forever."

"Redundant but heartfelt," Fiddle responded in his best English accent. "You are absolutely welcome, young lady," Fiddle's English accent was impeccable, and he had thirty distinctly different English accents, just as impeccable, should the need arise.

"Tommy is embarrassed; Josephine kissed him! Tommy is embarrassed; Josephine kissed him," Billy joked as he bounced around Tommy like an annoying talking pogo stick. "Are you gonna kiss her back?" Billy would not let it rest.

He was right, though; Tommy was embarrassed.

Josephine was now looking at him like he was the reason air existed. Anything else could vanish, but air had to be there so Tommy could breathe. Because of Tommy, everyone else who needed air was able to stay alive. It wasn't really true. Josephine knew that, but she remained staring at Tommy.

"Yeah," Agnes said, cutting right through the lovey-dovey mist. "I thought there was something weird going on the other day at school.

I was taking this test, and I could have sworn I had taken the test before.

It was like, I was looking at the questions and I knew all the answers without even thinking.

I didn't even have to like, do my work. I didn't need to write out anything; I just put down the answers. I was done in no time. I even got into a little trouble over that one. My teacher said, 'you got everything right on that test, but you didn't show any work; how am I supposed to give you any credit?'

" My point is, Agnes explained, "I just took that test and got everything right, without any extra work. My teacher got suspicious. He asked me how I could get everything right without writing anything down, and then he asked me one of the questions on the test. I answered right away, and it was right. Then he grabbed a piece of chalk and wrote a question on the board, the hardest one on the test, and he just looked at me, handing me the chalk. I wrote down the answer. It was right. Then he told me to show the work. I didn't really even have to try to figure out the work; I just wrote it down, superfast, and it was right. I got an A."

"Makes total sense to me." Fiddle stepped in. "Whenever we change things, we try to keep everything else as close to the same as possible."

"Does that mean that somebody else's dog got hit that morning?" Ralph asked Fiddle with concern.

"No, Ralph," Fiddle responded. "At least not because of anything we did."

"I am so blown away, Tommy." Josephine giggled. "You saved Bootsy; you're the best!" Her eyes were all glazed over like she was beholding a god.

Tommy lost his cool as he looked at her looking at him; he drooled a bit. "I'm happy you're happy," he awkwardly sprayed through a mouth too wet for consonants.

"Ralph is right though, everybody," Fiddle announced. "We must all be aware of how our actions might affect others. While it probably won't be an even swap of one dog's life for another, there may be a backlash to some of our actions, particularly when we're dealing with time."

"Speaking of that, Fiddle," Ralph said, "what do we tell our parents? We've been gone for a long time, and we didn't even go to school today."

"Don't worry, Ralph." Fiddle laughed. "Between Tommy and I, we're sure to work something out. Just think of our adventures as the world's longest field trip."

~ *Chapter 6: Dinosaurs* ~

"Cool," Billy said as he moved his legs so fast that they created a propulsion system, but not so fast as to fly; he just hovered inches from the ground, "I'm not telling anyone. Fact is, it's better to be somebody human who is amazingly awesome than it is to be a superhero."

Billy was having an epiphany. "Think about it, a human dude," he glanced at Agnes and Josephine and bowed. "or young lady, capable of running the fastest mile in history at the age of eleven, who is..." Billy looked himself over, flexing and twisting as if he had to see every inch of himself to utter the next syllable. "...stocky and would be a hero to all of the kids who have ever been called loser.

"The superhero, on the other hand, is expected to be able to beat the world record for the mile by at least three hundred percent and not break a sweat.

"I would most definitely like to be an awesome dude rather than Superman. But, Fiddle," Billy continued, "you can't tell me that in all your years of having powers, you never used them in a way that you thought might be pushing it just a bit?"

"I was an Englishman of some distinction at the time," Fiddle began, noticing that Tommy and Billy were keen on every word he was saying, motioning to the others to pay attention. "I went back in time to research the dinosaur, to discover places where dinosaurs might have died and to recover their bones. I was an astute archeologist, held in the highest regard." Fiddle paused.

"How *old* are you?" Billy was exhibiting a profound state of having his mind bent and his body was reflecting that state.

The pause was just long enough for Billy to accidentally tie himself into a knot. He just lay there on the ground in a complete knot.

Fiddle blew him off completely and said, accent still intact, "My findings were of the most significance for the time and regarded with the utmost respect in the field. I was able to do all of this because of my powers. I spent most of my summers on a journey in time, collecting facts and making sketches of dinosaurs both small and large.

"On one particular day, during the Late Cretaceous period, I found myself in a most awkward position. I was perched upon a rock, slightly taller than myself, when I spotted a particularly cute Microceratops. He was only a foot tall or so, and he seemed to be playing a game, kicking a rock around like a soccer player.

"As I observed the tiny creature, I felt the rock upon which I sat begin to lurch, back and forth, at regular intervals. Then I saw it, a Tyrannosaurus Rex, stomping its way toward the little Microceratops, which seemed to be unaware of the giant's approach. I was quite aware, however, that I would make a much more satisfying meal for the T. Rex than would my tiny friend, so I took the opportunity to hide in a small cave, just behind the rock I had been sketching on.

"The T. Rex arrived more quickly than I had imagined he could, and in a single motion he bowed his head to the ground and snatched the little Microceratops up in his teeth and gobbled him down. I gasped. The T. Rex heard me and scanned the area. He was so close that I dared not try to make a run for it. But the Rex wouldn't leave; he just stood there, waiting. I totally blew it and gave away my location. I was trying to peek out of the cave when my pencil tin was struck by a brilliant shaft of light, just inside the entrance to my hiding place. The shaft was reflected and struck the Rex directly in the eye. He turned with a fierce cry and batted at my cave with his enormous tail. My cave, as it turned out, was merely a collection of large rocks leaning against one another. As the Rex pounded the rocks, they separated; no longer properly balanced to create my shelter, the cave fell to pieces around me.

"I stood before the Rex, fully exposed, looking quite delicious in my explorer's cap and gear. He lunged down toward me in the same striking motion I had seen earlier; I was to be the supper after his Microceratops appetizer. Fortunately, the wormhole was quicker than the jaws of the tyrant lizard. I fell through the ground and out of harm's way; the Rex would have to find dinner elsewhere." Fiddle paused to accommodate the cheering and applause of all assembled, and then Billy piped up.

"But what did you do wrong?"

"I am coming to that, dear boy," Fiddle continued, still every bit the English gentleman.

"Whilst I was in the wormhole, the thought occurred to me that I could use my method of escape to save that little Microceratops. I reversed direction in time and space and traveled right through the arrival of the Rex, back to the moment I saw the little Microceratops. Only this time I came down from my rock.

"The tiny Microceratops was absorbed in his game. He kicked the pebble, and it rolled directly toward my feet. The Microceratops saw me. He looked as though he was about to run, and then he looked back down at the pebble and up at me again. I tapped the pebble with my foot, and it rolled toward the Microceratops.

"I knew that I only had minutes before the T. Rex would arrive. I had to get my new friend to trust me. In my pocket I had a small pouch of sweets. I crouched down low and pulled a sweet from my pocket. I held it out toward my new friend, who eyed it, sniffing the air around it. I felt the ground move. Suddenly the little Microceratops grabbed the sweet from my fingers. He held it in his little hands and licked at it with his tiny tongue.

"The T. Rex was in sight. I quickly scooped the little Microceratops into my field sack. The Rex was one step away, lunging for the both of us. The ground gave way beneath us as I fell through space with my new friend in tow. I arrived in the old farmhouse where I kept the articles I wished to hide from the public eye, things I have collected that people would want to put in a museum or study under a microscope. I named my new friend Mickey." Fiddle's voice returned to the voice they were all familiar with, no longer the English archeologist, "Mickey is still my pet to this day."

Tommy and Billy both said at the same time, "How *old* are you?"

Fiddle was slow to answer. "Well…"

"And how old is Mickey?" Agnes asked. "And how can you both still be alive?"

Fiddle knew that he wasn't going to get out of this one, and he addressed them honestly. "I am roughly eight hundred and thirty-four of your earth years old."

The whole group gasped in shock. They all looked more closely at Fiddle, sizing him up, trying to understand how he could be so old.

"What do you mean by our earth years? Are you an alien?" Ralph asked, almost afraid of the response.

"No, Ralph; I am human, or at least I started out human, but then I received my powers, and ever since I have been the same age and in relatively the same physical condition, except that I can do things I couldn't do before," Fiddle responded. "And as for Mickey, she is still alive and well because I keep her alive; it is one of my powers. Plus, she has to look after her babies."

"Babies!" Agnes and Josephine shouted for joy.

Agnes continued, "You have got to show us the babies, Fiddle; we have got to see them."

"Well, they aren't babies anymore, Agnes. Mickey was pregnant when I saved her, and I didn't know it. The fact is, I didn't know she was a female until after I got her out of my field sack."

"I don't care how old they are," added Josephine. "I want to see those babies *and* Mickey!"

"Eight hundred and thirty-four years old," Tommy said quietly, pensively. "Is there anything else you'd like to tell us, Fiddle? I mean are there more of you? Could my mom or dad be like you? Am I or are any of us also eight hundred and thirty-four years old?"

Fiddle looked at all of them with deep concern and answered calmly, "My dear children, I have asked you to join me because you were drawn to me, just as I was drawn to you. My purpose is to help you to understand and use your powers to the benefit of humankind, but it is also my responsibility to inform you of the risks. We will encounter a great many situations and life-forms—animal, human, and yes, alien—if we are to accomplish what I have been taught to understand as our destiny. I promise to tell you all that I can tell you, especially when you need it most, and yes, I will show you Mickey, Penelope, and Violet. But I must ask you now: Will you take on the challenge as I understand it? Will you defend humankind from whatever may come, even the actions of its very own members when the time comes?"

"Oh, man! I am totally into it," Tommy said without hesitation.

"Do we get money?" Billy quickly followed.

"Ah, um, I'm afraid not, Billy; you don't get paid," Fiddle explained. "But with the kind of powers you all have, making money isn't out of the question."

"You mean we can tell people we have our powers, like show off and get paid for it?" Billy was really excited at the proposition.

"Not exactly, Billy." Fiddle knew that he was sailing through treacherous waters when trying to provide the moral compass for his group of superpowered kids. "Let's take Tommy for example. He might use his powers to be in the right place at the right time and catch a bit of luck."

"Like the lottery? Eh, Fiddle, Tommy could bop ahead to next week and get the winning numbers, and bang, we're rich! Or a horse race—any kind of gambling really." Billy was really trying to figure the money part out. "But that would be cheating. Like my mom always tells me that there were kids who would sell the answers to tests, and all you had to do was get the cheat sheet and fill in the answers and you'd get a good grade, but that's cheating! She said that it's no fair to the other kids who did study."

"And your mother is right," Fiddle responded. "Keep in mind that she said it would be unfair to the other kids. Think about it that way. If you find a way to make a little money but you don't hurt anyone else or deprive them of their basic rights, then it is probably going to work out just fine. But you don't have to make any money at all if you don't want to. I have made plenty of money for all of us, a few choice investments here and there, helping certain world leaders gain an edge, so don't worry."

"I'm not worried about anything, Mr. Fiddle. I want to become famous! Like a famous skateboarder or a great athlete, y' know, somebody cool." Billy wanted to know just how far he could push it in front of the average human.

Fiddle tried his best to sum it up for Billy: "If you want to be a skateboarder or an athlete, that's fine; just don't break the laws of physics.

"If you begin flying or stop in midair and change direction, people are going to notice that something just isn't right, but if you keep your skills within reason, you could become a very inspirational young man. Think about it: if people knew what each of you can really do, then you would be just like superheroes, and Billy already said that he'd rather be a gifted human than a superhero. So it's up to each of you to determine what you let people know about and see and what you keep hidden."

"Hey, that reminds me," Josephine shouted out. "When I first discovered my powers, I went on a walk, right through town in broad daylight, and I even stepped on things like mailboxes and taxicabs, but no one saw me or got hurt. How did that happen, Fiddle?"

"You did that, Josephine," Fiddle explained. "Maybe not consciously at that point, but it was you who did it. Part of your power is the ability to shield yourself from those who you don't want to see you, to leave the places you walk through unaffected or to demolish everything in your path and send your enemies screaming in fear, whichever you choose. That first time an instinctual process occurred in your brain, enabling you to produce the shield by force of will without any real sense of knowledge. Now, however, you must consciously will it to happen, and you will be able to do it just as easily as you can change size."

"But why on earth did I crush Billy when he punched my toe but nothing happened to Tommy?" Josephine asked, trying to get a better handle on her power.

"That was your subconscious again, trying to protect you," Fiddle expounded. "You said that Billy punched your toe. I can only assume, based on what I have found him to be capable of thus far, that it hurt like the dickens." Josephine nodded as Fiddle continued. "Your subconscious saw Billy as an enemy, while Tommy was a friend. Your one foot became harmless when landing on Tommy, while your other foot hit with the weight of all fifty feet tall worth of Josephine. It's a good thing it was Billy; I'm not entirely sure that any other human being could have survived such a blow."

Josephine's eyes began to sparkle, and her face went all dreamy-dreamy, and then she spoke in a voice from an anime cartoon. "Does that mean that I could walk through a field of flowers and crush bad men in enemy tanks that are driving through the flowers without crushing the flowers while destroying the tanks?"

"Yes," Fiddle responded as Josephine's eyes began to tear up while she smiled from ear to ear. Had she been an actual anime character, her eyes would have taken up at least half of her face, the other half being her big smiling mouth, until she realized everyone was watching her and her eyes and mouth would instantly and simultaneously become two dots and a dashed line with red blushing cheek spots on either side of her totally embarrassed face.

"You see," Fiddle instructed the group, "you are now in control of your powers, and now that they are yours, only you can understand, expand, limit, explore, or control them. I can only advise you now, but it is up to you to define who you are. So I ask you once again: are you ready to become a team and will you dedicate yourselves to the role of guardians of humankind?"

~ *Chapter 7: Totally Awesome Dudes* ~

There was a long silence.

Each one of them looked at one another. A month ago they had been just friends, kids at school, trying to have fun, hoping to expend limited energy on the process. Today they were superheroes, or really gifted humans, and it was up to them.

Billy started to twitch. He was like a lightning bolt stuck inside of a taffy pull. Suddenly he began to hover, his legs doing that superfast motion thing again. "I am all in."

Ralph said invisibly, "me too, Fiddle man."

Josephine became the size of a capuchin monkey and climbed up on Fiddle's shoulder, whispering in his ear, "I'm in."

Inside his other ear he heard, "So am I," and he turned to find a real capuchin monkey, or rather Agnes, sitting upon his other shoulder.

"Hold on a second," Fiddle bellowed, waving his hands as if something important had been missed. In all the exuberance, it had. Certain members of the group, including all of them, had been feeling it, but none of them had said it. "We need a name for this group. We can't just keep saying 'where are Josephine and Agnes or Ralph and Billy and has anyone seen Tommy?' We need to be able to say something like, assemble the..."

"Magnificents." Tommy appeared directly in front of Fiddle despite being considerably farther away in a slightly downhill location engaged in the act of watering shrubbery only a second earlier. "We should call ourselves the Magnificents. It's not exactly the same as any other superhero group name, but it sounds good, and it covers everything that all of us can do."

"Including watering the local vegetation?" Fiddle laughed. It was one of those weird laughs that old people did when they were trying to be humorous. Everyone knew where trying to be humorous led to: if you had to try, then you just weren't.

Billy kicked the awkwardness under the rug with an abrupt, "I was thinking more of like something like the Totally Awesome Dudes."

Another moment of silence.

Until.

"Ahem, *hello*, Billy; we are *not* all *dudes*." Josephine started in low, and then her voice started to grow, and by the time she said "dudes" she was sixty feet tall. She looked down. She was towering over everyone again, so she deflated.

Before Josephine could regain her normal size, Agnes spoke. "Yeah, Billy, we're not *all* dudes. Maybe it should just be The Totally Awesome.

Ralph responded, "Eh, I kinda like the Magnificents better, but we could be the Totally Awesome Magnificents."

Fiddle tried to stop, guide, or at least influence the process: "Okay, okay, we can take our time, everybody. Let's all come up with names, and then we can share them and vote. So think of a name, and we can draw straws for the first pick and vote on each pick, all right? Also, are we all in agreement that each of you is responsible for your own perception in the public's eye?" They all looked at him with similar expressions, meaning that they weren't sure when they had agreed to that or what exactly he meant by that. Fiddle explained, "I can't police your every action, running around setting time back a few minutes if you really blow your cover and do something magnificent." He shot a quick wink at Tommy. "In fact, no matter how hard we try to hide your powers from the world, one day you may have to resort to costumes."

"I like the idea of a costume," Josephine said, as if she could picture it in her mind.

"But it must make you unrecognizable to the public, unidentifiable, invisible."

"I've got that covered," Ralph said from a special little place of emptiness, and everyone laughed.

Billy interrupted, "I'll wear whatever I have to, but that doesn't mean I'm going to be a mild-mannered little boy scout unless I have my costume on. No way, man; I am going to be somebody. I am going to go out for track and field, and I am going to set some new records—not school records, world records."

"That might be pushing it a bit, Billy," Fiddle warned. "The Elders might find it a bit too showy, arrogant, or self-aggrandizing."

They were all thinking it, but Billy took less than three seconds to deliver his response. "Elders? Oh great; we get magnificent powers." Billy traveled thirty feet in an instant to smack Tommy on the back as he corrected himself. "I mean awesome powers, and the next thing we find out is that we've got another set of parents to deal with? C'mon, Fiddle; is there really a group of elders who decide what we can and cannot do?"

"Yes." Fiddle answered, "And no."

Fiddle motioned to the group to gather in close to him. When Fiddle did this gesture, the arms out, hands out to embrace and then pulling in close to him, close to his heart, they all wanted to listen, they came to him, and they sat at his feet, precisely where his arms led them. "All of you. Your parents probably worry that you will hurt yourselves in some way, so they warn you to be careful or outright deny you access to something they worry might maim or destroy you. The Elders do care if you are maimed or destroyed, but they expect that you won't be. They know that you have a lot to learn, which is why they sent me. I know what they expect, most of the time, and if I tell you that you are walking a line, you had better be certain about your next step."

Billy burst from the group, a skyrocketing jump that made anything he had done before look like child's play.

Not one of them was hurt, but the ground pulsed for a moment and he was gone.

Off into the stratosphere he flew, and as he got about halfway up he began to think about a landing. There was time for that; he was still going up, and it would take a while to fall. He was starting to freeze on the outside. It was like his face was completely frozen on the skin layer, but everything below it was normal, and then he began to fall.

Agnes looked at everyone for all of a nanosecond, became a peregrine falcon, and headed skyward.

Josephine had acted even more quickly. Sensing that Agnes would assume flight, Josephine took a dive directly into Agnes's head—her ear, to be precise. And when she turned into a bird, Josephine became even smaller.

Ralph and Tommy just looked at one another.

"Looks like the girls have got it handled." Tommy said.

Billy, Agnes, and Josephine were gone, and suddenly a foot the size of a whale engaged the ground a few feet from Ralph and Tommy.

"Josephine," Tommy asked the moment she appeared. "Can you see him? And how tall *are* you? Your foot is *huge!*"

Ralph and Tommy were instantly swiped from the surface of the earth and placed into the middle of a field. Roughly two hundred feet away, a strange bird was turning circles in a field, pecking and pecking. Within seconds a small circle appeared in the turf. Suddenly the bird became larger, pecking and pecking all over again. The turf trimmed lower with each peck, and the cycle repeated. Within seconds a target appeared; the last band, delineated by the now giant bird, was etched just inches away from Tommy's foot. Tommy looked at the bird and then at Ralph.

"Agnes," they said in unison. Within seconds the bird stopped pecking, changing size and shape as it walked toward them as a fully reinstated Agnes.

"Billy will be here soon," she said, looking up in the direction that giant Josephine was looking. Ralph and Tommy looked at the same spot. All of them noticed that Josephine had begun to shrink. The other large foot had come into view and was drawing closer at an amazing rate. Before they knew it, Josephine was lifting the foot over their heads as she shrunk to her normal size, just clearing their heads before she planted it on the ground, directly next to her other leg, so that she stood just a few feet away from Tommy.

Her eyes were fixed just above the target as she counted down: "Five, four, three, two, one." All eyes were on the center of the target precisely when Billy hit the ground.

Actually, he didn't hit the ground.

He hovered just above the ground, his arms and legs moving so quickly they were nearly indiscernible.

Then, as suddenly as he had dropped from the sky, he stepped to the ground, out of his hovering state, at the exact center of the target.

"Woo-eee!" the group cried out with one voice as they ran to Billy.

They all cheered and clapped their hands, whistled, howled, and hooted as they bounced around in a circle with Billy at the center.

As the applause died down, one set of hands continued, clapping at a slow rate. "Yeah, yeah, bravo, everyone loves you," it was Fiddle. He was standing a few feet away from the group. None of them had noticed him there before, they had forgotten about Fiddle the moment Billy had left the ground. "Tell me Billy, were you just showing off?"

Billy smiled and the rest of them reacted like any group of schoolchildren did when they were caught doing something wrong. They hung their heads and walked around in tiny circles with each other as if it made them small enough to not be noticed. All except Billy, who said, "I was doing more than that."

Fiddle's eyes ignited, but his body, even his facial expression, remained unchanged. His hands still together from the final clap, Fiddle said in his most official and unamused voice, "Impress me."

"I know you think I'm the dumb one of the bunch, but I think that what you just said is dumb." Billy was stopping every urge he had to shoot off into the sky again because he was pretty certain that he would lose his powers at any moment. He couldn't explain it, but he felt like Fiddle was warning him more than anyone else in the group. "You told us that the elders would decide if we could have our powers or not, but you also told us that we are now in control of our powers. If that's true, then we should test our abilities and even the elders can't take away our powers for doing that. I don't care about being smart; I don't care about being right. I just want to do whatever I can, while I can, and if anyone messes with me or my friends, I will make sure they don't do it again!"

"I couldn't have said it better myself, Billy," Fiddle smiled.

"However, I do not think you are dumb. Furthermore, the elders *can* take away your powers, but that is *not* going to happen today. So, Tommy, let's see if Billy is right. Let's test our powers. Where are we going?"

"Really?" Tommy asked, half out of surprise and half because he knew where, or perhaps more appropriately when, he wanted to go.

"Yes," Fiddle responded. "I believe that Billy understands what we must do. It's time to learn to control your powers. How do you all feel about fitting into a time with which we might already be familiar, a time we may have already experienced?" he asked. Tommy wants to take us back in time, if I'm not mistaken," he smiled as he looked at each member of the group. They were all becoming aware of Fiddle's concern, six people in one place, each of them knowing what would happen next. If any one of them said the wrong thing to a classmate, parent, or teacher, their cover would be blown.

"Where are you taking us?" Josephine asked as she stepped in close to Tommy.

"Well, I was thinking that we might as well have some fun, not to mention the fact that I am super hungry." Tommy continued, "Do you guys remember the field trip to the amusement park?"

Both Ralph and Billy began to salivate like dogs.

Everyone got really excited. Josephine bounced up and down as she held Tommy's forearm with both hands; Agnes danced in circles with Billy, while Ralph continued drooling as he rubbed his belly.

"Dragonland, here we come!" Tommy concentrated.

"Excuse me for one second, Tommy," Fiddle interrupted politely. "I was wondering if you might deliver us to that little cotton candy stand, you know, the one that's tucked in behind the Dragon's Lair. I have a hankering for something sweet."

"It would be my pleasure, Fiddle." Tommy smiled as he concentrated again. "Here we go," he said excitedly as he opened a wormhole right before their eyes. He held out a hand to Josephine, who took hold of it just as he leaped into the wormhole.

Billy and Ralph dived at the hole while Fiddle bowed and motioned to Agnes. "Ladies first!"

She stepped into the wormhole, holding her hands out as if she were slightly raising her skirt over a threshold, closely followed by Fiddle, whose very next words were, "I'd like a large rainbow swirled cotton candy, please."

~ *Chapter 8: DragonLand* ~

Sure enough, Tommy was good to his word. Mr. Fiddle got his cotton candy. Ralph and Billy were eying the french fry stand.

"Don't run, Billy," Mr. Fiddle advised through muffled lips. It was all that Billy could handle, fighting the urge to run to the deep-fried goodness, but he walked at Ralph's speed, which was essentially running like an average boy. It took them less than a minute to reach the stand, five minutes to get their fries, and thirty seconds to eat them.

Josephine and Agnes went to the restrooms, and Tommy did exactly what he had the last time he had lived this particular second: he stared at the top of the Dragon's Plunge, which in this particular second qualified as the tallest coaster in the world, but this time he thought, "Eh, that's not so high." Tommy actually said it as he thought it, at the precise time that Mark Matheson walked by with a couple of his football buddies.

"Not so high, Tommy?" he taunted. "Then why haven't you ridden it yet?" He stepped in close to Tommy, feeling a little powerful with a couple of friends at his back. Suddenly Tommy had two friends at his back. Billy had grabbed Ralph, who had turned invisible out of instinct. He became visible just as Billy arrived behind Tommy; Billy had moved so quickly that he was practically invisible. It was as if Tommy had sent a distress call and the others had responded. All of the others, in fact. In a tree just above the bench where Tommy had encountered Matheson sat a crow, a large black crow with a tiny Josephine sitting on its back. Josephine was so small that she could not be seen. Billy and Ralph stepped out from behind Tommy.

"Hey, look who's here," Matheson laughed. "I didn't see you little shrimps behind Tommy here. Excuse me, one little shrimp and one fat one."

Matheson had a food tray in his hands. There were a burger, fries, a drink, and something that resembled a small throw pillow saturated with frosting. He held the tray in one hand and reached out to slap the top of Billy's head.

"Do shrimp even have fat?" Billy asked as he looked at Ralph while nonchalantly blocking Matheson's slap with ease.

Ralph responded as if nothing else were going on as Matheson attempted to hit Billy again. "You know, Billy, I think they do," Ralph cheerfully added. "But it's the good kind of fat, you know, the healthy, unsaturated type."

Matheson tried twice again to hit Billy, and each time Billy blocked it like he was shooing away a fly. Matheson was growing extremely frustrated and therefore quite angry.

"If I didn't have this stupid tray, I'd flatten you, you fat little shrimp," he yelled at Billy.

Tommy and Ralph stepped away from Billy and Mark Matheson, and Agnes squawked three times and flew away. For this the girls wanted to watch as girls. Agnes quickly dove behind an ice cream sandwich stand, where both girls changed back just in time to hear Billy's response.

"I'll hold it for you, then." Billy laughed and reached out for Matheson's tray.

Matheson didn't really reason it out. If he handed the tray to Billy, and if he was to be successful at pounding on Billy, that would probably make his food fall, but Matheson wasn't reasoning anything at the moment, so he handed Billy the tray.

Matheson took a giant swing at Billy's head, but Billy limbo danced so low, so quickly that Matheson's fist whiffed right over him. Billy still had the tray perfectly balanced. As he popped back up, he picked up the burger.

"Nice, juicy-looking burger, here, Mark; don't mind if I do!" Billy sunk his teeth into Matheson's burger.

Matheson became enraged and took a dive at Billy, who neatly scooted aside, too fast to grab.

Billy stood over Matheson, took a fry from its little bag, dipped it in some ketchup, and ate it with an "Mm" sound. Matheson bent his right knee and kicked out as hard as he could, directly into Billy's thigh. It hit with the force of an angry rhino, but it didn't budge Billy an inch. In fact, Billy licked his fingers and reached down for Matheson's foot, which he found with his free hand. Grabbing Matheson by the ankle, he twisted Matheson's entire leg, forcing him to roll over onto his face.

Billy took a long, slow sip from the drink on the tray as he lowered the tray to the middle of Matheson's back, where he set it down. He released Matheson's foot.

Billy pulled a ten-dollar bill from his pocket and dropped it next to Matheson's head.

"Thanks for lunch," he said as he walked away toward the Dragon's Plunge. Tommy, Ralph, Josephine, and Agnes filed in front of Matheson's football buddies and smiled.

"Going to take the plunge, boys," Ralph said as they left. "You're welcome to join us if you'd like," he added, knowing full well that they were not going to follow them.

Mark Matheson was lying on the ground, looking around to see if anyone had witnessed what had just happened. He stood up angrily, and the tray spilled its remaining contents onto the ground. He picked up the ten-dollar bill, shoved it in his pocket, and said, "Why didn't you guys do anything?" The two friends just stood there chewing, looked at Matheson, and shrugged their shoulders. Matheson pulled the ten-dollar bill back out of his pocket and said, "I'm gonna get another burger." Then he walked away in the opposite direction of Billy and the gang.

Billy was whistling to himself as the others caught up with him.

"That was awesome," Tommy laughed as he stepped alongside Billy.

"Maybe a little too awesome," Billy responded, as he saw Mr. Fiddle walking directly toward them. He wasn't smiling.

"I get that you think Mr. Matheson had it coming to him, Billy, but I urge you to do your best to ignore him and others like him as much as you can. We never know who's watching. Sorry; that's not entirely true. I have a pretty good idea of just who might be watching at any given time. Fortunately, Misters Matheson, Smith, and Reynolds were the only people from your school within a half-mile radius. Still, try not to hurt anyone." Mr. Fiddle continued in the direction he had been walking and entered a tailor's shop. As soon as he did, a hand reached up from within the doorway and turned the little open sign to the side that read "closed."

"Guess you got away with it," Ralph said as he slapped a hand on Billy's shoulder." And if I may add my comments, I would like to commend you on the eating his food while embarrassing him part of the whole event. I almost wish that everyone in the school saw it, but I'll be satisfied with Smith and Reynolds. You know those guys can't keep their mouths shut."

"That's what I'm afraid of," Billy said, without really sounding like he meant it.

"No, you're not, Billy," Agnes teased. "You know you want everyone to know that you defeated and humiliated Matheson—heck, I want everyone to know it!" She raised her hand, asking for a high five, and Billy happily obliged.

"There it is," Tommy said as he craned his neck to see the top of the Dragon's Plunge.

"I've been a lot taller than that," Josephine said as she placed a hand on Tommy's shoulder. He smiled at her, knowing that she was just trying to settle his nerves. Even if you had already ridden the coaster or faced a greater height, going up on top of the tallest roller coaster in the world got the adrenaline flowing. Even Billy, who had already jumped higher than any roller coaster in the world and landed without aid or anything to slow him down, felt a little nervous about riding the Dragon's Plunge. But it was a good kind of nervous.

They turned the corner to find a line that stretched past the two-hour point.

"Two hours?" Ralph cried out in disgust.

"There is no way I am waiting for two hours to ride that thing again." Billy was trying to think of a way to game the system. Now that he had superpowers, he wanted everything bigger, faster, and more awesome, and he was pretty sure that he could have it that way.

"We gotta think of something, you guys." Tommy was thinking about it too. He was thinking that this time he would keep his hands up the whole way, and he didn't want to change his mind. "I got it," Tommy said, as if he had just solved a complicated puzzle or a challenging riddle. Looking at Agnes, he continued, "We're going to need a wild animal."

It only took him minutes to outline his plan, and everyone agreed that it would work.

The group split up. Agnes went north toward the JungleLand theme area of the park, while Josephine went shopping at the most popular gift shop in the park, Snazzie's, where she purchased one of each type of clothing article available. She bought everything from the Dragon's Plunge jersey to the newest offering, Belfry Bats Baggies, the pants that scare the pants off ya. She even bought the Dragon's Head skullcap, a modified baseball cap that turned the wearer's head into a dragon's head. The clerk carefully placed all of her items into an ornately branded bag, which she recommended to Josephine might best be locked in one of the guaranteed safe lockers along the northeast entrance to JungleLand. Josephine thanked the clerk and promptly walked in the direction of the men's restrooms, where she shoved the bag into a trash can. She walked away quickly.

Seconds later Billy arrived. Opening the trash can, he rescued the bag and moved into the restroom. He took a private stall and changed his entire outfit. He emerged from the restroom looking like an advertisement for the theme park. He walked directly toward the Dragon's Plunge like he was going to cut in line, his oversized sunglasses with dragon wings popping out of the sides obscuring his identity, even to the kid with the big head who sat next to him in math. People started pushing him back out of the line. They were yelling at him to go to the back when a large bird unlike any of them had ever seen plummeted from the tops of the trees on the outskirts of JungleLand and scooped him up with talons like sickles. The bird dropped him at full speed into a nearby tree trunk. He crumpled to the ground as the bird circled back. Everyone ran. They ran in all directions. It took less than a minute for the line to clear. Billy tore the clothes off, stashed them in an abandoned stroller, and headed to the front of the line, where he was joined by the rest of the group.

The guy running the ride couldn't see what had happened from his post on the platform.

"What happened to everybody, man?" he said as he pulled back on the bar to let them pick their seats.

Billy, Agnes, and Ralph ran to the front, and Josephine and Tommy ran to the back.

Tommy liked having longer to dread the inevitable drop, while Josephine lived for the whoosh just before the big drop. The kind of whoosh you could only really feel if you were in the very last car. Usually there were lines within lines once you reached the platform, and those lines were longest on both ends. People always seemed to crowd into the lanes for either the first seat or the last seat of nearly any roller coaster. These kids weren't different, sick, or weird; they were just like everyone else, and they knew where they liked to sit. Sure, occasionally they would sacrifice their favorite seats to get a chance to ride again, but never when the seat they wanted was open or when the ride was new. Today it was both.

Even though each of them had ridden the ride before, the last time they experienced this day, no one else at this place in time had the same privilege. It was opening day, one week before summer vacation. This was epic, a trip backward in time to ride the world's tallest rollercoaster on opening day.

Phil, the guy who was running the ride, looked to the other park employees for some reassurance that it was okay to start the cars on their inevitable quest to the pinnacle of the world's tallest first hill. The girl who was working the end of the train searched the staircase for riders and turned back to Phil. She waved her hand, signaling him to go ahead and start the train.

He quickly said, "Welcome to the Dragon's Plunge, *the* world's tallest, fastest, and twistiest coaster. You will reach speeds of over one hundred miles per hour and experience zero gravity in at least two distinct parts of the ride. If you are riding, you have agreed to the terms and conditions and are quite aware that your brains may no longer be inside of your head when the ride comes to a complete stop. Just kidding."

A pre-recorded message about rider safety played through the speaker system surrounding the train.

Phil signaled to the controller, dropped his hand, and said, "Thank you for riding the Dragon's Plunge, and may you rest in peace."

The train ripped out of the platform, straight into a tunnel.

Even though each one of them had ridden the ride before, twice in fact, none of them could remember exactly how it was set up.

There was a slowing down and then a creaking as the cars suddenly lurched to the right. They were still in the total darkness of the tunnel as the train lurched back to center and gradually dragged its way up a long vertical climb. After what seemed like ages, the front car broke through to daylight, the top of the hill, still a good thirty feet away. Billy's hands were already up. Ralph and Agnes joined him. As their car reached the top of the hill, Tommy and Josephine were exiting the tunnel. Josephine reached out for Tommy's hand. Her lungs filled with excitement.

"Here it comes," she said, and within a breath all time stood still. They inhaled in unison as they whipped over the top, the plunge, so deep it made the train race at unprecedented speeds. Their minds were screaming with release, but their voices still had no air, until suddenly their lungs supported a single sound in perfect harmony: "Woo-eee!" And just as quickly they were climbing the next hill.

The three in front were high-fiving, congratulating one another on a hands-up plunge on the tallest hill in Earthendom, when Billy started to fidget. He collapsed his lungs and pulled his shoulder blades out of their sockets. He wiggled his way out from underneath his chest bar. He turned around and faced Agnes and Ralph.

"I want to try something," he said as the coaster climbed its way toward the top of the second hill. Incidentally, the second hill happened to be the fourth tallest hill of any roller coaster in the world at the time.

"What are you going to do now, Billy?" Agnes asked as they came closer to the top of the second hill.

"Watch!" Billy cried out as he stood on the front of the coaster. Mr. Fiddle was watching Billy. He didn't admit it to any of the group, and he would never share it with his superiors, the Elders, but on a certain level he envied Billy. Actually, it wasn't really envy; it was more like a life vicarious. He saw Billy as the boy he would love to be again, full of hope and imagination, a drive to have fun, and a quest for appreciation and love.

Billy had no idea that Mr. Fiddle was watching as he leaped from the front of the train, halfway down the second hill, and tucked into a triple somersault with a quarter twist that landed him neatly in the car in front of Tommy and Josephine. In a single motion, he collapsed his rib cage, sunk his shoulders into what small amount of space was left, and made his head turn in a thoroughly implausible fashion until he expanded again to occupy the seat immediately before Tommy and Josephine, chest bar in place.

"Hey guys," he laughed as he waited for their approval.

"Awesome!" both Josephine and Tommy shouted in response to Billy's acrobatics.

Suddenly everything went dark.

This was the best part of the new ride. It took a ninety-degree dive from a flat rail, in complete darkness, to a depth of 1,024 feet. When it reached this point, it flattened out for the length of the train and then rocketed straight back up. The whole time the train was underground, riders could see the earth that they were traveling through. The area of the ground that had been dug up was shored up by thick Plexiglas and steel, revealing the sedimentary layers, but there was hardly time to discern what was dirt rock or clay before the coaster whipped up to ground level. Once again the ride flattened out, cruising through a tube that was lined with people, waiting for their turn to ride. This time, however, there were a water bottle and a stuffed dragon that had been thrown by someone who had been trying to run from a giant bird. Billy laughed when he saw it.

"It's not that funny." Mr. Fiddle's voice came from the seat beside him. He whipped his head around and saw Mr. Fiddle, sitting securely beneath a chest bar, looking at him. "You're going to have to rein it in a bit," Mr. Fiddle added. "Amusement parks have cameras all over the place, you know. Ah, my favorite part." Mr. Fiddle smiled as the coaster wound its way up a tight counterclockwise spiral and then dove into a wider clockwise spiral. The train caterpillared over a series of progressively smaller hills until coming to rest back at the platform. A few people were now on the platform waiting to ride, and more were arriving.

"Can we go again?" Agnes asked the guy who was running the ride. He looked hesitant to allow them a second ride, so she said, "If you let us, I'll tell you a secret." Phil leaned in close. "The girl in the box up there, the one who starts the ride..." Agnes smiled and continued, "She likes you." Phil turned red as he looked over at the control booth.

"How do you know?" Phil asked nervously.

"We girls know these things," Agnes responded even though the truth was that she had already seen them together later in the day.

Phil let them stay on the ride as he motioned for the new arrivals to board the train.

"Go ahead, Phil, ask her out while we're riding again, and I'll bet you she says yes before we get back," Agnes coaxed as the last of the new arrivals got on board. Phil smiled nervously as he gave the signal to Veronica, the girl in the booth, to start the ride.

It was another awesome ride, but this time Billy kept his seat as Mr. Fiddle hummed "Somebody's Watching Me," a one-hit-wonder tune that Billy recognized without knowing how. He hummed it throughout the entire ride.

At the end of the ride, Mr. Fiddle said, "Billy, I'd like to show you something."

Agnes looked across the platform to see what had happened to Phil. He saw her looking his way and gave her a thumbs-up, shielding the gesture from Veronica for two reasons; one was that he was slightly embarrassed and didn't want Veronica to know that a young girl had told him to ask her out, and the other was that it was the signal to start the ride. Agnes smiled as she and Ralph met up with the others who were closer to the exit. Billy walked reluctantly along with Mr. Fiddle.

"When did you get here?" Ralph asked Mr. Fiddle. Billy turned and shot him a nasty face.

"I want you all to see this," Mr. Fiddle answered as he led the group to the photo shop that was associated with the ride. Snapshots of the last two rides were on display for every seat in the ride. Cameras had been placed at strategic locations to capture the expressions of riders on the world's tallest roller coaster.

Billy was afraid to look. Mr. Fiddle looked on as Billy surveyed the images from the previous ride. He studied each seat's photo carefully. There were mostly images of empty seats, and everywhere else the screen was black.

"How did you do that, Mr. Fiddle?" Billy asked in a stunned and humble tone.

"I covered for you this time, Billy, but don't make me do it again," Mr. Fiddle said in his most stern voice. "And that goes for the rest of you," he continued as he turned to the group. "No more little shenanigans." Mr. Fiddle softened his tone a bit and appealed to the hearts of the kids: "We have some important work ahead of us, and let's not blow it by messing around."

"Sorry, Mr. Fiddle," the group said in unison as they walked toward another food court.   "Anybody hungry?" Mr. Fiddle asked as he eyed the turkey leg stand.

"I am," was the unanimous response.

Mr. Fiddle reached in his pocket and nudged Billy with his elbow. In his hand there was a gift card with a fierce-looking dragon on the front. He gave it to Billy, who opened it. Inside was a photograph of Billy standing on the front of the Dragon's Plunge while Agnes and Ralph cheered him on. Billy looked at Mr. Fiddle, who made a secretive motion, instructing Billy to tuck the photo away someplace safe. Billy smiled as he stashed the photo in his buttoned pocket on his baggy shorts.

"Thanks, Mr. Fiddle," Billy said gratefully.

Mr. Fiddle just winked and replied, "Turkey leg?"

"Oh yeah," Billy shouted, full of relief and hunger at the same time.

The whole group grabbed a bunch of food. They really hadn't eaten anything of substance since the morning, but that morning hadn't happened yet, so they were even hungrier.

Josephine downed three "Dragon Scales" (tacos) in no time. Tommy polished off an "Excalibur" (Philly cheesesteak sub), while Ralph and Agnes went for a couple of "King's Crowns" (half-pound burgers with everything). Billy and Mr. Fiddle went for the "Mighty Mace Combo" (gigantic turkey legs, onion rings, and fries served on a shield).

All items were served with drinks that could be supersized for a dollar more.

If supersized, the drinks would be served in authentic replica steins, the kingdom's finest (cheap plastic, made in China).

They supersized.

It wasn't the best food, nutritionally speaking, that a superpowered group could consume, but it tasted good, and they were hungry. Tommy mentioned that fact to the rest of the group, and then he asked Mr. Fiddle something Billy had thought of right away but forgot to ask.

"Does it matter what we eat now that we have powers?"

Mr. Fiddle thought about the question for a while, and then he answered, "You should eat just like you would if you didn't have your powers. Things will happen to you, you know, like you might catch a cold or even break a leg depending on your powers. You might develop cancer for all I know, although in eight hundred years I have never known of one of us actually dying from illness." He looked far away and then snapped out of it. "Fighting! Fighting is usually what does it; that and rematerializing inside of a solid object, but I'm pretty sure that's an urban myth."

Tommy stopped drinking from his stein. "Thanks, Mr. Fiddle; that's very enlightening." He began to clean up his stuff and offered to dispose of Josephine's trash as well, and she nodded. "Hey everybody, let's go have some more fun," Tommy urged, trying to shake the vision of his future self, cancer ridden and half rematerialized into a large cement pillar under an overpass. Everyone stood up with a similar melancholy, as if struggling with comparable visions.

Mr. Fiddle happily stood up, brushed the crumbs from his lap, and smiled at the sparrow, who rushed for a chunk of french fry. "If you really want to have some fun, might I suggest the Fungeon? Lots of things can happen in a fun house. People will believe almost anything they see in a fun house, even if they can't explain it."

Synchronistically their moods changed as they realized what Mr. Fiddle was alluding to. Tommy's eyes lit up as he whispered with maleficent intent, "We are going to seriously mess with some people."

The others were laughing and nodding in agreement when Mr. Fiddle suggested, "I have a friend who is a medieval tailor.

He actually is, and he works in that nice little shop over there."

He pointed to a small house that looked far more genuine than any of the other attractions in the park. There was a sign over the door that read, "Ye Olde Tailor's Shoppe." "Everyone here thinks it's an act," Mr. Fiddle continued, "but he is over six hundred years old, and he's been sewing since he was a young boy."

Agnes turned to Billy and bared her teeth. "I vanna be a vampire, and I'm going to suck your blood!"

"You wouldn't hurt a simple friar, would you?" Billy joked as he held his fingers crossed in front of him, making a pudgy-fingered crucifix. Agnes backed away as if burned by the sight of a holy relic.

"Okay, everybody; let's get in the shop before we get all worked up," Mr. Fiddle instructed. "After all, I don't know what Chuck has on hand."

Agnes put her arms out wide as she snapped her hands into a ninety-degree speak-to-the-hand position and snapped, "Wait a second!" She snapped her hands a full 180 degrees and pointed her fingers at her feet. She was playing a wild hunch, but less than an hour ago she had been a giant bird, so she figured that nothing was impossible. "Chuck Taylor?"

Mr. Fiddle gave a slight smile, the kind that says yes as quietly as possible while trying to say "but don't freak out about it" at the same time. It didn't work.

"Chuck cluckin' Taylor? Are you kiddin' me? *The* Chuck *Cluckin'* Taylor? Oh my cluckin' dog. I am *not* going to meet Chuck *cluckin! Taylor* without my red pair." No one in the group could have seen this coming; not even Josephine, Agnes's best friend, had any idea how deeply Agnes admired Chuck Taylor.

Until that moment, none of them had had any idea who Chuck Taylor was—in fact, at that moment, they still didn't know who Chuck Taylor was.

And then suddenly the bell over the door was tapped into life as the group entered Ye Olde Tailor Shoppe.

Agnes's eyes glazed over as she gazed upon the man who had single-handedly marketed the most famous basketball sneaker of all time, the sneakers she had on her feet, the ones her dad had bought for her mom when they were little and he wanted to impress her, the ones he had never given her because he was too shy, and now that she was older and her parents were no longer together, she had rescued them from the trash her mother had dumped the day after her father kissed her good-bye.

~ *Chapter 9: The Fungeon* ~

"Chuck Taylor died in 1969, one day before his sixty-eighth birthday; he was sixty-seven years, three hundred and sixty-four days old. And I," Agnes stuttered on. "I am—I am standing in his medieval tailor shop in an amusement park nearly a half century later, looking into his eyes…"

"Hello, Agnes. Chuck Taylor," Chuck introduced himself. "Charles Zachariah Taylorson of Hampshire at your service, m' lady." He extended his hand, palm up. Agnes placed her hand in his, and he kissed the back of her hand. She began to sob. "Here, here, now, young lady," he consoled her. "I am quite sure that we can find suitable attire for any event her graciousness wishes."

Agnes looked up at him with dripping eyes. Warmed by the kindness of his voice, she felt almost embarrassed to mention, "I left my vintage red high-tops at home. I keep them in a special place so they don't get mixed up with these" Agnes pointed to the battered high-tops discarded by her mother. "These are faded," she sighed.

Charles Zachariah Taylorson of Hampshire rubbed his chin, scratched his head, and said, "Worn with love I should think, still, a vampire in vintage, pristine, red high-tops; sounds delightful. What are you exactly? About a size seven by today's measurements, I would wager."

Agnes stared at him for a minute and said, "Seven; yes, that's me; yes, I'm a size seven."

Chuck Taylor reached his hand up above his head and grabbed what looked like the bell end of a twisted trumpet that hung from the ceiling and spoke into it. "Classic canvas high-top, red, size seven, please." He released the trumpet. Looking at Agnes, he continued, "That should do it. Oh, hold on." He grabbed the bell end of the twisted trumpet thing once again and held it to his mouth. "And a permanent marker, please. Black, preferably," he said with a nod to Agnes's black leather skirt.

Mr. Fiddle was turning the "open" sign to "closed" and latching the door just as two fairies emerged from an otherwise empty air duct in the ceiling. They were carrying a box, suspended from shoelaces, and a permanent marker. Chuck reached up and retrieved both. He opened the box. Inside was a pair of size seven red, vintage, canvas, Chuck Taylor high-tops. He exhumed them from their corrugated slumber and uncapped the Sharpie. He wrote "from Chuck Taylor" from the ankle to almost the toe on the outside of each shoe. On the inside edge of each shoe, he wrote "4gnes." He handed them to her.

"That's so cool," Agnes responded. "Thank you! I can't—I mean—I mean it says 'For Agnes from Chuck Taylor.' Somebody *please try* to have more awesome shoes than mine."

Chuck was fast, blindingly fast—literally. He had to instruct the five to either keep their eyes closed or to wear goggles. Naturally, anyone who wasn't being worked on wanted to watch Chuck work so he and his fairies found enough goggles for the whole group. The person being worked on was instructed to stand still and to move only when repositioned by Chuck himself.

Within an hour the entire gang was suited up. Agnes was the vampire. Chuck had managed to convince her that a vampire in the Fungeon would be far more impressive in pointy boots rather than high-tops but he promised to keep the high-tops safe. Billy had indeed become a convincing friar; his bald cap made him look exactly the same but bald, but the wrinkled skin makeup that Chuck had applied was so convincing that even his friends had trouble recognizing him. Josephine had become the Queen of England. She was so convincing that Mr. Fiddle had a flashback to the time he had saved her from what would have been a nasty fall. He would have recounted the entire event if Chuck had let him, but Charles Zachariah Taylorson of Hampshire would stand for no chatter while he performed his costumery—a word he knew did not exist but loved so much that he used it anyway. This was the nature of Chuck; he was a man of considerable talents, not the least of which was creating drama.

Tommy had asked to be a knight, nothing special, just an "*I can slay dragons with my awesome sword*" kind of knight, a knight who lived in service to the queen. Chuck suggested a different costume, a different kind of knight, a dark knight, a dark king! Tommy was fitted with the most seriously "snaff" armor. *Snaff* was an Internet term; no one knew when it was first used, and no one knew, until recently, what it meant. Snaff was a fashion term. Snaff simply meant whatever was needed at the time. It could be argued that Charles Zachariah Taylorson had actually invented the term long before the internet came into existence but the words of a simple tailor were rarely transcribed in those days.

Ralph kept his request as snaff as possible; he wanted to be a zombie. Timeless, unavoidable, misunderstood, and terrifying—the zombie, the mummy, any undead being roaming its way around the world of the living making things just a bit uneasy. Sure, he could become invisible at will, but when he was seen, he wanted to be scary. Chuck obliged with shoulder-popping sockets and dripping flesh that made Ralph sick just wearing it, but he loved the idea so much he went with it anyway.

"Well, my friends, I would say that you are ready to put on a brilliant show, a right good scare, a presentation fit for a queen." And in saying so, Chuck Taylor kissed the hands of Josephine and Agnes and waved as he bowed to Ralph, Billy, and Tommy. The girls curtsied, and the boys bowed in response. "Now go, and by all means, Tommy, please provide the quick route; you don't want to miss the chance to mess around a bit with the younger kids." Chuck was right; field trips involving kindergarten through fifth grade generally left the park earlier than the higher grades, and it was nearing mid-afternoon. Tommy looked to Mr. Fiddle for approval. He simply tipped a fashionable medieval hat he had donned, and the five were gone.

"It's always such fun initiating a new batch, isn't it, Fiddle?" Chuck asked with a wistful expression. "It's really too bad we can't do the sort of things they do anymore, isn't it? That Tommy; he's so close, isn't he? And Agnes, all the promise of a new fire but something even more special with that one."

"You're just saying that because you are her hero," Fiddle responded.

"No, I am not, Bartholomew," Chuck corrected Fiddle, adding importance by using his first name. "You have seen her natural ability. No one so young has ever transmogrified so easily. She is quick and believes in nothing, no rules, no higher power. You remember the last time we encountered that explosive mix, that dynamic possibility."

Fiddle nodded and added, "It nearly cost you your life."

Charles Zachariah Taylorson of Hampshire stood up and said, "And I would gladly give it for another one like her." Fiddle and Taylor raised imaginary glasses to a beautiful memory. The two men sat in silence as they remembered a girl whom both of them had loved.

"Why can't we have a bit of fun, my old friend?" Fiddle asked as he fondled an outfit befitting a medieval nobleman.

"Why indeed?" Chuck responded as he flashed into action, adorning Mr. Fiddle with the fine outfit with puffy sleeves and sparkles of gold, topping it off with the splendid hat Fiddle had donned minutes before.

"And I will go as a funeral undertaker," Charles Zachariah Taylorson of Hampshire joked as he put on his most sullen face and donned a grim black full-length coat and a plain black hat.

Tommy, Josephine, Agnes, Billy, and Ralph stepped out from behind a long red curtain, just outside of the Torture Room inside of the Fungeon, the aptly named fun house. A small group of schoolchildren and their chaperones were working their way toward the Torture Room when they saw the five coming toward them.

A loud, obese blond chaperone was nearly face-to-face with Josephine, Queen of England, when she snarkled, "Look at the little queen. The least they could do is get a real grown-up to be the queen." The woman turned back to the whole group of kids and chaperones and laughed far too much at her own joke.

Suddenly she saw the expressions on everyone's faces change in unison as they all went blank and then dropped their jaws and pointed single fingers above and beyond her fat head.

She turned to find Josephine towering over her, barely fitting her majestic, eighteen-foot-tall self in the room. The woman screamed and dropped her supersized drink, which she was not allowed to have in the attraction, but she brought it regardless, hidden inside her supersized hoodie. She screamed, turned around, and nearly flattened half of the third grade at Dowry Elementary.

By the time the class recovered from Ms. Doughball's exit, Josephine had become her normal size and cut down another hallway to mess around elsewhere, and Agnes was the only one of the five left standing near the class. They stared at her. She smiled at the chaperones with her lips together and then at the children, showing her teeth. For an instant her incisors grew to fang proportions, and then suddenly she was a real bat, flying over their heads.

If a measurement device existed to calculate the number of ounces peed into various articles of clothing over a prescribed period of time, it would have been useful at this precise moment in time.

Still, the record had to go to the Fungeon, just outside of the Torture Room, for generating the most pee within a certain radius within a stated amount of time because there was a noticeable pool of the stuff within seconds of Agnes's transformation.

Perhaps the best illustration of the pee phenomenon was the front of Mr. Brunner's pants.

Mr. Brunner, in addition to being the physical education instructor, had the distinction of being the career-winning coach of record for the South Minneapolis district. That was what he put on his LinkedIn page, but as far as anyone knew, there was no career-winning coach of record for the South Minneapolis district. Regardless, he did have a large pee spot on his trousers.

The group left the Fungeon to tend to soiled garments, but that was only one class.

Altogether there were sixty different schools at Dragonland that day.

Mr. Fiddle and Chuck emerged from behind the same red curtain as the five had earlier.

Chuck noticed the pool on the floor in front of them and said, "Well, Fiddle, my friend, I think we missed a good show." Both men laughed as they headed down the adjacent hallway ready to perpetrate their own brand of mischief. Before they could get very far, a group of unruly high school students saw their clothes and started making fun of them.

"Hey, old man, what are you supposed to be, some kind of lord or something?" One of them started, and then the one-upmanship commenced.

"I think he looks more like a lady."

"I think he looks like a fairy. He looks like a plump little wingless fairy with a bad hat."

"It's a very fine hat, actually," Charles Zachariah Taylorson of Hampshire said in his most morose tone. "Far finer than your witless banter."

True, his feelings were a little hurt by the bad hat comment, but even he felt that he may have overstepped a boundary after he'd sent the teens screaming from the Fungeon once their temporary blindness proved itself to be temporary.

His inner tailor had sprung into action almost subconsciously; he moved with blinding speed, without warning.

Fiddle had been in so many similar situations with Chuck in the past that he had closed his eyes the moment the boy had said "bad hat."

Charles Zachariah Taylorson of Hampshire had effectively removed all nonessential ornamentation from Fiddle's outfit—yes, certain ornamentation is essential if one wishes to remain "in period," and he had placed those elements onto the annoying teens in strategic places that might indicate the very slander they had proffered upon Fiddle.

In other words, he made those nasty little boys look like little girls playing dress-up.

When the first boy to speak regained his eyesight he could see that his attire had been altered, but since it was on him, he couldn't really grasp what he looked like.

He quickly scurried through one hallway after the other while trying to remain unseen until he reached the place he was looking for, a bank of mirrors fun for all.

One mirror made you smaller, and one mirror made you tall, but each mirror that they gave you wouldn't do anything at all to help you see what you must see

As he gazed upon his reflection, he could see that Chuck had sewn the fluffy, pompous shoulder pads from Mr. Fiddle's outfit into his shirt. He was also wearing some of the braided gold cord. Moving his head around to get a better look only made him more upset as he saw sequins and ribbons flowing over the surface of the wavy mirror.

Just then the second boy came running to the mirror. He was dressed up in a much more ladylike fashion and was even wearing lipstick. They both started to laugh at one another, but their laughter faded quickly as they spotted their own reflections again.

Within seconds the third boy showed up wearing gold and sequins and some sort of wings, just like a fairy.

The other boys couldn't help themselves as they busted out laughing. Their laughter was short-lived again as a large group of teens headed toward them. It was a group of kids from their class.

"Hurry," the first boy said. "We gotta get outta here." He ran through the other two boys, desperate to leave the Fungeon in any direction other than one where people who knew him could see him. The other two boys left just as quickly, feeling every bit as humiliated.

Fiddle and Chuck stepped up to the row of mirrors. Fiddle patted his belly, adjusted his hat, fluffed up his overcoat, and said, "That's some fine tailoring Mr. Taylor; yes, indeed, some fine tailoring."

The two men laughed for a good minute until a little girl walked up and asked if she could see herself in the mirror if they didn't mind.

As she stepped in front of them, she looked up at Chuck and said, "Cool coat, Mister." Chuck plucked a button and some gold cord from Fiddle's overcoat and in an effortless series of motions fashioned a little flower pin that he gave to the little girl.

Her eyes lit up, and she thanked him graciously. He patted her head, and the two men strode off down another hallway.

They didn't have to go too far before they ran into a crowd, or more precisely the back of a crowd. At the front of the crowd stood Tommy, a dark scepter in his right hand, his other hand hovering over Ralph's head as if he were holding zombie Ralph in a trance.

Ralph looked just like a zombie held in a trance.

He looked like every other zombie you have ever seen. However, he was unable to move.

The crowd was standing in a Chamber of Horrors, which made the whole scene even creepier. Hanging above them were wax figures of people suffering various forms of torture, while eerie music played through speakers, sounding as if someone had decided to puncture them with a thousand needles. All around them wax figures were suffering in the stocks and on the rack; there was even a figure lying on a bed of nails. It was a truly gruesome scene. In fact, the Fungeon had suffered some minor criticism from a few of the nearby parent-teacher organizations, who claimed that the Chamber of Horrors was just "too darn scary for children and folks of good conscience." This had made the Chamber of Horrors ridiculously popular for the next few months following the exposé on the local news broadcast, but eventually the hubbub had subsided. The Chamber hadn't changed since the news report, but today it took on a new life.

"Ladies and gentlemen, or should I say subjects," Tommy proclaimed with authority as he eyed the crowd, still moving his hand over Ralph's head, "the time has come!"

"Stop!" a voice cried out from the crowd. A small, round friar emerged from the crowd. "This man has a soul. You cannot control him; he has free will; am I not right?" the small, round friar demanded.

Tommy answered, "Nothing and no one is free, Friar, not even you." Tommy made a sudden jerking motion with the scepter, and Billy was upside down, his entire body gyrating in a thousand different directions at once.

Actually, Billy knew exactly how much to gyrate in order to achieve such a hoax. The only thing Tommy had to do was to make a sudden jerking motion with the scepter, and the crowd was convinced.

Billy was hovering upside down using his ability to move at speeds that defied physics while appearing to be convulsing under Tommy's control. The crowd was in awe. The adults were busy looking for cameras and wires, talking with one another, trying to account for what they were seeing. The kids were either really excited or just plain frozen in fear.

"Release me," Billy cried out. Tommy set his scepter back down, and Billy fell to the floor, where he landed on his head and pretended to be unconscious.

A woman in the crowd took a step toward Billy, and Tommy shouted, "Do not help him!" The woman stepped back into the crowd as Tommy lifted his scepter in warning. He waved his hand over Ralph. "I have drained the life from this young man, and now that his energy is of no use to me, I will relieve my kingdom of his burdensome weight." With that he motioned with his scepter, closed the hand he held over Ralph, and cried, "Be gone!" Ralph turned himself invisible. The crowd gasped.

Billy, who had regained his feet, waddled like an old friar in the direction of Tommy. He held a crucifix in front of him as he neared the place from which Tommy presided.

"Do not come any closer," Tommy warned. Billy made a lunge toward him, and both of them disappeared. The crowd seemed to regain consciousness as they looked around to one another for an explanation of what they had just seen. Some teenagers thought the whole thing was awesome, while various parents debated the appropriateness of the show. Little kids were sobbing here and there while others were laughing, but all agreed that it was not what they had expected from a visit to the Fungeon.

Meanwhile, the girls had found one another again, and Josephine suggested an idea. "Hey, Agnes, you remember that one room for little kids that had all sorts of toys, dolls, and stuffed animals?"

Agnes nodded.

Josephine spun her plan, "We could go in there and become toys. I'll be a Queen of England doll, and you could be any animal from any storybook ever written, like *Stewart Little* or *Puss in Boots*."

Agnes looked at Josephine for a full minute before she answered with a question: "And what's fun about that?"

Josephine realized that Agnes wasn't just like her anymore, but she hoped that Agnes hadn't lost all of the joy they used to share from simple, imaginative play. "Do you remember when we were little girls, Agnes?" Josephine reminded. "We would make up fantastic stories about our dolls and our stuffed animals, and it was as if they really came to life. Well, we could actually do that for some kid who plays with us in that room!"

Agnes seemed to soften a bit as she got a faraway look in her eyes.

Josephine continued, "You could be the White Rabbit from *Alice in Wonderland*; you love that book!" It was true; Agnes did in fact love that book.

"All right, I'll do it, but if one of those kids tries to put me its mouth, I'm going alligator on the snotty little brat."

Josephine laughed in agreement, but inside she worried that Agnes might really go alligator. Still, it was worth the risk, and she was fairly certain that Agnes wouldn't really eat a little kid.

When they reached the Royal Playroom, they found themselves surrounded by all sorts of dolls and stuffed animals from every time period imaginable.

It was an oversight when it came to theme, but the kids who played there didn't understand that one bit. As long as they could find something to excite their imaginations, they were happy.

There were about half a dozen kids in the room and four adults.

Josephine walked over to the area where the dolls were stacked on shelves and began organizing them as if it were her job. She waited until all eyes were focused away from her and instantly transformed to doll size. As she did so, she managed to leap onto the second shelf, a rather prominent place to appeal to a kid in preschool or kindergarten.

When Agnes saw that no one was paying any attention to her, she simply changed to the white rabbit and lay down in the middle of the floor. It was a good way to get stepped on or noticed, and fortunately for Agnes, the latter occurred. A young woman saw her on the floor and picked her up.

"Wow," the young woman said as she lifted her from the floor and held Agnes up to her friend. "This bunny looks so real!" Her friend's kids, four-year-old twin boys in matching outfits, cried out, *bunny!*" The woman who found Agnes gently handed her to the two kids, who flopped down to the floor as she handed over the bunny.

They sat on either side of her and stroked her fur, saying things like "Hi, bunny" and "What's your name, bunny?" and "Do you like carrots, bunny?" while Agnes tried to remain immobile. Meanwhile, across the room, Josephine was being eyed by a little girl who had just been playing tea party on a nearby table and realized that she had no one with whom she might share tea.

"Oh, your highness," the girl said brightly, "would you do me the honor of sharing tea with me?"

Josephine nodded slightly, and the girl rubbed her eyes and said, "Did you just nod your head?"

Josephine remained motionless. "I must be seeing things," the little girl continued as she picked up Josephine and carried her to the table, where she sat her down in a tiny high chair so Josephine was at the perfect height for tea. The teacups were the perfect size for Josephine and a bit small for the girl.

There wasn't really any tea in the teapot, but this didn't stop the girl from pouring for the queen and asking, "One lump or two?"

While the girl seemed extraordinarily precocious, it came as no surprise to Josephine, who used to fantasize elaborate royal parties, weddings, tea parties, and games when she had been this young girl's age.

"And I'm sure you take cream, your highness," the young girl continued. She smiled as she poured imaginary tea and cream and spooned imaginary lumps of sugar.

Josephine felt incredibly happy as she recognized the pure joy within the young girl's eyes.

Meanwhile, on the other side of the room, the twins were beginning to argue over ownership of the bunny. One of them was pulling at Agnes by the ears and the other by the tail. Agnes wasn't going to sit for it. She felt that she had every right to go alligator on them but opted for something far less harmful. She simply hopped away from the twins and ran for the table where Josephine was sharing tea with the little girl. The girl had poured for the queen and felt obliged to introduce herself. "I am Lilly, your majesty." Lilly was quite certain that it was Queen Victoria she was serving and knew without a doubt that the queen must also love toast and jam with her tea as much as she did. Lilly was happily spreading imaginary jam on the toast and did not notice the arrival of Agnes in the seat next to Josephine until she raised her eyes while presenting the toast to the queen.

The twins arrived shortly thereafter to find the bunny sitting quite still next to the queen at the table with Lilly. "That's our bunny," one of the twins said as he pointed to Agnes. Lilly was quite happy to acknowledge that the bunny was not hers but proceeded to invite the twin boys for tea. The boys, who imagined that there might actually be something real to eat and drink, promptly sat in two empty chairs on either side of Lilly. They stared into the little cups as Lilly pretended to pour.

"Hey! There's nothing in there," the first twin said.

"I'm thirsty," the other twin shouted as he held the tiny cup upside down and looked up into it, trying to shake something drinkable out of it. The twins' mother heard the second twin's plea for something to drink and walked to the table.

"Are you thirsty, Buddy?" she asked as she searched her bag for a drink bottle.

"I'm sorry. Buddy thought that my tea was real," Lilly apologized as she gestured to the pot in the middle of the table.

"Oh." The woman laughed as she lifted an empty bottle from her bag, "His name isn't Buddy; it's Fred. C'mon, Fred," she instructed as she pulled on the little boy's shoulder. "Let's get you a drink. You too, Bud," she said to the other twin, who hopped down from the table."

"Good-bye, Bud." Lilly smiled as the other twin turned toward his mother and then stopped and said, "I'm George, not Bud," as if Lilly had insulted him. "Excuse me, George," Lilly said innocently as she turned her head back toward the table and spoke to the queen. "Now where were we?"

"We were having tea," Josephine answered, "and I would like more."

Without missing a beat, Lilly responded, "I thought you were alive." She proceeded to pour tea for Josephine. Lilly pretended to add the cream and sugar and looked at Agnes. "You probably just want the sugar, don't you, little bunny?" Lilly asked as she pretended to put sugar into the tiny teacup in front of Agnes.

"I'll actually have a little tea, but you can skip the cream, please," Agnes, the white rabbit, responded.

"Oh, my, a talking bunny; how delightful." Lilly smiled as she poured a bit of tea for Agnes. The three of them had quite an enjoyable tea time, laughing and talking while oblivious adults and future diabetic children milled about around them, illegally consuming all sorts of high-fructose-laden concoctions and transferring the sticky goo to the assorted toys in the Royal Playroom.

"C'mon, Lilly, it's time to go," Lilly's mother said as she headed toward the exit.

Lilly pretended to dab her lips with her napkin as she said, "Thank you for joining me, your highness, and Agnes the bunny; that was very lovely."

"Thank you," Agnes and Josephine said in return.

Lilly skipped away toward the exit and took hold of her mother's hand.

Lilly turned back toward the table just as she was leaving to see Josephine return to her full height.

Agnes returned to her "normal" girl dressed up as a vampire form.

They waved to Lilly as she turned the corner and waved back at them.

"Cute kid," Agnes said as matter-of-factly as she could.

"Yeah," Josephine responded, "I haven't felt like that since we were little girls."

Agnes put her arm around Josephine's shoulder and said, "What now, your majesty?"

Josephine responded, "I had my turn; this one's all yours, Agnes."

Agnes smiled with eyes that told Josephine that someone was going to get very frightened very soon.

Agnes pulled Josephine around two turns and up a staircase, and then they saw it: the Hall of Horrors. Agnes had been planning this from the moment she put on the black boots. She wasn't about to let those tap dancing lessons go to waste. She remembered the floor of the Hall of Horrors. It had a crisp sound like a marble floor, but it was cheap linoleum at best.

"Do you have heels on whatever he put on your feet?" Agnes asked. "I can't see anything under that skirt; it's enormous."

Josephine nodded and looked at the floor. "Thinking of tap? Because I'm pretty sure..." Josephine lifted her skirt over one leg and showed her heels. "...that these will do just fine." And then she tapped *tuh dum dum*.

"Tom Sawyer?" Agnes and Josephine said in unison.

Their tap instructor had shown them a video of a very gifted tap dancer performing to "Tom Sawyer" by the instructor's favorite band, Rush.

The dancer was able to emulate changes in melody and even capture some of the incredible beats laid down by Neil Peart, one of the greatest drummers in rock 'n' roll. In class they experimented with all sorts of combinations to try to achieve a reasonable simulation of the performance despite their lack of experience. In class it sounded a bit like fifty thousand marbles dropped from a three-story balcony onto a hard marble floor.

Today, however, when Agnes and Josephine performed it, something magical happened. They didn't dance like children; they danced like Eleanor Powell, a truly extraordinary tap dancer from the 1930s and 1940s.

They started slowly, Agnes creating a beat with only her heels while Josephine joined in, magnifying the beat.

The dance evolved as one girl played off the other: a stomp here, a tap there, a ball change here, a paradiddle there, until it sounded like Rush, but there were no guitars and no drums, and Neil Peart was nowhere to be seen.

A crowd had gathered. They were enthralled. At the front of the crowd were Tommy, Billy, and Ralph, only now they weren't doing anything crazy. They were just watching and listening in amazement. Even the crowd was ignoring the Dark Lord, the Friar, and the Zombie as they gazed upon the girls who were, at this point, generating actual sparks from feet moving far too quickly for the brain to process. Josephine ripped her skirt off to avoid catching fire; fortunately Chuck had had the foresight to tailor in a sort of subskirt should she feel the need to lose the extra bulk of the larger skirt. Over six hundred years of hindsight had paved the way for a good deal of foresight.

"She's beautiful," Tommy gasped as he looked at Josephine.

"Makes me want to run so fast I bounce off of everything in this place," Billy said aloud, although he didn't know it until Ralph said, "Ugh! The way you guys look at those girls, I mean, I might as well be invisible. But seriously, how in the world are they *doing* that?" Ralph was just as captivated as anyone in attendance.

Fiddle and Chuck had found their way to the front of the pack of spectators.

"They're discovering some of the finer aspects of their powers," Fiddle said quietly to the three boys, who looked back and forth at one another.

It was clear what was on their minds, but there would be plenty of time to make those discoveries later.

For the moment the spotlight was on the girls.

With the ending notes of "Tom Sawyer" ringing out from shoes that seemed to be not only well crafted but also tuned, the girls suddenly stopped, precisely in unison.

They looked at one another with sheer delight, and then they looked at their shoes.

Their eyes drifted over to the crowd, which had burst out in spontaneous applause, to find Chuck looking very pleased with himself.

Fiddle patted him on the shoulder, and the girls curtsied.

The crowd assumed they were curtsying to them, so they grew even louder. Seconds later the girls were mauled by the crowd. People were asking for autographs because they thought the girls were working for the park and had to be famous, except for the kids from their school, who all came up and said things like, "We are so going to have lunch together tomorrow" or "So, like, I know you're in sixth grade and I'm like in eighth, but I can like totally hook you up with everybody, literally everybody."

Tommy walked up to Josephine and said, "I have never seen anyone so amazing before in my life." Everyone who had been talking before suddenly stopped. "Anything! I meant anything, anything so amazing as what you and Agnes just did; that was like, totally cool, especially like the sparks and stuff."

Everyone from their school started laughing.

The cool eighth graders and the wanna-be-cool seventh graders had seen Tommy and Josephine together before, but now, he had no right to be with her.

Now she was in and he was out.

Agnes and Josephine had transcended a firmly established rite of passage by virtue of their amazing performance, but inclusion did not come by methods as meaningless as friendship.

Just because Josephine was in, it could not be subsequently assumed that Tommy would be in as well. As far as Billy was concerned, many kids would agree that his chances of acceptance were hovering around zero but far more frequently dipping into the negative numbers. And Ralph continued to be as he had always been: invisible.

"You are so totally not talking to our friend like that, are you?" One eighth-grader named Belle stepped beside Josephine and put her hands on her hips. "You boys had better find something better to do. Obviously these two extremely talented friends of ours have no interest in wasting their time with losers."

Josephine looked at the eighth graders and smiled.

She walked over to Tommy and put an arm around his shoulders.

Turning back to the eighth graders, she said, "We'll let you know if we need you for anything, although it's rather unlikely."

The group of eighth graders did their very best to act cool as they slinked away like vampires from the sun.

Agnes couldn't help but stand in between Billy and Ralph, adding, "You eighth graders are in for a big surprise."

The five stepped together, facing the retreating eighth graders, as Agnes continued, "You're going to wish you didn't dump on Tommy," she continued, "and Billy and Ralph are pretty awesome too."

The eighth graders turned away and brushed her off as if they didn't care. They kept looking back at the five as they neared the staircase, and Agnes could tell that she had made them curious and interested.

"You know that Belle is one of the most popular eighth graders in the school," Agnes said. Josephine nodded as Agnes went on. "She's the type who either loves you or hates you, and right now I think she's trying to figure out how she feels about us. Things could get pretty weird at school."

"Things have always been weird at school," Billy said with a shrug. "Ever since we started sixth grade. Seventh and eighth graders act like they are so much better, especially the eighth graders, like they rule the school. You know what's funny though? Next year they are going to be freshmen in high school, and they will be back in the same place we are now, only worse because they will have to deal with real teenagers, high school teenagers."

Fiddle and Chuck had been having their own private conversation while the middle school kids were busy sorting things out.

"That's a very good observation, Billy," Fiddle interjected, "but it isn't something that happens exclusively in school. It happens in life, all around us. People seem to feel the need to differentiate themselves from one another, either by financial or social status, through the titles they earn or give themselves, within their careers, even within families."

Chuck stood very close to Fiddle, towering over him, and said, "Even between us, you see. I am quite a bit taller than Fiddle, but it is he who is the master. I learned everything I needed to get started from Fiddle, and after I had learned all I could from him, he disappeared, and I had to learn for myself, or with my friends. You see Fiddle with me now, and it seems like we are of the same status because of how he treats me, but I will always know him as my teacher, just as you will. He and I have been talking about the five of you, and there is something we want to share with you, but I will let the teacher speak." Chuck bowed a little and motioned with his hand toward Fiddle, who stepped up very gallantly in his lordly attire.

"What Billy said is very important to understand if you are to manage your powers appropriately in front of others. I believe that you will do a fine job of that. As you begin to exhibit skills beyond the capabilities of those around you, remember to remain gracious. It was right for Josephine to defend her friendship with Tommy and understandable the way that Agnes hinted at what I can only imagine will be a remarkable few years at Stamford Middle School. Just one last word of caution," Fiddle leaned in close so as not to be accidentally overheard by anyone passing by. "Just as you five comprise a remarkable force for good, there are forces that are quite the opposite. I would rather we had time to train before we run into them. So watch out, and try to control your level of achievement. We don't want to draw any undue attention."

Fiddle smiled and looked at Chuck. "What do you say, old friend? Care for one last prank with the whole group?"

Fiddle changed his voice until he sounded like a growling beast. "Something a little spooky. And maybe a little magical?"

Chuck obliged as he whirled into action, his movements so fast they were nearly imperceptible.

The five had instinctively closed their eyes.

Tommy turned to the other four kids and said, "Wait here." Before they could ask where he was going, he was standing right in front of them with a stack of Chuck's special goggles in his hands.

"Grab a goggle," he said as he shoved goggles into their hands.

The kids all put on the goggles as Chuck's movements raced to a blinding symphony of motion. With the goggles on, they could see how Chuck was pulling elements out of thin air and layering them together as if weaving strings of energy into matter. He was turning Fiddle into something: something massive, a dragon. Before the light could dissipate, Agnes tossed her goggles to Josephine and changed herself into Fiddle's twin. Chuck's hands were ablaze with energy as he changed the very makeup of the costumes he had created for Billy and Ralph, simultaneously dressing them as knights.

Tommy looked on, feeling a little disappointed; after all, it had been he who had asked to be a knight. Just as that thought solidified in his mind, he heard a voice in his head. The voice belonged to Chuck. The voice told him that it was in need of his help, and if Tommy could kindly dip into his shop, the two stunt swords by the back door would be truly appreciated. Tommy looked at Josephine, reached over, and grabbed the goggles Agnes had tossed and disappeared. A second later he was standing right where he had been a second earlier, holding two stunt swords that looked more like real swords than he had thought possible. They really were stunt swords.

He took the time to test them on the scarecrow Chuck had conveniently displayed next to the swords.

Chuck stopped suddenly, and the blaze of energy vanished. Billy and Ralph were standing before him. Chuck looked at them a little longer than it seemed he wanted to, held his chin, tilted his head, and said, "Could be better."

"Fantastic! Really, you guys look amazing," Tommy said as he handed them the swords.

Anyone else who had shown up in the area was still rubbing the blindness from their eyes when Chuck said, "Right, the swords do make the look, thank you, Tommy" and then swirled into action again.

This time he recovered Josephine's large skirt from where she had tossed it earlier and transformed Tommy's outfit into kingly robes, while he changed himself into an old wizard.

The dragons took up a quarter of the space in the Hall of Horrors, and Agnes and Fiddle found themselves knocking over a variety of cheap props with their tails.

People were starting to flood into the Hall of Horrors because a kid who had been in the bathroom down the hall when Chuck was blazing around had come out just in time to miss the blindness but see the dragons and the knights. He had taken off through the Fungeon, screaming that there were real dragons in the Hall of Horrors.

"Your highness," Chuck began over the din of new arrivals. "Your majesty." He bowed to the king and queen. "I have warned you for far too long that one day the dragons would break through the magical chains with which I was able to hold them, and here they are." With that Fiddle breathed a column of fire at Chuck, who raised his hands, causing the fire to deflect away from him as if bouncing off a protective invisible globe around him.

Chuck moved effortlessly away from the dragons and disappeared down the hallway. Tommy heard Chuck's inside his head again, telling him to order Ralph and Billy to fight the dragons.

Tommy motioned to Ralph and Billy and called out, "Attack!"

Billy rushed toward Fiddle at slightly faster than normal kid speed, while Ralph tried to work his way behind Agnes.

"Only one thing can stop this," Chuck had returned.

Agnes and Fiddle shot plumes of fire directly at Josephine and Tommy while Ralph and Billy deflected the shots with fake swords made by Chuck.

"The king and the queen must once again rule!" Chuck shouted as he swirled brilliant particles of light throughout the space.

At this, the dragons blew fiery death upon Billy and Ralph, who held their swords up to reflect it back, causing showers of hot sparks that turned to glitter as they fell upon the crowd that had now assembled in the Hall of Horrors.

A barrage of texts and tweets hit the data stream like a hurricane.

Tommy took Josephine in his arms, waved a hand over the crowd, the dragons, the knights, and the wizard, snapping his fingers, and only the crowd remained.

The five plus Chuck and Fiddle found themselves back in Chuck's shop.

"Fiddle I must say, that was the most fun I have had in twenty years," Chuck said. "Well, Mon'Ami, I suppose it's *au revoir*." Chuck continued in his finest French accent.

Fiddle looked at Chuck and said, "I don't think so, friend." Chuck looked at Fiddle inquisitively. Fiddle continued, "We are in need of a tailor."

Chuck's eyes welled up with tears. "I haven't worked in the field since," his voice choked off. Fiddle extended a hand and placed it softly on Chuck's shoulder. "We need you," he continued. "I know it's hard."

Chuck looked at the five and then slowly turned to Fiddle. "These are good kids, Fiddle." Chuck wiped a tear that had rolled upon his cheekbone. "I'll do it!"

None of the five could have known what had happened to Chuck, but each one of them could sense the magnitude of his commitment. Something had happened to him or someone very close to him, or both.

Before anyone could process their own emotions, Agnes transformed into a lovey, snuggly, living teddy bear and hugged Chuck. She was the size of an inflatable display rack at a superstore but considerably more cuddly.

"I am so happy you are going to join us," she said through teddy-bear lips. "I can tell that it isn't easy for you to do."

The entire group looked at one another, acknowledging the same perspective.

That perspective was that Agnes was super weird as a teddy bear.

Chuck smiled through a slight sniffle. He walked to the cupboard behind him and pulled out the vintage pair of red Chuck Taylors and placed them at the teddy bear's feet.

Agnes returned to her normal form, except that she was still, mysteriously, a vampire.

Chuck moved like lightning and suddenly the Taylors were on her feet. Agnes smiled.

Chuck placed a hand on her shoulder and hugged her into his chest, gently saying, "This is going to be fun!" He looked at the rest of the group and said, "Now close your eyes."

All five of the kids closed their eyes, and so did Fiddle. Chuck sprang into action. His entire shop was glowing from the outside, and then, suddenly, nothing.

Inside he whispered, "Now open them." One by one the group opened their eyes. They had all been changed back into their regular clothes. "There you are, back to normal." Chuck quickly changed his expression to a deep frown and said apologetically, "Not that a single one of you is *normal*."

Fiddle chuckled, "Not these kids." Turning on his heels toward the door, he continued, "But they are going to have to do their best to fake it. And now it is time for me to grab a funnel cake or maybe a bit of taffy. C'mon, kids; we only have an hour until the bus leaves, and I'm sure you'd like to try another ride or two." Without looking back, Fiddle cried out to Chuck, "See you soon, Charles Zachariah Taylorson of Hampshire; there is much to do, and we will need you along, so listen for the call!"

"Will do, Fiddle," Chuck responded. "Have fun, kids. I will see you soon."

With that the group left the shop and headed out into the amusement park.

Billy started bouncing up and down and pointing to a spinning ride just beyond the train tracks that wound throughout the park. Tommy and Ralph saw him pointing and started walking in that direction.

Josephine pulled Agnes in the opposite direction, saying, "Let's go this way; there's something I want to check out that we didn't look at the last time we were here." She squinted a bit and continued, "I guess that's right now, isn't it?"

Agnes rubbed her chin in thought. "It's gotta be right; otherwise there would be two of each of us right now." The girls discussed the complexity of time travel while walking for several minutes until Agnes looked up in front of her and saw the Tunnel of Love.

"Oh no, Jo," Agnes blurted out. "I am *not* going in there with you."

Josephine grabbed Agnes by the arm. "C'mon, Agnes; we don't have to go in together. I just want to see what it looks like."

Agnes followed along reluctantly. As the girls reached the Tunnel of Love, they could see a few girls from their school milling around the entrance. They were pointing at boys who were milling around close to the Tunnel of Love but not getting close enough to look like they were going to the Tunnel of Love.

"Look at them, Josephine," Agnes said. "Why don't they just go ask the boys they like to go for a ride? Everybody knows who they like; it's totally obvious."

"Maybe they're shy," Josephine responded as she inched her way closer to the entrance, trying to get a look inside without committing to getting in line.

"Like you are with Tommy?" Agnes asked as she jabbed an elbow into Josephine's ribs.

"I don't know, Agnes. I mean, I guess I just don't know *how* to ask Tommy," Josephine confessed. "I mean, I'm afraid he'll just think it's stupid."

"Just tell him you think there's a wormhole in the tunnel!" Agnes suggested.

"A wormhole, are you kidding? Tommy can sense wormholes. He's not going to believe there's a wormhole inside of the Tunnel of Love. He's going to laugh at me."

"No, he's not," Agnes responded. "He likes you, and he'll believe anything you tell him."   "Well, I'm not going to lie to him," Josephine said quietly.

"Then I will," Agnes answered, "because the two of you have got to get over it and just be together. Heck, even Fiddle knows you guys like each other." In an instant she was gone. She didn't even wait for Josephine to approve her plan; she simply implemented it.

Agnes became a hummingbird. She flew to Tommy, who had just finished riding what the young kids called the vomit saucer, which was really the Cosmic Saucer, but it did spin very quickly. As she hovered near Tommy's ear and spoke to him, no one else could hear, "Hey, Tommy, Josephine says she found a wormhole in the park."

Tommy snapped around to see Agnes. She hovered for an instant and then shot off toward the Tunnel of Love. Agnes hovered until Tommy caught up to her, and then she flew off again, hovering when needed, leading Tommy to Josephine. As she got close to the Tunnel of Love, Tommy slowed down.

"No way," Tommy barked. "I am not going to go in there with anybody, even..." His eyes drifted over to the empty seat next to Josephine on the car that was next to enter the tunnel. Josephine patted the seat next to her. The girl who was running the ride motioned for him to hurry up, and so did Josephine. Tommy ran to the car and got in.

"Wow, that was quick," the ride girl said. "Someone really knows how to train 'em. Keep your hands and feet inside the car at all times, please remain seated, and enjoy your journey through the Tunnel of Love!" The girl winked at Josephine, who leaned into Tommy as the car jolted toward the entrance.

Billy and Ralph didn't even notice that Tommy hadn't joined them for another spin on the Comet Saucer until they were on the ride. It was the kind of ride in which the passengers could turn a wheel, making the saucer-shaped seats spin as quickly as the riders were capable of.

Each of the five was beginning to discover that they had more energy and were generally more capable physically than they had been previous to their own transformations.

It wasn't just Billy who had gained physical strength and speed; they all had improved a small percentage, whereas Billy's improvement was downright epic.

So when Tommy, Billy, and Ralph were on the Cosmic Saucer, it was all that they could do to go as fast as possible and remain within normal human expectations.

With Tommy gone, it was just Ralph and Billy. When the two of them were alone together they hardly ever made fun of each other.

What they did, however, was far more dangerous.

They played the stupid bet game.

That was precisely what they did.

"I bet I can make this thing go as fast as you can," Ralph said to Billy as they boarded the ride.

"Betcha can't," Billy challenged.

"All right; this is how it works," Ralph said. "I know a way we can test it for sure."

Billy nodded. He actually didn't mind when Ralph came up with how to test things because he was too busy figuring out how he would beat Ralph in the stupid bet game. Now that he had superpowers, he wasn't about to worry about any of it. It didn't matter what kind of test Ralph came up with. No matter what, he was going to spin that saucer faster than ever.

"I am going to spin first, as hard and as fast as I can," Ralph started, "and then when I am totally going as fast as I can, I will stop and you grab the wheel." If you make it go faster than the speed it's going when I pass it, you win."

Billy agreed. Ralph grabbed the wheel as the speaker crackled a reminder to riders that the park was not responsible for lost or damaged items, sickness, or death. Pregnant women were warned, as were pacemaker owners.

The ride hydraulically lifted to life, and Ralph began spinning the saucer. He made remarkable progress in a very short amount of time. The grease on the bearings of the saucer was hot enough to make a nice tea if one had the desire for tea made from oil. He could barely hold on to the center wheel because the centrifugal force was pushing his back against the seat cushion while his arms stretched out for every inch to increase the speed until he had hit his limit. Ralph tried to give Billy a look that would tell him that it was his turn, but it ended up being more like a look that told Billy that Ralph couldn't hold on to the wheel anymore. Billy didn't waste a moment. He bent forward from the stomach, easily besting the centrifugal force. He grabbed the wheel and started turning it, equalizing the speed so it remained constant at Ralph's maximum. Then, with a devilish grin, he kicked it up a notch. The grease began to boil.

~ *Chapter 10: Tunnel of Love* ~

Across the park Tommy and Josephine waited to enter the tunnel.

As they boarded the swan boat and sat down Tommy became a little uncomfortable until they entered the tunnel and Josephine snuggled in close to him.

"There isn't really a wormhole, is there?" Tommy asked, already knowing the answer.

They passed through a couple of sharp turns and sliding doors with angelic cupids painted on either side, and then they were surrounded by darkness.

"Nope, just a tunnel," Josephine responded as she snuggled in even closer.

They felt the boat dip a little as above their heads an enormous furry heart was illuminated from within, pulsing with warm red light.

"Oh, man," Tommy said. "That is so sappy."

Josephine held his arm and sighed, "Sappy."

Another turn and they found themselves in a room full of hearts and flowers.

"Hey, Josephine," Tommy asked emotionlessly, "do people really go for this sort of thing? I mean, do you like all of this hearts and flowers stuff?"

Josephine was looking up into his eyes, "It's kinda nice, y'know, kinda pretty," she answered, still gazing into Tommy's eyes.

He mumbled, "I just don't get it."

Josephine just smiled. "That's 'cause you're a boy, but that's okay; you don't have to think it's pretty. The Tunnel of Love isn't just about what's in the tunnel; it's about who you are in the tunnel with!"

Tommy looked at Josephine and had no idea what to say. He smiled, remembering how he had gotten there, and said, "No wormhole. I can't believe I fell for that." Josephine whispered quietly in his ear. Tommy replied out loud, "I don't know if I can *do* that."

"You can just try it," Josephine suggested. "We just won't go anywhere if it doesn't work."

"That just seems a little scary. What if we aren't together?" Tommy worried.

"Of course we'll be together," Josephine reassured him. "We have to be. We've got these powers now, and we are part of a team; that isn't just gonna end."

"Okay, Josephine." Tommy took her hand. "Hold on."

The boat seemed to dive into a hole. All around them hearts and flowers swirled magically through the air, bouncing off their faces like little snowflakes. Their speed increased as the spinning grew faster until suddenly everything changed.

They were there—there meaning that they were twenty years in the future. Twenty years from the day they got into that boat in the Tunnel of Love. There was no boat and no tunnel. They had both imagined that they would still know one another, but they couldn't be sure of much else. The one thing they hadn't considered was that they might actually be married. Josephine had thought about it, but she had never shared the thought with anyone. Tommy thought marriage was for old people, and he wasn't ready to be old. So for Tommy what came next was not only shocking but also a bit repulsive.

He was sitting in the bleachers of a gymnasium watching a grade school basketball game, holding a baby who had apparently just puked all over his shoulder. Tommy was twenty years older. Josephine had just turned from her spot on the floor, with the same hair and the same mannerisms, only now she was a full-grown woman who happened to be the coach. Tommy had another rather unsettling moment as he looked at his paint-stained pants. Three things flashed through his mind. Either he was married to Josephine or he was her boyfriend, and if he was married to her, then the kid who had puked on his shoulder was his son. The vomiting continued. Tommy nearly gagged as he looked around for something to help him clean up. On the seat next to him, he saw a bag. Upon opening the bag, he realized that this was the bag for taking care of the baby. It was the ComPlete Parent backpack. It had everything in it. It had diapers, milk in a bottle with a nipple, a small teddy bear, and most importantly towels, wet and dry. There was a box of wipes that he ripped open for the vomit and cloth towels for drying himself off.

Then he looked at the baby. There was a little dribble on his chin, which Tommy wiped with a wipe and disposed of in the convenient garbage compartment on the ComPlete Parent backpack. The baby burped directly in his face and then farted. The combination was not only close range but directed, and to top it off, the air conditioning was not working, so the gymnasium air hung like a wet sock, steeping the smell in like the corpse of Earl Grey. It was a ridiculously obscure fact that Earl Grey was indeed a very odiferous man due to his constant traveling to far-off exotic regions in search of the perfect blend of tea leaves, while the more commonplace fact that a simple bath now and then might have relieved such a stench had never quite reached his ears.

Tommy was now suffering the full potency of an Earl Grey Vomit Fart. He was consumed by a sudden urge to chuck the baby onto the court but thought better of it. Tommy thought that it was unfair that he had ended up here, taking care of a baby, while Josephine was the one in charge both on the court and probably off the court, when suddenly something beautiful happened. His baby, the one he held in his arms, smiled at him and giggled.

"Oh, you are so cute," Tommy blurted out.

The whistle had just blown on the court. One of the girls was down.

Josephine heard Tommy's exclamation regarding the cute baby in the bleachers and stared at him with eyes that said only one thing: "I am so in love."

The girl who was down was a spitting image of Agnes. Josephine turned to the bench. A girl who looked exactly like Tommy in girl form was sitting in a slightly oversized jersey on the end of the bench. Josephine realized it was her own daughter as she called out, "Billie, get in there."

Tommy looked past his baby boy to witness the interaction between Josephine and his daughter Billie. The girl looked so much like him that he was stunned.

She gave the young, injured Agnes a high five as she left the floor.

A man who looked like an older Billy moved to the bench to help the child.

The referee blew the whistle for the jump ball, and Billie whacked the ball to her teammate, from an entire foot higher up than the taller opponent could reach. The girl she slapped the ball to was a young female version of Billy. As she dribbled through the opposition, she cried out, "Nobody injures my sister." Her name was Sally.

She was a good five feet off the ground when she slam dunked the basketball. At least twenty phones, eye sets, and wrist displays sent the video instantly across the web; forty retina implants instantly encoded the whole event and marked it for general consumption to all pathways on the GIS (Globally Integrated System). Billy and Agnes' daughter, Sally, who looked far more like Billy than Agnes, poor girl, had gifts that could simply not be explained. Karen, Billy and Agnes' other daughter was more like Agnes, truly gifted yet far less likely to make a show of it.

Tommy had seen enough. He quickly exited the moment and hovered in a space of "no time," willing himself to a position directly next to Josephine. He whispered, "Let's go" directly into her ear. The eleven-year-old part of Josephine looked for Tommy in the empty space that spoke with his voice.

Suddenly Josephine and Tommy were rocketing back to the amusement park. Their boat emerged from the Tunnel of Love. Now that they were back, they looked at one another differently than they ever had before.

Billy and Ralph found Agnes waiting at the exit of the tunnel; she was watching Tommy and Josephine, who were ignoring everything around them, staring at one another, even while climbing out of the boat as they exited the Tunnel of Love.

"Take a picture, and get on with your life, you two." Agnes opened the exit gate as the two continued to walk with their eyes locked on one another. "What is in that tunnel?"

Josephine snapped out of it and turned to answer Agnes. She was absolutely beaming as she replied, "A wormhole."

Agnes had a sudden fit of tennis-audience head as she looked from the tunnel exit to the love-struck duo and back again, over and over, trying to guess what might have happened. A slow feeling of dread crept over her.

"Where did it lead?" she asked, worried that whatever they saw had to include her. So now they knew more about her than she knew herself. That was simply unacceptable, so she added, "C'mon, spill it."

Ralph had mysteriously materialized between Tommy and Josephine and looked back and forth between them, suffering a similar head affliction to Agnes. "Yeah, you guys look..." He wanted to say "super weird," but instead he settled for "different."

They stopped walking. Tommy looked at Josephine, and she smiled.

"We end up getting married, and we have a couple of kids." Tommy said like it was a weight that he was absolutely certain he would not be able to continue holding.

Josephine shot a wink to Agnes, who felt happy for her friend. Agnes was terrified at the proposition of finding out what she would be like in the future.

Billy quickly followed up. "What about us? What happens to the rest of us? Do you know anything about what happens to people other than you in the future?"

Tommy and Josephine looked at one another and then back to Billy. The tennis-audience head was contagious. There were at least five tennis balls of thought bouncing around at any given moment. They couldn't decide how much they actually knew about the future versus what they might just be guessing at.

Tommy spoke first. "We saw people who looked like you guys in the future, but we didn't stick around long enough to talk to anybody. I spent most of the time cleaning barf off of myself."

Josephine added, "And I was the basketball coach. I saw kids who looked like you guys and adults who looked like us, grown up."

"Normal?" Billy barked.

"We are going to grow up to be *normal* people, living average, everyday lives? What the heck is that all about?" He was noticeably disturbed by the thought that they would end up like their parents.

"What was I doing?" Ralph asked as Billy fumed over his disappointment.

"I didn't see anyone who looked like you, Ralph," Josephine said as she looked to Tommy.

"Me neither," Tommy added with a shrug.

"Oh, great," Ralph responded. "I'm probably dead."

Billy and Agnes continued to pump Tommy and Josephine for information even though they had very little to go on. Ralph looked on as the scene continued, Billy trying desperately to find some shred of SuperBilly in his future, while Agnes struggled with the implication that she and Billy would be married in the future. She liked Billy, and she could tell that he liked her, but they had been very careful to maintain a safe distance, and any talk of love or romance was promptly cut off by a gesture of mutual disgust. Ralph felt more like the fifth wheel than he ever had before.

"Feeling a bit like the fifth wheel?" Fiddle asked as he walked up to Ralph, who hadn't noticed him coming.

Ralph nodded. "Don't worry about it, Ralph; you have a very interesting future in store for you," Fiddle reassured him as he placed a hand on his shoulder, leading Ralph back toward the other four.

"So Tommy, it seems you decided to take a little glimpse at the future, am I right?"

Tommy and Josephine turned toward Fiddle, feeling embarrassed and a bit shameful.

Billy was about to open his mouth, desperate to discover what had become of his powers, but Fiddle stopped him with a hand and a calm voice. "The future is always changing."

Fiddle paused just long enough to let the thought sink in, resuming quickly enough to keep Billy silent.

"It is affected by what we have done in the past and what we are doing at this very moment. It is affected by elements outside of our control and those that we guide with our words and actions.

To understand how all of the elements come together, one must exercise great wisdom and forbearance.

I have only known one individual capable of truly walking through time without causing the slightest ripple, but he is not himself right now." They all looked at Fiddle with eyes that burned to know the truth.

Once again Billy stepped forward.

Fiddle looked directly at Billy and said, "I hope to reveal him to you all when the time is right."

Fiddle turned to face Tommy. "I understand why you created that wormhole, Tommy."

Fiddle's eyes moved to Josephine with a smile.

"However, Tommy, I suggest you wait a little longer before trying it again. You were lucky to get out without causing any trouble. In fact, your exit plan was quite brilliant; leaving your future self and grasping Josephine from hers in the way that you did was terrific."

Fiddle looked at each one of them for a moment.

"Ralph was concerned that neither one of you saw him during your brief stay in the future. His mind went to a thought that he had died.

Billy was upset that you all turned out 'normal,' and Agnes felt trapped." Billy's head whipped around to Agnes as Fiddle revealed what Agnes had not shared with any of them.

Agnes wanted to say something to Billy but couldn't find the words." Seeing into the future can be quite hard to assimilate into one's current mentality," Fiddle went on to explain, "because we are often not ready to find things out about ourselves without the understanding of the life experiences that triggered the decisions leading up to the people we may become."

Fiddle could sense that he had not been clear enough.

"For example," he continued, "Billy thinks that it is some sort of failure to end up like his parents. He imagines being a father as something odd and can't see himself in that role. I don't blame you at all for that, Billy. If you were really excited about being a father at the age of eleven, I would have serious doubts about whether or not you allowed yourself to enjoy your time as a boy.

Honestly, if I could have waited to assemble you all together and delay the onset of your powers, I would have, because childhood is a great gift and a truly magical time.

So just a word of caution to all of you: As we spend more time together, it is important to not lose sight of your own selves. It will make you more capable if you understand yourselves more fully. A stronger you makes a stronger team."

Ralph started pacing between the group and Fiddle. "I don't get it, Fiddle," he said, scratching his head and rubbing his temples as if the action would shake a broken piece of his brain back into place. "How do you know what happened in Tommy's wormhole?"

"You see, as a different sort of human being, a more evolved, more connected, energy-based organism sort of human being than your average mortal, I can do some things that other beings cannot. I do have limitations, however."

"You mean that you can't run like me or turn into creatures like Agnes, or get all big like Josephine," Billy guessed. "Or turn invisible like Ralph. Because we all know you can like pretty much do anything Tommy can do."

Tommy slugged Billy's face as hard as he could. It was ineffectual. Billy laughed.

"No, Billy; it's not like that." Fiddle chose the shortest distance between two points. "Actions speak louder than words, so here we go."

Fiddle did everything Billy described and more. While he was doing it, he dragged all of them along throughout every size change and time remap, only to come to rest in a classroom, the very classroom in which he had introduced them to the wormhole. Fiddle stood before them, each of them in his or her proper seat facing his desk. Fiddle looked at them with eyes that burned from centuries of devotion. In their eyes he saw the reflection of a lesson he had truly hoped they all would learn.

"We all start out so differently, yet we reach the same end."

While the five soaked in his words, Fiddle brought them back to the amusement park. Jumbled images of Fiddle, the size of a skyscraper and diving into Lake Calhoun, twenty times the size of any walleye they had ever seen, swam through their heads as he pulled them along.

The buses had arrived to take the kids back to school. Fiddle returned to normal. He turned away and walked toward the buses.

Today's lesson had been taught. True, they had jumped into the past, so time was barely affected, but the entire cycle of time for the five was taking its toll, seemingly at the exact same time. They drudged their way toward the buses, climbed listlessly onto their bus, and slunk into seats too uncomfortable for sleep, and fell into dreams of everything, and nothing.

~ *Chapter 11: Record Breaking* ~

Tommy woke up late. He barely ate anything. Not because he wasn't hungry; he was ravenous. His mother managed to tell him in six different ways how time works and that "you can't remain in bed for the entire morning and expect to have a leisurely breakfast, as if time will just stand still because you want it to." She was quite certain of that. "And you can't get to school on time if you try to eat your entire breakfast, when your classes start in less than half an hour," she added as she took his bowl out from under his mouth after hoisting his backpack, which weighed more than his father's bowling ball, onto the table next to him. In a single motion, she dropped the bowl into the sink and spun Tommy's chair to face the door. "Go," she finished as she turned away, grabbing the laundry basket and a family-sized bottle of detergent on her way to the basement. Tommy dashed to the sink, threw down another three mouthfuls of cereal, grabbed his backpack, and headed out the door.

Tommy saw a wormhole.

Tommy saw Billy skate like a god.

Billy and Tommy saw Josephine step gigantically through town.

Ralph spoke invisibly.

"I think we should go to Agnes right now and save her from that cat," Tommy said as he pointed to a wormhole, dust still in the air from Billy's "Ralph Detection System."

His aim was magnificent. Tommy had connected with Agnes at the precise moment of her encounter with the cat. Billy scooped her up in his hands so quickly that Tommy hadn't yet created the return wormhole. He quickly did, and the five rode the wormhole to their favorite meeting spot behind the old tree, just off school grounds.

Agnes changed back to her true form and summed up what everyone else was thinking. "So we're back to the day we discovered our powers." They all nodded. She continued, "And we really did all of that stuff like you guys flying on my back and Billy jumping off the hill?"

Tommy pulled out his smartphone and showed her the pictures.

"Hey, man," Ralph interjected. "You're not synced to the cloud or any other autosave service on that thing, are you?"

Tommy quickly checked his settings; sync was off. "Good thinking, Ralph. I'm guessing the NSA might be a little worried about five kids with superpowers." They all laughed, nervously, because they had all heard of the NSA but none of them were actually sure what it did.

Josephine wanted to be sure of everything before they went into school. "So we *did* go back in time to the field trip, right?" Everyone nodded. "That means that the eighth graders who saw Agnes and me dancing are going to be weird about stuff."

"Eighth graders are always weird about stuff, Josephine," Ralph offered. "But the part I don't get is Fiddle. First of all, he can do anything we can do, so why does he need us and why did he bring us back forward in time to today?"

"Maybe he thought it would be easier for us to just continue from here, y'know, instead of having to go to all of those same classes over again." Tommy put his phone back in his pocket. "And that's just fine with me. That's three tests I don't have to take again." He turned away from the group and began to walk around the enormous tree trunk toward the school.

Suddenly Fiddle was standing right in front of Tommy. "Hello," Fiddle said with a huge smile. "Did you all sleep well?"

"Fiddle!" They all cried out in unison.

Fiddle looked over his shoulder at the school.

"Mr. Fiddle," Josephine said in a much quieter voice. Fiddle gave her a wink, acknowledging that she had gotten the point.

In a hushed voice, Fiddle spoke to the whole group. "It's time you guys had a name." They gathered around closer as he continued, "Tommy came up with one that I like. It was The Magnificents. Do any of you have one that you like better?"

Billy spoke up right away. "I had some ideas, but I keep thinking of us as the Magnificents in my mind; it's like it just stuck there."

"Me too," Josephine added.

"Yeah," Ralph agreed.

"How are you spelling that, Tommy?" Fiddle asked, just to be sure. "Is it the Magnificence with a *C* and *E*, or does it end with a *T* and *S*?"

Tommy paused because he had only considered one way, but Ralph jumped in quickly. "It has to be the Magnificents with a *T* and *S* because there are a bunch of us and we are all magnificent. If we did it the other way around it would be like we embody the spirit of magnificence rather than being a group of superheroes."

"Magnificents with a *T* and *S* for sure then," Agnes chimed in. "Because we are a group of superheroes! But why did you stop us here, before school? Why is it so important that we pick the name now?"

It was a reasonable question, and Fiddle was delighted to answer it. "Because, my dear Agnes, you have your first assignment!"

Her reaction was not what he had expected. "Assignment? I don't want an assignment. Are you kidding me?" Agnes was totally bugged by the word *assignment*. "We just became superheroes, and now we have an assignment. That's like going to school twice!"

Fiddle had been at the game long enough, but it had been a while since he had worked with pupils who were still so young. "I'm sorry," he said gently. "It isn't really an assignment. You see, assignments you can pass or fail; assignments you can be graded on. No, Agnes; this is a mission! We cannot fail; a lot is riding on this. Will you accept a mission?"

He had used the right approach this time. It took less than a second for Billy and Agnes to both shout out "*Yes!*" The other three Magnificents looked at one another and said together, "We're in."

"Great," said Mr. Fiddle as they walked toward the school. "Now for the best part: we are meeting after school at a special location."

"The park?" Josephine guessed.

Fiddle shook his head no.

"The movie theater?" Ralph tried.

Again no.

"I know," Agnes said in a quieter voice than usual. "Is it the ice cream shop?"

Mr. Fiddle nodded his head. "Yes! How did you know?"

"I remembered." Agnes said as everyone stared at her with apprehension wondering if she had time traveled without them. It couldn't be, that was Tommy's power.

"When I was a little girl, before my parents got a divorce, we used to go to get ice cream all the time. We don't do that anymore." She paused, and the group remained silent as she worked her way through the memory. "But every time we went there, I saw a man in the corner of the ice cream shop. I noticed him because he always had the hugest ice cream. It was twice the size of anything I ever saw anybody else get. He was you!" Agnes squeaked as she pointed to Mr. Fiddle.

He smiled and nodded as she jumped at him with a hug. It was as if just holding him could bring back the way she felt in that ice cream shop, when her mother and father could still enjoy one another's company, when both of them had loved her at the same time, together.

"That's right, Agnes; it was me," Fiddle explained. "I have been watching out for you for quite some time. In fact, the same is true for each of you. If you search your memories, you may see me somewhere within, on a park bench, or riding by on a bicycle. I am so proud of all of you. You truly are the Magnificents! I will see you all after school; meet me at the ice cream shop!" Mr. Fiddle turned toward a door at the other end of the school as the five headed toward the main doors.

It was the longest school day ever.

The five waited as patiently as possible, but it felt like every teacher in every class had conspired to teach the most boring thing possible on the very same day.

Mr. Fiddle had handled everything with their parents between emails, phone messages, and typed letters which he had personally delivered to each of their homes; the five wouldn't have to worry about getting home at any reasonable sort of time.

The explanation letter went something like this:

"*Dear Parent, your child has been hand-chosen to participate in a special field trip.*

The trip requires after-school participation that may run into the later evening.

I will be personally responsible for the well-being of your child. Should you feel the need to contact me directly, please call me or send an email or text.

Thank you for your understanding. Bartholomew Fiddle."

The most fun of the whole day, by far, had to have been gym class. In the past it had been the day that Billy couldn't stand, Physical Fitness Testing Day. It was the day that nearly every kid ran faster and climbed the rope higher than him. They did more push-ups than he could, and the teacher counted so loudly that everyone in the gym knew what number he was on.

Today was different. Ralph was the first to break a school record for the fastest lap in the gym.

Josephine shattered the rope climb record by not only reaching the top but by also doing it twice as fast as anyone else.

Agnes did over one hundred pull-ups and then decided to stop because she was making it look too easy.

Tommy performed a little better than usual but with one-tenth of the effort, but Billy needed to go just a little further.

He outscored everyone who participated that day, but his best performance had to be cut short by the gym teacher. Ms. Rashburn blew her whistle after calling out "five hundred and thirty-seven." Her voice had begun to trail off after he had completed three hundred push-ups in a row, and class was ending, so she stopped Billy at 537. Billy looked disappointed and hadn't even broken a sweat.

Tommy said, "Do a thousand, Billy!"

Billy stayed on his hands and said, "You know I can!"

Matheson, surrounded by his cronies, scoffed, "You'll drop out before six hundred."

Ms. Rashburn was already walking away when the class started chanting, "One thousand, one thousand, one thousand."

She blew her whistle, and everyone stopped and stared at her and then at Billy. "Hey, it's your lunch," she conceded, and the kids all cheered as Billy continued. "Five hundred and thirty-eight," Ms. Rashburn counted.

At about 550, Billy looked over at Tommy. "Did she say something about lunch?"

"Yeah, man," Tommy said. "It's lunchtime; better speed it up."

Billy looked at Ms. Rashburn and said, "Try to keep up."

Before she could adjust, he fired off another twenty-five push-ups, and she blew her whistle. "Okay, I have you at five hundred and seventy-five, but I'm going to use my clicker from here on in." She pulled a number counter from her belt, adjusted the count to 575, and said "Go."

Billy went up and down so quickly it became hard to see him. Poor Ms. Rashburn's finger was having a terrible time trying to keep up.

Only a couple of minutes had passed when she blew her whistle and announced, "One thousand push-ups, a Stamford Middle School record!"

The class went crazy; even Matheson and his buddies were cheering.

Billy popped up from the floor as if he had only done a couple of push-ups, dusted off his hands, and said, "Let's get lunch!"

Tommy put an arm around Billy's shoulder. "Way to keep a low profile, man," he said quietly as the entire class filed behind them toward the cafeteria.

"Keep an eye on what he eats for lunch," Matheson said to his friends. "There has to be some explanation." His ego was still stinging from the amusement park.

The Magnificents shared a lunch period surrounded by Billy's new fans. They couldn't talk about Fiddle or the ice cream shop, being magnificent, or anything they usually talked about because nearly half the class was grouped around Billy, asking how he had done it.

"Clean livin'," Billy joked as Lisa Johnson parted her way through the crowd until she was standing right across from him at the table.

"I am a big supporter of clean living," she said with an air of smugness that came from having lots of money and a wardrobe the size of most kids' bedrooms. "You should come by my house sometime and I'll show you."

Billy laughed. "Do you even know my name?" he asked, fairly certain that she did not.

Lisa Johnson looked at him and tried to remember his name. He was in a couple of her classes, but she had never paid any attention to him, unless it was to make a joke about him or what he might be wearing. Suddenly she remembered the clamor in the hallways as he emerged from gym class.

"Billy; your name is Billy," she said as she pulled a glittering business card from a small pocket in her phone case and placed it in front of him.

He looked up at her with a strange feeling that this was going to be the first in a long line of proposals. He quickly glanced at Agnes, who was wearing a face that she reserved for moments of extreme disgust or excruciating boredom.

Lisa Johnson noticed Agnes's reaction and made her next move. She leaned across the table, getting closer to Billy than she had ever been to anyone who didn't have their own chauffeur. Reaching down for her card, she flipped it over to reveal a QR code printed on the back. Her eyes still glued to Billy's eyes, she said in a voice that made syrup seem bitter, "Scan the code for a free download of my absolute favorite song. I only give it to my best friends." With that she turned and left the table. The crowd was still pretty thick, but they made way for her to walk through, as she had become accustomed to.

Her head held high, she passed through them untouched until she walked behind Agnes's chair. Although she was a good ten feet from the table, she could not escape the power of Agnes, who managed to transform just enough to produce a long tail that slithered through the legs of the crowd undetected. The arrogant and haughty princess Lisa tripped over the tail at full speed, dropping her precious smartphone, injuring her pristine body. The lunchroom erupted with laughter. Lisa Johnson recovered her feet, picked up her phone, and scanned the crowd for the culprit.

"Who did that?" she screamed in a voice that could turn syrup to motor oil.

Mr. Cooligan walked over to investigate the disturbance.

He placed a calming hand on Lisa Johnson's shoulder and instructed the students to break it up, clean up, and move on to their next class.

The day dragged on.

There was a fire drill shortly after lunch. The entire school emptied out and waited for the fire trucks to arrive.

Ralph was practically pulling his hair out. "When is this day going to end?" He was pacing back and forth in front of Agnes and Josephine while Tommy helped to manage the crowd that had once again formed around Billy.

Some of the kids were actually lining up to feel Billy's muscles. Billy was getting used to the attention and even starting to feel like he was letting his audience down. At one point he turned to Tommy and asked him if he should do a quick run around the school to entertain the bored students. Tommy advised against it, reminding Billy again that they were not supposed to be drawing too much attention to themselves and that they had no idea what the consequences of being discovered might be.

The fire trucks showed up, and the principal made an announcement regarding the importance of having a plan and knowing where to go in case of a fire, and then everyone went back into the school.

The school day was almost over when it happened again. Another fire alarm rang out throughout the halls and in the classrooms. Students filed out with their teachers and assembled in the main parking lot, just as they had done earlier that day, only this was less than a half an hour before the final bell. It would have been perfect if the drill went off without a hitch but it didn't. The fire trucks did not arrive in the usual three to five minutes. In fact, they did not arrive even after fifteen minutes had elapsed.

Ralph was pacing again, and only a handful of kids were trying to buddy up to Billy.

It was beginning to look as though they would be staying late at school.

The policy was that the fire department had to arrive and pronounce the building safe before anyone could enter once the alarm had been sounded.

The principal made an announcement that the fire department was delayed because they were fighting a real fire on the other side of town, helping out a neighboring department, and both trucks were busy.

Ralph stopped pacing and stared at Tommy. "Ice cream," Ralph said in a firm voice. Tommy patted Ralph on both shoulders in an attempt to calm him. "Ice cream," he said again in a much more desperate voice. "I just want to go and get some ice cream," Ralph said. This time his voice sounded like that of a mafia hit man. "What's a guy got to do to catch a break around here?"

"I got it!" Billy said as he pulled the Magnificents close to him. "We can do it. We can put out the fire." The other Magnificents stared at him for a minute. "Don't you guys get it? All we have to do is go put out that fire, and then the fire department can send a truck over here and we can all leave and get ice cream!"

The group agreed that his plan did have some merit, and they began discussing strategies for putting out the fire when they heard the sound they had been waiting for. The fire trucks were on their way.

The fire department wasted no time declaring the building safe, and the principal even hurried through the safety reminders. It was Friday.

The Magnificents were respectful of Fiddle's warning to use their powers only when necessary. They walked to the ice cream shop, no wormholes, no giant bird rides, and even Billy walked at the speed of any normal eleven-year-old who was on his way to get some free ice cream, which was easily five times as fast as that same boy would walk on his way to school.

On their way to the ice cream shop, they all shared theories regarding their upcoming mission.

Billy thought they had been chosen because they had to save their school from a disaster, like a fire.

Tommy pointed out that an increase in imagination was most certainly not one of Billy's new powers.

Josephine thought they had been chosen because the mission had to do with kids. It seemed only natural to her that they would want kids to help out other kids who might be in danger, and Agnes agreed.

Ralph thought it must be something top secret because you needed an invisible guy if you were going to do something top secret.

Tommy reminded everyone that Fiddle worked to protect the entire universe so it might not even be a mission on Earth.

They all did their favorite imitation of an alien in need.

Billy's was by far the funniest because it made absolutely no sense. He started jumping around like a monkey; he even made little monkey sounds, and then he stopped and spoke in a voice that sounded like SpongeBob SquarePants. "I am an alien; I need help. Ooh aah ooh!" They were all still laughing about it when they reached the ice cream shop.

True to his word, Fiddle was waiting for them, seated at his favorite corner table, the one Agnes had seen him sitting at all those years ago.

"Hey, Fiddle," Billy blurted out. "Howdju beat us here?"

Fiddle smiled calmly as he surveyed the shop, recognizing that, so far, they were the only customers. "You don't actually think I sit through those infernal fire drills, do you?"

"So what's the mission?" Tommy asked before he even sat down.

"Slow down, Tommy," Fiddle said as he signaled to the server that they were ready to order. "The first order of business is the ice cream."

The girl behind the counter grabbed her order pad and headed over to the table. As she arrived Billy asked Fiddle if there were any limitations on the type of ice cream treat they could order. Fiddle told him he could have anything he wanted from the menu.

The shop had a little jukebox on every table.

It actually had music that you could order, just like old-fashioned jukeboxes did, but this one also served as a menu. By turning the menu knob, you could scroll through images of each treat that was available, along with a selection of toppings and a price.

Billy had started scrolling the moment he hit his seat. He stopped at the Ultimate Avalanche, a concoction loaded with ice cream and toppings ranging from sprinkles to nuts, all topped with a cherry.

"I'd like an Ultimate Avalanche, please," he said politely. "And can you give me three cherries on top?" The server nodded as she wrote down his order.

"Okay that's one Ultimate Avalanche with three cherries. Who's next?" the server asked as her eyes landed on Ralph. She smiled at him, and he forgot what he was going to say. She was about his age, but she didn't go to his school; he was sure of that.

"Ralph." Billy nudged Ralph. "Are you going to order or just stare at her all day?"

Ralph snapped out of it. His voice sounded like an adult soul singer. "Hot tin roof sundae with extra nuts, if you don't mind." She wrote down his order and looked at Agnes, who quickly ordered a banana split, followed by Tommy, who asked for a dipped cone rolled in nuts.

"Do you have any of the red dipping sauce?" Josephine asked.

The server nodded and added, "We have red strawberry and cherry, plus butterscotch, chocolate, and root beer."

"Root beer?" everyone at the table said in unison.

"It's new," the server responded as she held her pad out in front of her, waiting to add Josephine's choice.

"I think I'll try the strawberry with chocolate sprinkles, please."

Fiddle smiled at the server and said, "Hello, Candy; I'll take my usual."

"Sure thing, Fiddle," the girl responded.

She turned on her heels, walked a few feet, and then lifted the hinged counter top as she called out, "One split, two dips, a chocolate and a strawberry, nuts and chocolate sprinkles in that order, one tin, an ultimate with three cherries, and a Fiddle."

"Did she just say a Fiddle?" Agnes asked Fiddle in disbelief. "They have a sundae named after you?"

Fiddle laughed. "It's not actually on the menu. It's just something they do for me; you'll see. While we're waiting, however, I'd like to ask you all if you would be ready to leave first thing in the morning tomorrow. Well?"

"Leave for where, and for how long?" Josephine asked. She hadn't been away from her family much in her life, and even though she thought it was super cool to have powers and go to different places, she wasn't sure how ready she would be to be gone from home for a very long time.

"Up north for a couple of days," Fiddle said as he passed around a sealed envelope to each of the kids. "I have prepared permission slips for your parents. Please give these to them when we are finished here. If they have any questions, they can call me, or I can drop by, whatever. We need to get going by nine o'clock, so I will pick you all up before then.

Wear clothes you can get dirty in; we might have to play it rough.

And don't worry about the cold. I will provide all of the gear and anything else you'll need. After all, the Arctic can get a little frosty."

~ *Chapter 12: Ice Cream* ~

"The Arctic?" The Magnificents were shocked for a second, and then Billy said, "Hey, we live in Minnesota. How much colder can the Arctic be?"

"Actually, it's the other way around sometimes," Ralph added. "You all remember last winter, that stretch of record lows; they even closed the school for two days in a row. It was thirty below zero without wind chill here and seven degrees above at the North Pole. How's that for frosty?"

"How's this for frosty and hot?" Candy had a tray of treats in her left hand as she placed Ralph's hot tin roof in front of him. She placed a long-handled spoon in front of him as he stared at the way she balanced the tray and moved around effortlessly. Ralph saw his reflection in the large end of the spoon. He was drooling. He quickly grabbed a napkin, wiped his lips, and, regaining his soul voice, said, "Thank you. Thank you very much."

Candy delivered the ice cream quickly and accurately; she even had the cones balanced inside of long glasses, perfectly fluted to follow the contour of the cones. Everyone thanked her for the treats until Tommy mentioned that she hadn't brought Fiddle's sundae. Fiddle and Candy began laughing at the same time, and Candy walked away. Tommy looked surprised. The whole group was slightly mystified. Fiddle continued to laugh and then motioned with his eyes toward the hinged counter top. Candy opened it and then walked away, farther into the kitchen.

Seconds later she returned, pushing a cart with a large glass bowl on it. Inside of the bowl were roughly thirty scoops of ice cream, each one a different color and flavor. It seemed to grow as she guided it toward them, as did the smile on Fiddle's face.

"Ah, the Fiddle, one of every flavor. How many flavors are there this time, Candy, thirty-five?"   "We've added one, Fiddle." Candy smiled. "You are looking at number thirty-six." At the top of the stack of scoops was a bright pink scoop with flecks of crystals. "We call it Pom-Mite because it's made from pomegranates and our own habanero hard candy."

The Magnificents all looked at the scoop. Billy was salivating, and Agnes was too. Tommy and Josephine each raised an eyebrow at the exact same time and left them there.

Ralph said, "I prefer ghost peppers to habaneros, but it sounds interesting."

"Okay, enough about ice cream; it's time for me to tell you all why we are here." Fiddle rammed his spoon into the mound of scoops. He shoved a huge spoonful of ice cream into his mouth and said, "Mmnnffghhm mhhnnfffgg hgfmmmmn."

They all stared at him in dismay.

"Mm, ah, well, I guess you're right. I can't exactly tell you any more while I'm trying to eat." Fiddle wiped his lips with his own fabric napkin. They stared at the napkin. "I like to conserve on paper products—good for the planet, kinda my job really." Fiddle put down his napkin. He looked at all of the ice cream on the table and noticed that drips were about to happen on every sundae at his table, including his.

Fiddle looked at the whole group, threw his arms around his bowl like he was blocking off his territory, and said, "Whaddya waitin' fer? Eat!"

They all dug into their treats.

They didn't speak.

They ate.

Tommy finished off his large cone and wiped his mouth with his napkin. He was so absorbed in his own treat that he hadn't noticed anyone else around him. None of them noticed each other. It was as if they had been enclosed in an ice-cream-induced isolation chamber. He looked at Billy, who was tilting his head back to catch the final drop falling from the overturned, oversized parfait glass he was shaking over his open mouth. Ralph was scraping the last vestiges of hot fudge from his parfait glass as Josephine was cleaning up with a wet-nap.

"Oh yeah," Agnes said as she dropped her spoon into her empty bowl. "Wet-naps; let me have one of those."

Tommy's eyes moved to Fiddle's bowl. It was empty. "How in the world did you do that?" he asked Fiddle as he stared into the enormous empty bowl.

"Do you want another one, Fiddle?" Candy asked as she returned with her cart and started clearing the table.

"Not today, dear," Fiddle said with a satisfied grin.

"What? You can eat two of those monsters?" Tommy was staring at Fiddle's belly. "You're not even that big. Where does it go?"

"Sometimes I do have two Fiddles at a single sitting." Fiddle said, massaging his temples. "It helps me think. And sometimes the brain burns through that energy faster than the body can...at least that's what I tell myself. Anyway, we have a mission to plan."

"Okay, Fiddle." Tommy wanted a full explanation. "Are we different, physically, from everyone else? Like, do we get zits?"

"Everyone gets zits, Tommy." Fiddle put a thoughtful finger to his lips. "Maybe yours will be superzits!" The whole table burst out laughing, spurred on by the rush of sugar in their veins.

"Is Tommy right, though? You know, are we different?" Josephine wanted to know something specific. "If I keep growing and shrinking, using my powers to help others, stuff like that, will I be able to eat anything I want and still keep my girlish figure?"

"Most likely," Fiddle said. "But in your case even more so. After all, you can make any part of you any size you want it to be."

Josephine looked shocked and a little creeped out.

Tommy was staring at her.

Billy jabbed Tommy with an elbow and whispered, "I know what you're thinking."

"I am *not!*" Tommy said out loud as he purposefully looked at anything other than Josephine.

"Boys!" Agnes huffed, showing her disgusted/bored face. "I'll stick with being any animal I want, and I'll still be more civilized than they are." She patted Josephine on the shoulder. "Stay strong, sister." Agnes looked directly at Billy. "You gotta be careful with them. Give a boy what he wants, and before you know it...*bam*, you are stuck with him."

The whole table fell silent. The comment was a little on the spiteful side, even for Agnes.

Josephine knew her friend well and could tell that Agnes was upset that Billy had even said anything at all regarding her and not Agnes. Even though she never acknowledged it, Agnes was slightly jealous of Josephine for a number of reasons, and Josephine always tried to downplay their differences, but with Billy a whole new sort of jealousy was emerging. Suddenly a thought occurred to her.

She leaned in close and cupped a hand to Agnes's ear, whispering, "Watch Billy's head." She sat back up. Agnes looked at her with a puzzled expression and then at Billy. "Ready?" Josephine said out loud.

"Ready," Agnes returned, and instantly Billy's head was twice its normal size. Agnes gasped at first and then broke out laughing. The whole table soon noticed, all except for Billy.

Just as quickly as she had changed him, Josephine returned Billy's head to its normal size. The group was still laughing as Fiddle said, "So you can impose your transformations on others, Josephine. Very funny, but be careful with that. You know, that may come in handy." Billy was still sitting with a puzzled look on his face so Fiddle clued him in, "she made your head twice as big as it really is, Billy." Billy grabbed his head. "Don't worry; she changed it back already." Billy turned his head to catch his reflection in the window glass.

"I didn't do anything," Billy pleaded.

"It was for what you were thinking," Josephine answered.

"Oh, so now you're a mind reader too?" Billy asked sarcastically.

"No one has to be when it comes to seeing inside of your head Billy," Agnes said as she gently laid her hand on his. Billy was at once offended and comforted, and the combination of those two feelings shut him up better than a whole roll of duct tape. Josephine's little joke also calmed Agnes's feelings, creating the perfect environment for a little pep talk from Fiddle.

"The first mission for the Magnificents is top secret."

"Yeah! Top secret!" Ralph jumped up and hooted with his hands over his head. "I was right."

He saw Fiddle's eyes telling him to be quiet, so he lowered his voice. "I told everyone that our mission was going to be." Ralph's voice was now at a humiliated whisper. "Top secret."

"Right; thanks for announcing that, Ralph," Fiddle said sarcastically as he waved a hand, and they were suddenly top secret.

What anyone who may have looked their way, from any angle, including from the street, would have seen were one middle-aged man, sitting in a booth, in an ice cream shop with five middle school kids, all of them engrossed in their mobile devices.

What was really going on was a conversation about a top-secret mission to the Arctic in which Fiddle explained that the Magnificents were operating on a whole new level of top secret. "You probably think we're going to do some work for the government of the United States, right?"

They all nodded slowly as they began to realize that the moment they'd heard "top secret" they had all pictured themselves in black coats and sunglasses, SWAT gear, or fatigues.

"Well, we are not working for the United States." Fiddle paused just long enough for the five to become concerned. They weren't military kids or scouts, but they did enjoy a barbecue and the fireworks on the Fourth of July. (During the summer before sixth grade, Billy had found out for the fourth year in a row that the Fourth of July and Independence Day were actually the same thing.) None of them wanted to work against their own government.

Fiddle continued, "We aren't working for China or Japan, Germany, or any other country. We are not working for any religious group or organization like anything you have ever known. We only have to answer to ourselves, humanity, the planet, and the universe."

There was a long silence while the Magnificents thought about what that meant.

"How do we know if we're doing the right thing?" Josephine asked, breaking the silence.

"You'll know, Josephine; you'll know," Fiddle reassured her as he smiled at each of them. "You will all know; just trust yourselves."

The Magnificents looked at one another in a more serious way than they ever had before, and Fiddle sensed that the time was right to ask, "Are you all ready to take on your first mission?"

"*Yes, we are!*" They all cheered in unison.

"Great!" Fiddle responded. "Now a few quick details. We cannot be late, so be ready for me early. As far as your parents are concerned, we are off for a little camping trip. Remember, don't be afraid to have your parents call me. I'll come to your houses if necessary; whatever it takes. Besides, they'll probably be happy to get rid of you for a weekend."

"Mine will for sure," Billy interjected.

"So will mine," Agnes added. "Hey, wait. I'm at my mom's house this weekend; who did you write the letter to, Fiddle?" Fiddle made a gesture to the envelope in front of Agnes. She turned it over and read the front; it had her mother's name written on it. "How did you know which house I'd be at?" The moment she said it, she smacked her own skull with her fist and said, "Duh, never mind. I know. Heck, my mom would probably be happier if I moved out, except that I'd go live with my dad and that would burn her insides up. She'll probably think this letter is a stunt that my dad is pulling to get an extra weekend with me."

"Whatever it takes is what I said, Agnes. I will visit your mother if proof is needed," Fiddle announced reassuringly.

"I'm awright, Fiddle." Agnes picked up the letter and flipped it up into the air by the corner so it rotated end over end, perfectly straight up, perfectly straight down. She kept her eyes on Fiddle and let the letter fall almost all the way to the floor. At precisely the moment before the corner of the envelope was to strike the floor, she snatched it out of the air and said, "I'll be ready."

"So will I," the other four said in unison.

"Hey, Fiddle," Ralph said both in fear and spite. "Are you pickin' us up in a short bus?"

"In a manner of speaking," Fiddle responded so matter-of-factly that it took Ralph and the rest off guard. Then he squinted his eyes and said in his best Clint Eastwood voice, "It's been modified."

~ *Chapter 13: The Short Bus* ~

The next morning Fiddle was up bright and early. His dinosaur was up before him and had already let the cats in. Well, some of the cats—a couple of them had decided that going out was a bit too adventurous for their blood, so they were already inside of the house. Mickey was quickly followed by her two "babies," Penelope and Violet, hungry for their daily breakfast stroll through the garden. Fiddle quickly counted his cats, refilled the communal cat food bowl, popped a bagel in the toaster, and cracked a few eggs into his favorite frying pan. It had nice rounded sides that sloped to the perfect height for flipping eggs, mushrooms, onions, and anything you could imagine cooked up perfectly, and the best part was that it had only cost him fifteen bucks. He added a dash of salt and pepper to the eggs, caught the bagel as it popped from the toaster, and opened the refrigerator to grab some cream cheese when he noticed the clock. It was 8:30 a.m.

He checked his smartphone. He had forgotten to turn the ringer back on after silencing it when his Twitter app went nuts after a Tweet he'd sent the night before went critically viral. He didn't know what had gotten into him, but he'd decided it would be funny to Tweet a picture he'd taken of Mickey, Penelope, and Violet playing Twister together. These days you could put up a picture of just about anything and no one would believe it was real: cats with laser-beam eyes, the face of Jesus in an oil spill, double rainbows, and now dinosaurs playing Twister. Fiddle was rethinking that decision and more. He knew he could just start the whole thing over again, go back to the moment before the Tweet, keep his ringer on, and wake up with plenty of time, but he decided against it. If he was going to ask Tommy to strictly control his use of wormholes, then it was only right to set a proper example.

Fiddle had to act fast.

The dinosaurs always spent at least a half hour in the garden, and he still hadn't showered.

He bolted his breakfast down and moved on to the dinosaurs.

Only one thing could lure them away from the garden: watermelon. He grabbed two big watermelons from his "dino" fridge, pulled a machete from its sheath on the wall just above the fridge, tossed a melon in the air, and in a single motion, sliced it into six even wedges. He repeated the action for the second watermelon and ran from the kitchen.

The cats did the same, sensing imminent danger.

Just as the last cat cleared the kitchen, a thunderous clamor arose as Mickey, Penelope, and Violet came running into the kitchen. Mickey made the turn from the garden fairly well, followed closely by Violet, who would have made the turn if Penelope hadn't lost her footing, plowing into Violet, slamming both of them into the doorjamb. They quickly shook off the blow and joined their mother in a gluttonous feast upon the watermelon wedges. Fiddle kicked the door closed and threw the latch, the one Mickey couldn't open, and then bounded up to the shower.

Less than ten minutes later, Fiddle was on the road, teeth brushed, shower completed, vehicle packed. Actually, the vehicle had been packed for a couple of days. He had even remembered to fully charge the "bus" before he hit the road, which meant that he'd left it outside where its solar panels could soak up the rays of the sun for a few hours.

A minute later he was sitting in front of Tommy's house. Tommy emerged from his house, laughing. His mother was standing behind him, blowing kisses, as Tommy ran to the bus. Fiddle waved to Tommy's mother as he swung the door open for Tommy.

"A UPS truck?" Tommy couldn't believe he was climbing into a UPS delivery truck. "Our bus is a UPS truck." Tommy laughed, his eyes still on Fiddle. "I can't believe we are going on a secret mission in a delivery truck. Why aren't you wearing brown?"

Fiddle laughed and said, "Welcome aboard, Tommy. Take a seat."

"Don't you mean a box?" Tommy joked. He nearly choked on his own laughter as he turned toward the back of the truck. His breath was cut off by the signals his eyes were sending to his brain.

The inside of the truck had been completely redesigned; even the shape seemed to defy its exterior boxlike constraints. Eight captain's chairs had been placed evenly throughout the space, while TV monitors were sunk into the walls on either side. Each chair had its own laptop and mobile device, as well as independent lighting, fan, and position controls. The chairs even had speakers built right into them, as well as heating controls. There was a water dispenser next to each chair that featured a unique straw-like attachment, one for each seat: no glasses, no spills—at least theoretically.

"Awesome," Tommy said as he slowly stepped into the back.

"Pick a seat; we're in a hurry," Fiddle urged kindly. The moment Tommy was seated, a seat belt hugged him into the seat at just the right tightness, and Fiddle hit the pedal. The truck seemed to glide down the streets. It wasn't like any ordinary delivery truck at all. There was no sound related to the shifting of gears, no smell of exhaust, and it handled like a sports car. "Next stop, Josephine's house," Fiddle called out, and within a minute or two they were there.

"Lemme go get her," Tommy shouted, excited to show her the bus.

"Go ahead," Fiddle replied. Tommy realized that the seatbelt had withdrawn itself from around his body. "Nothing keeping you here." Fiddle swung the door open.

He bolted out of the door and ran to Josephine's steps, leaping all of them at once until he was standing on her porch, face-to-face with her dad. "Hello Mr. Connors," Tommy said quietly. "Is Josephine ready to go?"

Josephine stepped out sideways from behind her father and said happily, "I'm ready, Tommy." Her father gave a rather grumpy and disapproving look at the two of them. He even growled slightly until suddenly Fiddle stepped sideways, out from behind Tommy.

"Bartholomew Fiddle, sir." Fiddle smiled and offered his hand.

"Pleasure to meet you. I always enjoy meeting the parents of my pupils, particularly the truly gifted ones like your daughter.

"But I don't have to tell you how great she is, do I, Jim? Mind if I call you Jim?" Fiddle shook Mr. Connors hand with one hand and turned him back into the house with the other. "She's going to have a great time, and I'll keep an eye on them during our entire trip. Be sure to let Alice know that." Fiddle slowly backed out of the doorway and pulled the front door closed as he said, "Take care now."

"What're you two waiting for?" Fiddle asked as he scooted past Tommy and Josephine and headed to the truck.

"A UPS truck?" Josephine looked in disbelief at the truck.

Tommy grabbed her hand and said, "Wait until you get a load of the inside of this thing; it will blow your mind." He pulled her toward the truck.

Inside the house Mr. Connors was still feeling strangely about the whole thing, but he couldn't quite express himself. He just stood in a sort of fog as he pulled the curtain on the front door window to one side and peeked out at the truck.

"Did Josephine get off all right?" Alice Connors asked as she walked out of the kitchen to find her husband peering out the window.

"Strange little man," he said, still in the fog. "And why a UPS truck? They're going on a field trip for school in a UPS truck."

Alice Connors walked over to her husband and took his hand. "Maybe the school got a deal on the truck, or maybe it's a donation. You don't look right, Jim," she added. "Have you had your coffee yet?"

"Coffee," he said. "Maybe you're right; maybe I just need my coffee."

Inside the truck Josephine just stood in awe for a second, and then her hands sprung up as if pulled up by strings at the wrists. Then she began to bounce up and down in excitement. "This is *so* cool!"

"Seats!" Fiddle announced. "Places to go, people to see."

Tommy and Josephine grabbed seats across from one another and were simultaneously hugged by seat belts as Fiddle sped off toward Billy's house.

They arrived in no time, and Billy was already on the sidewalk waiting. He was making good use of his time by breaking his own record for number of push-ups in a row. He was fairly certain that he had done it at least three times over but had lost track numerous times. As soon as the truck arrived, he stopped.

The vehicle door swung open, and Billy made a joke about the truck, "What did you bring me, Fiddle?"

"Step inside and I'll show you," Fiddle replied. Billy hopped in quickly and turned to the back of the truck. He stopped in his tracks and fell backwards throwing both arms out to the side for balance as the shock nearly knocked him over.

" Awesome! Totally frickin' awesome, man!" he shouted as he rushed to the seat in front cf Tommy and dove into it. He swung his butt around into the seat and called out to Fiddle, "Let's go!" His seat belt hugged him in close as Fiddle slammed down the pedal.

At the next intersection, an old lady stepped out onto the street with her dog. She was one of those old ladies who thought that because she was really old she should be able to walk out into the street anytime she wanted, regardless of what the traffic light was telling her to do. It was telling her to stay on her side of the street.

Fiddle was driving at the speed limit but still didn't have time to stop before hitting the old woman or her dog, so he neatly created a wormhole on either side of her.

A young couple who had been sitting at a corner coffee shop was looking out the window at the precise moment it occurred. They got up and ran out of the shop toward the old woman, expecting to find her crushed on the pavement. To their surprise she had crossed the street unscathed.

"How did you do that?" the young man asked.

"Do what?" the old woman snarled, pulling her dog away from the offensive young man. "What?" She snarled in a voice that clung to her old, entitled distain like a wet windbreaker. "DO you think that just because I am elderly I can't even manage walking my Wilbur across the street?"

"We saw that truck heading right for you, but it seemed to pass right through you," the young woman explained.

"What truck?" the old woman snapped. "You must be all high on that marijuana all you young people are smoking these days. Now leave me alone."

The young couple looked at one another and turned away from the woman, their eyes drifting in the direction of the truck, which was now turning right, six blocks away. They returned to the coffee shop and decided not to mention what they had witnessed to anyone.

Fiddle pulled the truck up to the curb in front of Agnes's house. She was already waiting even though nobody could see her.

Fiddle swung the door open and said, "C'mon in, Agnes." A grasshopper leaped onto the first step of the truck, and Fiddle closed the door.

Agnes transformed right there on the step. "Will I ever surprise you?" she asked Fiddle.

"I'm not sure," he replied. "But please do keep trying."

"*Agnes!*" a cry went up from the back of the truck, and Agnes turned and saw the others, kicking back in their plush captain's chairs.

She nudged Fiddle with an elbow and winked. "Nice ride, old man." She headed back and took the seat across from Billy. "Hey, everybody." She smiled as the seat belt hugged her, and Fiddle headed for Ralph's house.

A minute later they were at Ralph's house. Ralph came running out, and Fiddle swung open the door.

Ralph said, "Good; just making sure it was you. Be right back." He ran off behind the house and returned unbelievably quickly, especially for Ralph. He stepped onto the truck, and Fiddle swung the door closed. Fiddle was waiting for a joke about the truck.

"What?" Ralph said, identifying that Fiddle looked expectant.

"Well," Fiddle urged. "Aren't you going to say something about the truck?"

"Oh yeah, great cover! Nobody thinks it's weird to have a UPS truck around pretty much anywhere you go in the world." Ralph looked at the steering wheel. "Except you'd have to be able to change the side that the steering wheel is on if you were in England or something."

As he finished speaking, the interior front end of the truck reversed its sides. Fiddle d dn't even have to move; his whole seat moved, along with the steering wheel, and even the door changed to a window and the window to a door, but it did it almost magically. The essential parts that made up the structure of each part of the truck moved in such a way as to be completely fluid. The parts actually moved Ralph to the other side by the soles of his shoes and then back again because they weren't actually in England.

To say that the truck was intelligent enough to change itself into the new configuration for roads European would only cover the first change. What is more startling in this instance is that the truck actually knew that was time to change back to its original configuration, and quickly.

"*Cool*," Ralph shouted.

"*Ralph!*" exclaimed the other Magnificents. Ralph turned to see them all smiling at him and waving.

"Get in here!" Billy shouted as Ralph hooted and ran all of the way to the back, the last seat, driver's side.

"I like it back here," Ralph cooed as he settled in to the hug of his safety belt.

Fiddle drove the truck toward the edge of the city. "We'll be heading out of the city in a minute, and then we'll be on open road.

Tommy! Feel free to zap us out at any time once we hit the long stretch of Ninety-Four West." Fiddle instructed. "But real quick: have any of you heard of the abominable snowman?"

There was a silence.

"Are you not hearing me back there?" Fiddle started playing with a knob while saying, "Testing, testing; are you hear—"

"*Yes!*" they all shouted.

"Do you mean the abominable snowman from 'Rudolph the Red-Nosed Reindeer'?" Billy asked as he sipped on his water straw.

"Yes and no." Fiddle began to explain the true story behind the abominable snowman.

"He actually kinda looks like that snowman, believe it or not, but he's significantly larger, and he grows. He actually gets bigger when he gets madder, so he's very dangerous.

Also, he has a hibernation thing he does where he is awake for a long time and sleeps overnight, and then all of a sudden he's out for fifty years or sometimes longer.

Sometimes his hibernation is shortened if he senses a disturbance.

He is very connected with the wildlife population, and likewise so are they connected to him.

I am connected to them and to him as well, and I can tell you that he is awake and it is early. He's only been asleep since 1979."

"Excuse me, Fiddle, why do you want me to get us there?" Tommy asked. He quickly added, "I mean you already know him; you can feel him, so why don't you do it?"

"Of course I can do it, but I want you to do it." Fiddle explained. "It's good to exercise your power, and I do plenty of that. Also, Bombi will respect you for doing it."

"Bombi?" the Magnificents all said in unison.

"You call the abominable snowman Bombi?" Ralph said quietly from far in the back, but the communication system made sure that it was audible for all to hear.

"Yes," Fiddle answered. "He's really quite gentle unless he feels he must defend against you. The problem here is that the polar ice caps are indeed melting; miles upon miles of glacier are breaking off, floating away, and melting down, and entire ecosystems are changing.

This will be perceived as an immediate threat by Bombi.

It will be our job to convince him to allow humanity to continue to exist."

"Is he really that powerful?" Billy asked, feeling suddenly weak and small.

"It all depends on the level of threat he faces," Fiddle explained. "For instance, if a guy on a dogsled yelled at him, he would just ignore him.

If the guy shot at him, he would release the dogs and throw his sled several miles away.

If the guy was in a tank and attacked him, Bombi would grow large enough to crush the tank or swallow it whole." Fiddle paused. The Magnificents were silent; they were beginning to understand that they were about to face a power they had never dreamed of before or since their own transformations. "Try not to worry; we come in peace."

Ralph broke the tension with a spot-on alien voice. "Fear not, oh great Bombi; we come in peace!" Everyone laughed, including Billy, who was already imagining how he would outrun the abominable snowman.

"Anytime now, Tommy," Fiddle instructed as they hit a long stretch of open highway.

Tommy looked at Josephine, and she smiled in encouragement. He concentrated on an image of Bombi and the feeling he'd had when he'd first learned about global warming. The deeper he thought, the clearer the vision of Bombi became. He saw Bombi walking along the edge of a vast body of water and said, "Here we go."

The truck vanished from the highway.

~ *Chapter 14: Bombi* ~

Fiddle drove the truck along the edge of the large body of water that Tommy had seen in his vision. Bombi was not in front of them, so Fiddle checked his mirrors: nothing.

"Nice work, Tommy. He's right here. I can feel it, but I can't see him." Suddenly the truck shifted slightly and then tilted skyward as it rose from the ground. A second later a large eye was looking directly in through the windshield. Fiddle smiled and waved. The truck continued to rise and just as quickly came to rest, facing the body of water, roughly two hundred feet up from where they had landed.

"Stay here," Fiddle said as he grabbed a coat from a closet behind the driver's seat. He left the vehicle through the front door, motioning to the five to remain in the back of the truck. They could tell that he was looking out for them, but they were curious.

"I wish we could see what's happening," Billy said after a couple of seconds.

"No problem, Billy," Ralph said. "Come check this out. I discovered it while we were driving."

"I'm stuck in my seat belt," Billy said. "How do I get out?"

"Try thinking about getting out," Ralph responded. "I wanted my cushions to be soft, and they became softer."

"Really?" Josephine asked.

Agnes quickly thought about a couple of things and was in the back, perched on Ralph's shoulders, within a second or two.

"Got it," Billy exclaimed as he jumped from his seat and headed back to Ralph. As he stepped past Josephine's seat, it moved slowly over until it was right next to Tommy's seat. Billy hardly noticed, but Tommy started to get a little nervous. He quickly stopped thinking of what he wanted.

"Hey, that's awesome," Billy said. "Look at this, you guys. Ralph has a camera pointed right at Fiddle and the big guy."

"Never mind, you guys," Ralph said as he punched at his laptop. "I got this."

A second later the large TVs on either side of the vehicle burst to life with the image of Fiddle and Bombi standing face to whole person. The truck, Fiddle, and a field full of caribou were perched on a bluff while Bombi stood just next to the bluff looking at them.

"Let's see if we can get sound," Ralph said as he managed a few settings on the laptop. Sure enough, seconds later, they could hear Fiddle talking to Bombi. Agnes flew back to her seat, regained her form, and thought about how nice it would be to put her feet up. As she reclined, Fiddle's words became clear.

"I know they all seem like idiots, Bombi, but not all of them are," Fiddle was pleading.

"Is he talking about us?" Billy wondered out loud.

"Shhh." Ralph put a finger to his lips.

"There are actually a lot of good people who are working on the problem." Fiddle was pacing back and forth in front of Bombi. "If I were you, I would want to do the same thing, but in my heart I would know it was wrong, just like you do. You can't wipe out an entire species simply because the individuals who control that species are self-indulgent, arrogant, and cruel." Bombi folded his arms across his massive chest and grunted. "Not to mention the whole fabric of the universe thing. How ya' goin' to explain that one to the elders? Listen, give 'em another chance." Fiddle turned toward the truck. "I've got some really nice kids I want you to meet."

He started to walk toward the truck and then stopped. He looked directly at the camera and said, "Grab some coats and come out here, you guys."

"We're never going to be able to get away with anything," Ralph said as he closed the laptop.

Josephine's chair slid back into position, and the Magnificents descended upon the closet. Inside were sets of coats, hats, gloves, boots, scarves, and backpacks with each of their names on them. They each quickly grabbed a coat and rushed to the door. As they ran from the vehicle and headed over to Fiddle, the sheer massiveness of Bombi hit them. They slowed to a walk as they surveyed his features. He looked like a combination of a fierce gorilla, a polar bear, and a handsome middle-aged man.

"Bombi, I would like to introduce some new students of mine," Fiddle announced joyfully as he waved his hand in the direction of Josephine and Agnes, who had huddled together for warmth, friendship, and security. "These lovely young ladies are Josephine and Agnes." Josephine attempted a curtsy, fighting a slight shiver. Agnes did more of a bow and began to move her feet back and forth for warmth. "And these three gentlemen are Ralph, Billy, and Tommy." Ralph hardly seemed affected by the cold and took a deep bow, as did Billy, and Tommy was feeling quite cold but felt it important to actually say something to Bombi, so he shouted, "Hello; it's a pleasure to meet you."

Fiddle placed a hand on Tommy's shoulder. "He's big, Tommy, not deaf."

Bombi's face moved into a grin and then a laugh: a huge, warm, deep laugh. "Hello," he said with the voice of a mountain. His voice made them feel safe, not frightened, and his eyes shone with the radiance of the sun.

For a moment none of them noticed the cold, but only for a moment. Josephine and Agnes began to shiver, and Tommy started stepping back and forth, right and left, in order to stay warm.

Bombi raised his right arm and laid it down upon the ground before them. It was so thick that they could only see his eyes over the top of it.

Fiddle called out, "Follow me," as he took a run at the arm, jumped up, and grabbed a hold of Bombi's fur.

The five quickly got the idea and did the same. Bombi rotated his forearm slightly, bringing them to the top. They were instantly warmed by his dense yet soft fur and were now sitting less than thirty feet from his enormous face. From where they sat, they could see that the caribou herd stretched farther than they had imagined.

"Why are they all just standing there?" Josephine asked.

"Their home has changed, and they are confused," Agnes answered. "They have come to Bombi for help." Josephine could see that Agnes was right.

Bombi made a deep sound of approval.

~ 189 ~

"But what can you do to help them?" Josephine asked Bombi.

"Bombi help," he said in a big, deep, simple voice. "Bombi find new place."

"We can help too," Josephine said.

"Yeah!" they all cheered, each one excited to help but none of them quite sure how.

"Fiddle help Bombi," Bombi cooed like a young child, his voice deep but so gentle. "Fiddle's friends help Bombi, so nice." Bombi rolled his forearm back down, and the Magnificents jumped off. Fiddle landed first and took a few steps toward the truck. "I'm going to check a few things in the truck," Fiddle said to Bombi. "Things I think might help us figure out what to do."

"Fiddle and friends help good," Bombi said.

"I love it when you talk like that," Fiddle said to Bombi. "It's cute." The abominable snow man laughed to himself.

"We're just going to go warm up a bit," Tommy said as he pointed to the truck, waving to Bombi with his other hand. The Magnificents all headed to the truck as Bombi nodded in understanding.

Once they were all inside of the truck, Billy said, "Fiddle friend, Bombi good." His imitation of Bombi was as good as the vocal cords of an eleven-year-old boy could do. He got a good laugh. Then he asked Fiddle, "Is Bombi slow or something?"

Fiddle looked at Billy and asked, "If he was, would that be a reason not to help him?"

"No," Billy replied. "I just wondered because of the way he talks." Billy felt like he was saying something bad but didn't know why, so he continued, "I didn't mean anything bad."

"I would only be concerned for you, Billy, if you had," Fiddle explained, "because you are all going to face many situations as the Magnificents where you will not be able to tell how intelligent or powerful your foe may be. Fortunately for all of us, Bombi is a friend, and I can assure you, he is quite intelligent and also very old. In fact, he usually only talks like that in front of animals and occasionally the military. It calms the animals and confuses the military."

While the Magnificents, guided by Fiddle, scoured for resources in the truck, Bombi placed a hand on the plateau where the caribou had assembled. He pulled himself up with that single hand as his body transformed to a much smaller Bombi, still quite large, roughly twenty feet tall. He patted a few of the caribou and walked over toward the truck. He walked around to the front of the truck and looked through the windshield. Billy had his face in the closet; he was looking for some gloves. Suddenly he felt a presence. He closed the closet and looked out through the windshield.

"Bombi," he gasped, stumbling backward slightly as he said it. "Hey, everybody; Bombi's right outside the window."

Fiddle turned and gave Bombi the internationally known one-minute sign. Actually the sign was known intergalactically. It just meant something different in a variety of places. Knowing what it meant could at times be lifesaving. In this case it meant one minute, and one minute had passed, putting Fiddle on his way out the door, equipped with a backpack with compartments for a map of the region pulled from an active satellite directly overhead, a GPS device that provided a wealth of information in addition to the coordinates, a first aid kit, and a variety of snacks.

"Magnificents, it's time to have some fun and help out our friends. We're going to put the bridge back, starting from the edge of the bluff. Let's get out there and get this thing going!" He was hoping for a huge hooray or something like that.

Nothing.

The Magnificents were all getting suited up to go outside, but none of them looked like they had any idea what they were going to do.

"What thing?" "A bridge?" "How?" "With what?" "Huh?" said Tommy, then Ralph, then Josephine, then Agnes, and then Billy.

"*Oh right.*" Fiddle started banging his own skull with his fist. "You don't know the plan. I am very sorry. Let's go outside, and I'll explain it to you." Fiddle stepped toward the door.

"Hey, Fiddle," Billy snapped. "Forgetting something? You don't have a coat on."

Fiddle turned only to look and said, "I don't need one, and neither do you. We're on a mission; turn those cold receptors off." He opened the door, and while he was stepping out said, "Don't worry; you're the Magnificents. Little things like cold and heat won't affect your bodies. In fact, you can withstand a great many things. How far that goes is up to you. So come on out; I need my team." He left the door open, turned his back, and walked toward Bombi.

"Heck of a pep talk," Billy joked. "But what the heck, he's been right all along." He tossed down his coat, took off his boots, and pulled off his socks. He turned to Josephine and Agnes. "Girls, do you mind? I have to change," he said as he reached for his zipper. They turned their heads with a little laugh. Billy bent over and unzipped the lower portion of each leg of his pants. He was now wearing shorts. "Okay, you can look now," he laughed. The girls were mildly amused, and then Billy ran out onto the cold ground in nothing but a T-shirt and shorts.

The Magnificents all crowded into the doorway to watch. Billy was halfway to Fiddle when he realized that there were patches of snow here and there and he had been colder than he was willing to admit when they had first arrived. He stopped walking for a minute and turned back toward the truck, holding his arms out to the sides, palms up. Then he scrunched up his shoulders and looked at the rest of the Magnificents.

"I don't feel cold at all! Woohoo! Let's go!"

The rest of the group momentarily forgot that Billy was the guy who had gotten punched hard in the face by Tommy and hadn't even acknowledged it. Fueled with Billy's excitement, they all rushed outside, expecting an epiphany, a shining change from being cold to not being cold. What they got was an instant realization that they were not being affected at all.

Ralph reached down to pick up a clump of snow. He could still feel it, but it wasn't cold. The group stood around him and looked at the snow. It wasn't melting. Fiddle and Bombi had moved up behind the group and were peering into Ralph's hand.

"Hand the snow to me," Fiddle said calmly. Ralph turned the snow over in his hand, placing it in Fiddle's palm. It did not melt. "Watch now," Fiddle said, and all eyes were on his palm. He looked at the snow and said, "Feel my warmth." Nothing happened at first, and then slowly and steadily, small beads of water formed along the edges of the snow. It was melting. Still, there was no effect on Fiddle. He looked at each one of the Magnificents and said, "But if you want to feel it, just tell it." He looked at the snow again and said, "Let me feel you." They watched as his hand started to turn from his normal pale skin tone to a pink and then a red.

They were all still staring at his hand until his face said, "Okay, show's over." Fiddle's hand returned to normal, filled with a small pool of water. He held it there, as still as could be. Gradually a skin of ice began to develop on its surface.

"Wow," said the Magnificents.

"A wonderful capability to have, is it not?"

The Magnificents nodded in agreement. Fiddle stood up straight, dropped the icy water, and said, "Particularly useful when you're being attacked with heat-seeking missiles—isn't that right, Bombi?" Bombi laughed a big, deep, "ha-ha-ha" sort of laugh and scratched his head.

"So let me get this straight," Bombi said in a voice that sounded more like Samuel Jackson as Sergeant Fury than Barney the big purple dinosaur. "These kids are *those* kinds of students."

"Yep," Fiddle said with a hop in his step.

"Howdju keep that secret from me? Wait a second," Bombi said as he turned toward the Magnificents. "One of you is a wormholer! That's why I didn't feel you comin', Fiddle." Bombi loomed over the Magnificents. Then he knelt down to get a little closer and said, "Don't tell me." He rubbed his huge hands together like a little boy excited to pick his favorite candy. He paced around the outside of the ring of the five. They all watched him circle them, and then he said, "Tommy, you're the wormholer." Bombi looked at him closely. "You can be of great use if Fiddle has taught you the Tosser. Bombi turned to Fiddle. "Didju?"

Fiddle turned to Bombi and said, "This is our first mission, Bombi."

Bombi grabbed Tommy around the ribcage out of the circle of five and walked off with him toward the edge of the woods, saying, "It's time for you to learn the Tosser."

Tommy blurted out, "Why don't I just take this whole place back in time to before the melt?" Bombi stopped walking, dropped Tommy, turned to Fiddle, and asked, "He can do that?"

Tommy pulled himself off of the ground, brushed himself off, faced Bombi and said, "I can do that."

Bombi looked at Tommy with an expression that skydiving instructors give their students a full minute after they say jump and said, "Well, then, why haven't you done it yet?"

"Because he shouldn't," Fiddle said while walking toward Bombi. "You know it as well as I do, Bombi, that even if Tommy did that, the same thing would happen again."

Bombi agreed, and Tommy was once again picked up.

"What are you *doing*, Bombi? I can walk by myself!" Tommy shouted. Bombi did not let go.

"I really want you to learn this, Tommy, and in order to do that, we have to be right here!" Bombi planted Tommy next to a pile of boulder-sized rocks.

Tommy looked at where they were versus where they had been. "I guess your way is a little faster," Tommy admitted. "What's a Tosser?"

Bombi looked at Tommy very thoughtfully and said, "Well, I've seen Fiddle do it, so I figure I can tell you what he did, and then you can do it."

Tommy gave him a less than optimistic look.

Bombi turned with a grand gesture and said with a booming voice, "Picture a wormhole." He motioned to a spot roughly thirty feet ahead of them, and then there was a small flash.

~ *Chapter 15: The Pen & The Tosser* ~

Fiddle and the rest of the Magnificents walked out of the wormhole toward Bombi and Tommy. "I think it would be better to leave the wormhole training to the wormholers," Fiddle said. "Besides, we need a plan." With this Fiddle pulled a pen from his pocket.

It was no ordinary pen.

"I need you all to take a look at this diagram," Fiddle said as he waved the pen in the direction of his backpack. A tube jettisoned from the pack, following the sweep of Fiddle's pen tip. It looped through the air and landed in the center of the group. Fiddle clicked the pen once, and the tube opened, revealing the map that opened like an accordion, stretched to its maximum. With another click and a twist of the pen, Fiddle made the map topographical.

"Awesome," Ralph said as he stepped closer to examine the details of the topography.

"I'm glad you like it, Ralph, because this is your job," Fiddle said as he handed Ralph the pen.

"I don't know how to use this thing, and what's my job, looking at a map?" Ralph tried to refuse the pen, but Fiddle was persistent.

"This is your job, Ralph; we need you to do this." Fiddle put one hand on Ralph's shoulder and in his other hand held the pen vertically, twelve inches from his nose. "That laptop is not at all intuitive for your time, Ralph, yet you made it do what you wanted it to do. You gravitated to the tech in the truck before testing because you saw that the rear section of the truck was loaded with extra tech."

Ralph was about to interrupt but realized that Fiddle was right. Fiddle recognized it in his eyes and felt it strong as daybreak. "You probably don't even need instructions on this pen, if my guess is correct." He bobbed the pen up and down in front of Ralph's face, and Ralph took it quickly.

"Let's see," he said as he turned his head toward the backpack.

"Let's see what else you have in that bag, Fiddle."

Ralph began to speak a little more triumphantly as one of the tubes launched from the pack. It shot up. "Let's see what's inside." The tube did a little turn in the air at its peak and then began to drop.

Ralph was a little stunned that it had worked in the first place and left his pen just pointing up in the air. He quickly focused as he watched the tube seemingly hasten its descent toward the ground. In a swift and single motion, he aimed the pen at the tube, spun on his heel, whipped his arm around as if he were throwing a sidearm pitch, and then tapped the pen when the tube was directly over and roughly a dozen feet higher than the topographical map. He clicked the pen, and the tube opened. It was a GPS, a very well articulated GPS that had somehow manifested out of thin air with coordinates and details about the entire area.

"Well done." Fiddle slapped Ralph on the back. "Well done."

The entire group cheered. Bombi let out a hoot that would have passed for a train whistle, and Billy jumped about a mile into the air.

Roughly thirty seconds later, Billy landed his jump in a perfect three-point stance, ten feet to the right of Bombi, who said, "I didn't know you could do that!"

Billy stood up and stepped toward Bombi. "I didn't know you could talk right."

Bombi looked him in the eye and said, "Bombi talk right," in his most cuddly bear voice, and both he and Billy cracked up.

While Billy was still holding his gut from laughing, Bombi swatted him sideways and into the air, propelling him so quickly they all lost sight of him. Bombi turned to the group, shrugged his shoulders, and said, "He'll be awright."

They all laughed.

Ralph shouted, "I got an idea; watch this." He raised the pen and pointed it at the center of the map and the center of the GPS. He double-clicked it, and the map and GPS closed.

The tubes began to drop until Ralph quickly twisted the pen slowly and the tubes were held in their positions by the pen. He twisted some more, and they drew closer together while moving toward him. A second later he caught both tubes as he moved the pen to his mouth, where he held it in his teeth. Ralph shoved one tube under his arm and twisted the end of the other tube until it glowed. He drew the other tube out from under his arm and fused it into the other tube, gently gliding it into the glowing end. Without wasting a second, he tossed the tube out and up into the air, retrieved his pen, and guided the new tube to a spot where they all could see.

A click later, the tube burst open revealing a mash-up of map and GPS elements hovering a few feet off the ground.

Another click and the map and GPS separated, but not entirely. The coordinates from the GPS were registering in real time on the map. There were clusters of numbers making shapes of color outlining the dimensions of everything from trees to caribou to Fiddle, Bombi, and the Magnificents, even the one who was currently arcing his way through the sky.

Ralph pointed to the arcing spot that represented Billy and said, "There he is."

Agnes ran a few steps and said, "I'm going to find him." She transformed into a hummingbird and shot off.

Bombi said, "Oh, look at that; she becomes a hummingbird." He turned away from watching Agnes fly away. "She'll never catch up with him."

Josephine, who was now standing face-to-face with Bombi, pointed at the sky. "Wait for it." Bombi got an amused expression on his face and turned his eyes to the sky. He was chuckling to himself. A few seconds later, at a point far beyond where they had lost sight of Agnes the hummingbird, a tremendously large bird seemed to grow out of nowhere. Agnes had become the largest peregrine falcon you could imagine.

Bombi looked at Josephine and said, "She just changed into a much bigger bird, didn't she?"

Josephine smiled.

"There she is," Tommy called out, pointing to the GPS, "on the GPS map thingy, it's Agnes."

Josephine became her normal size again and watched as the large bird shape gained ground on the catapulted Billy.

Ralph stepped in closer to the GPS. "Let's call her Gypsum," he said as he twirled the pen a bit, "after all, she's more than just a GPS," and Gypsum sparkled and expanded.

"Agnes is going faster than the speed of sound." Ralph said in amazement.

The entire group watched as Agnes went even faster. Suddenly both the small dot assumed to be Billy and the larger mass of Agnes stopped, and the larger dot blended with the smaller dot.

"Zoom in," Josephine said with urgency.

Ralph flipped the pen in the air like a small baton. It twirled a thousand times, into a blur, and then flashed with the sound of swords clashing. Two rings burst out, in opposite directions, from the center of the flash. They fell back to earth, flipping end over end as they fell. Ralph put his hands up, fingers together, as the loops slid over his hands and onto his wrists. As they hit they expanded into intricate tiles that mapped themselves around his skin, gloving each hand.

"Nice," he said as he waved the hands over Gypsum. Miles of data flew by as he dug his way in deeper. As he neared the single dot, it began the separate into two. Then suddenly it was one again. Then two.

"What's going on down there?" Josephine wondered out loud as the dots became one again and suddenly grew. The large dot was now a shape, and it was headed back in the direction of the group. "They're coming back," Ralph announced. Everyone cheered except Bombi, who just added, "See, I toldja he'd be fine. Oh, and is that all you got, little girl?" he said challengingly to Josephine.

She walked over to Bombi and said, "Sorry, it really takes a lot out of me," her voice getting quieter and quieter. "Can you come a little closer?" Bombi picked her up and held her next to his ear. She whispered, "No," and then she disappeared. Bombi gasped. He looked all around him. He started pulling through his fur with his massive hands.

"Where'd she go?" he said to the group, his arms out to the sides, palms up.

Suddenly Josephine became a good seventy-five feet tall and was standing on Bombi's shoulders. He lost balance and fell beneath her weight. A half second later he was standing up to her full size. Fiddle whistled by putting his fingers under his tongue. It was amazingly loud but necessary. The two giants looked down. They were in danger of crushing everything. No room was left on the bluff for anything.

"You kids take your game elsewhere," Fiddle called up to them as he pointed over the edge of the bluff.

"Fine," Bombi said as he leaped up into the air in the direction of the bluff's edge, growing as he did. Within a second or two, he was standing on the ground below the bluff with his head high enough to be eye to eye with Josephine, who was still on the bluff.

Suddenly Josephine felt something, an overwhelming sensation she couldn't ignore. She jumped directly into the air, first using a boost from a sudden growth spurt and then shrinking to her normal size. The result was like a cannon shot. She burst into the sky, and as she cleared the top of Bombi's head, she was gone.

A large fast shape had cruised overhead, taking with it any sign of Josephine.

Bombi turned in the direction of the shape and saw a large peregrine falcon zooming toward him.

Something was falling his way, getting bigger by the second. It was Josephine, who at this point was now a good eighty feet taller than Bombi but was flying at him too fast for him to escape. She plastered him up against the bluff, pushing the edge back a good twenty feet, making a mound form so that now there was a small hill with a bluff at the edge rather than the previous bluff. Even the pile of boulders was pushed back from the force of the blow. Bombi was surprised and even a little dazed by it. He looked up to see Josephine towering over him with Agnes and Billy standing on her shoulder.

"He looks a little out of it," Agnes said with a smirk.

"Aww, he'll be fine," Billy said as he took a big leap at Bombi, bounced off his nose, and flipped up and landed on the ground next to Gypsum.

Josephine leaned forward as she began to shrink, placing her hands on Bombi's shoulders.

Agnes became an eagle and soared down toward the group, changing back and landing next to Fiddle. "He'll be cool about this, right?" she asked, slightly worried.

Fiddle watched as Josephine gave Bombi a little kiss on the forehead and then continued shrinking as she walked over him and joined the group.

Bombi stood up, brushed himself off, turned to the group, and said, "The kid's right. I'm fine." He began to shrink, and as he did he caught the edge of the bluff with one foot. Stepping past the edge, he became his usual height, took a couple of steps, and towered over the group once again.

"They're a good group, Fiddle," Bombi continued. "They're smart, talented, and they stick up for each other. Only one more lesson to learn, and we can get started. Will you do the honors?" he waved a hand toward Tommy.

"Right, the Tosser," Fiddle exclaimed.

"Okay, Tommy; follow me," Fiddle said as he bounded toward the pile of boulders. Tommy ran to keep up but was falling behind. "C'mon, Tommy; move faster," Fiddle cried out as he mounted the pile. Tommy tried a leap, and to his surprise was able to clear about twenty feet. He tried again and leaped thirty feet in one bound. Moments later he was standing next to Fiddle at the top of the pile of boulders.

"Right then," Fiddle said as he patted Tommy's back. "Let's get started." Fiddle faced a large boulder and pointed past it to a point roughly a hundred feet away. "Keep your eyes on that floating block of ice, Tommy," he said as he waved his arms in a clockwise circular motion in front of him.

A small patch of swirling light appeared above the ice block. It began to expand, and then a deep darkness of space appeared within the swirl.

Fiddle stopped his circular motion and pulled his arms back toward himself evenly

The deep space seemed to advance toward them. When it reached the boulder, Fiddle made a slight motion inward with his hands, and the boulder teetered

Tommy took a step back

Fiddle lifted his hands in unison, and the boulder rose from the pile. He looked over his shoulder at Tommy and said, "The Tosser."

Fiddle pulled slightly back with his hands and then flung them forward.

The boulder moved toward the pair and then ripped off into the deep space, toward the ice block.

The deep space was actually pulling the rock through the swirling ring above the ice block. When it reached the ice block, there was a sound like a tennis ball machine, and suddenly the back side of the swirling ring burst open with a projection of deep space accompanied by a boulder rocketing through the air at incredible speed. The boulder landed nearly a mile away with a splash.

"Whoa!" Tommy exclaimed. "Just how exactly?"

Fiddle smiled and held Tommy by the shoulders. "It's easier than you think. Okay, imagine a two-sided wormhole with each side just inches away from the other, allowing time and space to increase the impetus of the object you are tossing, and that's it."

Tommy was not convinced. "How do you make the hole, y'know, the hand motions, the way to grab the thing?" Tommy pressed his forehead in an effort to unblock his understanding.

"All you are doing is extending space in both directions and using the energy of your hands to guide the object. You make yourself a gravitational force to pull the object back toward you, then reverse your intent, power through the hands, and thrust forward through the center of the hole, amplifying the momentum using time over distance acceleration." Tommy still looked mystified. "Trust me, Tommy. Better yet, trust yourself." Fiddle smiled. "Start small; what can go wrong?"

Tommy consented and resolved himself to give it a shot.

He stepped over to the smallest boulder on the pile and planted his feet roughly ten feet behind it. He began to lift his arms, a look of determination on his face, when suddenly Fiddle interrupted.

"Maybe start just a little smaller," Fiddle suggested as he picked up a rock about the size of a baseball from the crack between two monstrous boulders and held it out to Tommy.

"Or not," Tommy replied as he finished a full circle with his hands and a spark of lights flashed a full hundred yards from the place they were standing.

The circle burst open to reveal deep dark space and advanced toward them at a stunning rate. The moment it made connection with the boulder, Tommy brought his hands closer together and lifted. The boulder rose from the pile and moved toward the pair as Tommy pulled his hands back.

When the boulder was less than five feet from their noses, Tommy snapped his hands forward, and the boulder shot off with a puff. Small particles of the boulder were shorn from its exterior from the sheer force of Tommy launch. The boulder reached the hole inexplicably quickly and popped out the other side with the sound of a cannon being fired. The course of the boulder's flight could not be followed with the naked eye. The other Magnificents and Bombi were watching from below.

Ralph called out, "Gypsum has a lock on it."

Fiddle shouted down from the top of the boulder pile, "Let us know where it lands."

Ralph waved his gloved hands over Gypsum and soon was tracking the boulder as if he were flying in formation with the meteoric projectile. It slowly started to descend and then hit the ice, skidding for roughly a mile.

"Got it," Ralph yelled. "It's right about twenty miles from the North Pole."

Fiddle turned to Tommy and said, "Very impressive; now can you control it."

Tommy smiled, his heart racing with the thrill of his initial launch. "Where do you want the next one?" he asked Fiddle as he surveyed a stack of four larger boulders in front of him.

Fiddle looked for a landmark.

There was a rocky peak sticking up out of the water nearly a mile from the edge of the bluff.

He instructed Tommy to hit the top of it with whichever boulder he wanted. The top boulder in the stack of four was calling to him. He ran up behind it and got into position. Tosser wormholes disappeared after they were used unless the wormholer consciously kept them open. Tommy waved his hands in a circular motion and formed the Tosser. He pulled back and engaged the top boulder from the stack. Pulling it back very gently, he fired with a flick of his wrists. The boulder shot off and fired from the Tosser with a pop. Seconds later the top of the far-off peak was shattered by the boulder.

"Hooray," went the cry from the entire group. And then *pop pop pop*—three other boulders shot from the Tosser, lodging direct hits upon the rocky projection, nearly flattening it from the blows.

"Woo-eee," Billy shouted above the other hoots and hollers.

"That boy is ready," Bombi cried out as Fiddle and Tommy bounded their way down from the boulder pile to join the group.

Everyone gathered around Tommy and congratulated him until Fiddle said, "It's time."

~ *Chapter 16: The Rescue* ~

The group gathered around Gypsum.

"Ralph, I need you to show us what's out there. I want to know what's ice, how thick, how far away, and what's land? Also, we need resources, trees, boulders, anything you see out there that we can use to construct this bridge."

Ralph said, "Okay, Fiddle; no problem, but aren't caribou great swimmers? Why do they need a bridge?"

"Good point!" Bombi answered. "But you see, Ralph, the caribou are not the only friends who have come to me."

Bombi motioned with his tree trunk of an index finger toward the wooded hills. "We have the arctic fox and hare, the Dall sheep, and the wolverine to help. For many of these creatures, that ice bridge, which is now lost, was their route between the vast stretches of ice and this wooded area in which we now stand.

Replacing the bridge will open up that route once again, enabling these creatures to choose where they want to be, to find lost members of their herds, to bring back together families who have been separated through no fault of their own."

"Yeah, Ralph; we gotta have that bridge, man," Billy said as he slapped Ralph on the back and moved alongside Fiddle. "So what's our plan, Fiddle man?"

Fiddle smiled broadly at Billy and asked, "How far can you throw one of those boulders over there, Billy?"

Billy looked at the boulders like Fiddle was nuts and then remembered all of the things Fiddle knew he could do before he even knew he could do them.

He walked backward a few steps and said, "I will go find out." Before Fiddle could say, "You do that," Billy was at the top of the pile, hoisting one of the larger boulders over his head. From the ground it looked like a tremendously oversized golf ball on a ridiculously small tee. Suddenly the boulder shot into the air and flew all the way to the previously pummeled rocky peak, where it flattened the peak once and for all.

"Woo-eee," the entire group hollered in unison as Billy flipped back down to the ground and landed back next to Fiddle.

"That'll do, Billy; that'll do." Fiddle laughed.

"So that's where we begin. I want Billy and Tommy piling rocks from here to the ice ridge.

Ralph will get us coordinates and monitor the buildup.

We need to make sure that all of our stacks are reinforced. I want two lines of boulders roughly a half mile apart from one another from the edge of this bluff to the ice.

Billy, you take everything from here out to halfway. Tommy, you hit the ice ridge and work your way back to meet Billy at the halfway point.

The rest of us will work with lumber. I want Agnes and Josephine to work as a team to gather any fallen trees first. They're all over this place.

Bombi and I will also work as a team. If we need to bring some trees down at the end, we will, but let's work with what we can find before we damage anything.

Ralph will keep all of us in touch." Fiddle looked at Ralph, who hesitated for only a minute before thrusting his hands toward the backpack and pulling back, causing the backpack to leave the ground and fly into his hands.

He waved his hand over the pack, and seven rings rose from the pack and clung to his gloved hand. He turned to the group and started throwing the rings at their heads. As the rings drew close, they opened into an almost fluid matrix of tiles and wrapped themselves to the ears and down the jaws of each member of the group. Even Bombi's headpiece was perfectly wrapped to his face. The last ring rose from Ralph's hand and wrapped itself to his head.

"Testing, testing, one, two; all right, Magnificents, just nod if you can hear me." Ralph watched as each of them nodded. "We are good to go, Fiddle."

"Okay, everyone, you know what to do." Fiddle was excited, almost too excited. "Wait!" he said a little too loudly for the headphones.

"I can't forget to mention the importance of our next moves, directly after finishing the bridge.

I need you, Agnes, to take on the form of an alpha male caribou and lead these caribou across to the other side safely. Billy, I need you to grab the snacks from the backpack and make a trail through the wooded hills surrounding us, leading down to the bridge. Do your best to make the snacks last. You have a lot of ground to cover. Then we will all help Bombi to get the other animals heading in the right direction. Billy, Tommy, Josephine, and Ralph will monitor our progress and deal with any difficulties that arise. Are we ready, Magnificents?"

This time Fiddle got the reaction he had wanted earlier: "Ready!" they all shouted as numerous high fives were shared. Josephine smacked a strong high five with Agnes and then turned and grew quickly to give a high five to Bombi. He was overjoyed to have someone his size along for the mission.

"Ralph, where are we, where is the ice, and what are the best places to begin to look for lumber and rock?" Fiddle asked as the group gathered around Gypsum.

Ralph used his gloves to show close-ups of each place Fiddle had asked about. He zoomed in and out to show where each spot was relative to the others. After Ralph finished pointing out every spot, he said, "Remember, if any of you need anything, just talk to me. I'm here."

Fiddle had been teaching students for so long that it was easy for him to pick up the clues, but everyone could tell that Ralph felt like he wasn't doing anything to help the cause: he wanted action.

"We are going to need you here, working with Gypsum, keeping us informed. Remember, Ralph," Fiddle reminded him, "we don't want the rest of the world to see what we are doing here."

Ralph responded without enthusiasm, "Yeah, I kinda figured that already, so the first thing I did was to capture an image of the entire Arctic region and feed that image back up into the satellite. Everything will look as though it hasn't changed until I remove that image. C'mon, Fiddle; there has to be something I can do."

Fiddle spoke in a calming and appreciative voice. "You are already doing a fantastic job of it, and no one else here can do it." He looked around at the others in the group, and they were all nodding their heads.

"Yeah, man," Billy said. "You're the man for this sort of thing; we need you." Ralph looked encouraged.

"Ralph," Bombi said in his most military voice, "you have a duty to protect the other members of this team." Then in a softer voice he continued, "Besides, the moment all those yahoos who monitor this stuff realize that *nothing* is changing up here, they are going to send airplanes. Airplanes from China, airplanes from Russia, airplanes from your home, the United States of America, are going to be flying in low to get a look at us." Bombi continued, "I am going to have to hide so they don't get me angry, and everything we are doing here will have to be hidden. Do you know what you're going to do then?"

Ralph looked with concern at Bombi and said, "No, Bombi; you're right. I didn't think this all the way through."

Ralph suddenly became a great deal more interested in Gypsum. "We are going to have to work on this one a bit, aren't we, Gypsum?" Ralph waved a hand over the center of Gypsum, and a voice responded, "I suppose we are, Ralph; how should we begin?"

"Whoa, it can talk," Billy exclaimed.

"And you can spit when you say your Ts," Gypsum responded. Everyone, including Billy, burst out laughing until Ralph said, "Okay, then; we have a limited amount of time. Let's review the locations of all critical points to the project."

"Tommy, you start here," Ralph said as Gypsum highlighted the region. He continued through the entire plan until, minutes later, everyone was sure of it. "Break," Ralph said, like the quarterback in a huddle, and the team went to work.

Billy was the first to action. Faster than the eye could see, Billy was on top of the boulder pile.

He tossed three boulders before Tommy could bound up next to him, and then two more, while Tommy said, "I'm going to catch up to you."

The motions Tommy made were so quick they were invisible, and the Tosser was created. He had an immense boulder lined up. He pulled it back and gave it a wave forward. It cruised through the Tosser and flew unwaveringly through the air until it came to rest, lodged perfectly into the forward edge of the ice shelf.

"That's one," Billy said as he fired one after another off, moving between them so quickly it made his voice sound like it came from everywhere.

Then Tommy demonstrated why a wormholer might choose to keep a Tosser open. Instead of lining up the Tosser, Tommy levitated the boulders around him by distorting the space between the Tosser and the boulders. As the space folded itself around a boulder, Tommy would gently nudge it, the Tosser sucking it into its center and then blasting it out the other side. Tommy looked like he was directing an orchestra as he would nudge and then pull back to control the flight of each boulder.

"Hey, Ralph," Tommy said over his headset. "Would you mind keeping a tally over here?"

"I'm on it already," Ralph responded. "Billy is up by twenty."

"Oh yeah!" Billy said as he continued to move between boulders like some highly charged particle.

"Let me know when I pass him," Tommy said with certainty, and Billy sped up even faster.

Meanwhile, Agnes and Josephine were far more cooperative.

Without a word, Agnes took off into the sky, circling the woods, indicating the location of fallen trees.

Josephine was looming over the entire forest, reaching down wherever Agnes indicated, picking up trees like toothpicks.

Just beyond and below the bluff was an area that stretched for a half mile and then dropped off into icy waters left by the receding, melting glacier. It was there that Josephine piled the massive fallen trees. Her pile was growing quickly. It extended from the spot where Billy had started his wall to the area Ralph had indicated for the other wall within minutes.

Agnes noticed the problem right away. "We need the other side of the wall over here quick, Ralph. How's Billy coming?"

"They've almost completed this side. Billy's still up by a few boulders." Ralph continued, "It's a race to the center."

Agnes and Josephine stopped what they were doing and moved to watch the boys finish the west wall.

"Billy's up by one," Ralph said, "but Tommy's been catching up the whole time. It's a race to the finish, and these two stalwart warriors are battling head to head. Who will be the first to capture the prize and who knows what exactly the prize is..."

Suddenly there was the sound of thunder. It was the final two boulders coming to rest in the center of the wall.

"It's done," Ralph exclaimed. "Time to move to the east wall. Oh, and just in case anyone's counting, it's a tie. I guess you guys will have to determine the winner on the next wall."

"Nice job, Tommy," Billy said over the headset.

"You too, man," Tommy said.

"Yeah, guys, great job, but we need the other wall to move ahead," Agnes said, fully in control of her voice even though she was now a bird.

"Josephine, you can start filling in along the west wall and work your way over now that the wall is complete," Ralph instructed.

"Sounds good," Josephine answered as Agnes and Josephine continued to forage.

"Where's Fiddle and Bombi?" Billy said as he set his sights on the east wall.

"We're here, Billy," Fiddle responded. "Keep it up, everyone; you are doing great. Bombi and I will have a surprise for you shortly."

"Bombi like," was the next thing they all heard through their headsets. It was hard to perform feats of magnificence when the real abominable snowman sounded like a kiddy program host in a big purple costume.

After the laughter died down, Billy started launching again.

Tommy started at the same time.

Agnes was already flying high above a prime stretch of fallen timber. Josephine was on it instantly. She filled in along the close edge of the west wall until the crossfire from the boys made it impossible.

"I'm going to have to fill from the other side," Josephine said. "But I can't keep stepping around these guys."

Agnes circled around. "Group the trees into stacks, and then get to the other side," she said as she darted away.

"I have an idea." Josephine quickly made the stacks, which was no easy task considering it was a bit like stacking toothpicks. Small, remaining parts of branches helped the stacking, and Josephine was ready to leave the woods. She stepped over the boys as they continued firing off massive boulders, neck and neck in a macho game of "boulder-ball."

As Josephine reached the opposite side, she turned and saw the biggest bird yet.

Agnes had changed herself into a gigantic snowy owl. She swooped down into the wooded area, which now had piles of fallen trees stacked in rows of two. Josephine was extremely tidy, even under pressure. Agnes lifted two stacks simultaneously and with great ease. She lost one tree from the stack on the right but brushed it off as an acceptable loss.

One of Josephine's earliest questions about being a person who could grow and shrink had been about clothing, but she had never found the need to ask it

Every time she transformed, so would her clothes.

She really wasn't thinking about the clothes specifically while she was doing the thing in her brain that made her change size, willing herself to grow or to shrink.

About an hour before Fiddle had picked her up for the mission, Josephine had had a question and then an idea.

She wondered whether or not she could change the size of her clothes if they weren't on her.

She had tried every combination she could think of, from wishing, to thinking, to trying to quickly take her sweater off while she was big or small, to see if they stayed the size she changed into.

They didn't.

They always returned to their original sizes.

The best combination she had found was moving the sweater to a spot it normally wasn't worn, like just around her neck, and then changing her size. If she left the sweater on her body, it remained the size she changed to, perfect for the baggy look or just to have the nice, comfortable oversized warmth of a big sweatshirt.

She wasn't sure why she had spent so much time messing around with that idea until now.

She had a giant snowy owl headed right for her, hankering to let fly a couple of bundles of trees, and she had no way to catch them.

"Agnes," Josephine said through the headset. "Come around again. I need a second." "No problem," Agnes responded as she banked for a second run. Josephine became even larger than she already was. She was wearing a hoodie she had borrowed from Tommy on one of their walks to school. She pulled it up to her neck and shrank back down to her bridge-building size. The hoodie remained significantly oversized. Quickly Josephine spun the hoodie around backward so the hood was facing her face. She slipped it down around her waist and opened up the hood.

"Fire when ready, Agnes," she said as she readied herself to catch both bundles. She thought about suggesting doing one bundle at a time but was fairly certain that Agnes would find that less than challenging and a bit of a time waster. Agnes came swooping in fast, headed directly for Josephine and a head-on collision, when suddenly she used her gigantic wings to stop and glide up slowly as the wings pumped down, lifting her giant talons over the makeshift basket where Agnes had gently delivered the bundles of trees. For Josephine it was a bit like being hit by a single, sudden gust from a hundred-foot freezing blow-dryer set on high. Fortunately, Josephine felt no cold, and the wind was a mere distraction.

"Thank you," she said as Agnes rose higher into the air above her and then turned to get another load. Josephine packed the bundles in tight to the edge and prepared for another delivery.

Meanwhile, the boys were all in a private conversation on the headsets. Billy had wished he could find out the stats, secretly, so he knew how he was doing against Tommy, and Ralph didn't think that was cool, so he dropped in on both of them privately.

"I'm telling you guys, it's neck and neck. I'm busy running shields and working on close-quarter cloaking. That's right, boys; you heard it here first. I am working on making *all* of you invisible. Well, sort of."

"Hey, Ralph, I could use a little help here." The voice broke in on their private conversation.

"Who is that?" Billy asked as he continued throwing an even more incredible number of boulders. "Ralph, are you there? Ralph," Billy continued. "Who's the girl?"

"Uh, well, I mean," Ralph stammered. "It's me, boys: Gypsum," the magical map/GPS system said in a voice that sounded like Jennifer Lawrence as Katniss in the movie version of *The Hunger Games*. "Ralph thinks I sound better this way."

Both Tommy and Billy agreed that Gypsum's new voice was way better than the original voice, which had sounded a bit like it had tinfoil vocal cords.

Plus, now they could refer to Gypsum as *her* rather than *it*. She had a very good reason for interrupting, and the boys were taking the conversation in the wrong direction, telling her how good she sounded and how they could see her running through the woods whenever she spoke.

"Seriously, Ralph," Gypsum stated, "we have a bit of a problem. There's chatter on the security channels for all of the major players: China, Russia, Japan, the United States, and even Canada are noticing the anomaly."

"Gotta go, guys. Keep up the pace," Ralph said as he popped out of the private chat and started a new one with Gypsum. "What is the anomaly?" he asked urgently.

"Weather patterns," Gypsum responded.

"Duh, I should have thought of that right away," Ralph confessed. "No problem. Let's tap into the nearest Doppler radar feed we can get a signal from and map it over our projection." Ralph surveyed the feeds while Gypsum ran a quick search.

"Got it," they said simultaneously.

"Do it," Ralph said as they both laughed at the coincidence. Immediately the weather map was fed over the static transmission of an unchanged Arctic. Seconds later the chatter stopped as words in English, Russian, Chinese, French, Japanese, and German, as well as a host of other languages, meaning "it must have been a glitch," chattered their way through the security channels.

"Thanks, Gypsum," Ralph said with true gratitude. "It's a good thing you're here."

"Slow down there, Ralph," Gypsum replied. "You're starting to talk to me like I'm a person. They cart boys your age who talk to objects away."

Ralph looked puzzled and said, "I talk to my action figures all the time, and my computer, like, 'where did you put that picture?' or 'for crying out loud, how long are you going to take to boot?' and my backpack: 'you stupid thing, why do you have to weigh a ton? I'm going to kill you.'"

Gypsum made a sound like the old computers used to make when working on an answer, complete with the sound of the tape heads.

Ralph got the joke as she replied, "Very well, then; continue to address me as a person if you wish. Just don't be mean if I take a while to answer. Or else you will have to do the calculations instead."

Ralph waited a second or two before responding, "So you're actually telling me that I shouldn't be so hard on my computer and my backpack, right?"

"Exactly, Ralph," Gypsum explained. "Those objects are just objects. It isn't the computer's fault that it is slow. I am sure it was faster when it was first purchased, possibly the fastest of its kind, but someone had to put a whole bunch of stuff on it to make it slow down, and that person was most likely you." Gypsum didn't stop. "And your backpack. It is just a backpack, a place to put things. Until you put something in it, it is very light and easy to carry. Someone had to put a lot of stuff into that backpack to make it heavy, and that person was most likely you." Gypsum had finished, and Ralph had listened, and then something occurred to him.

"Hey, Gypsum, you aren't anything like my computer or my backpack. Since you began speaking to me in this voice, you have referred to yourself as 'I' and have provided insight into things without an instruction to do so. You have artificial intelligence far beyond anything I have seen being developed in my science and technology magazines, but you aren't just technology, are you?"

Ralph was staring directly into the center of Gypsum where a light was pulsing. He had noticed it before but always thought it was a reflection or an odd combination of the units that made up the data stream overlapping. As he stared at it more closely and moved around Gypsum, he realized that it remained in the center of everything from the coordinates to the map and anything else that Gypsum displayed.

"Is that your heart?" he asked.

Suddenly the sound of thunder struck again as Billy and Tommy completed the east wall.

"What'd we get?" Billy said into the headset.

Ralph quickly checked the girl's progress and said, "Josephine and Agnes are just about to finish; Get down here, Billy and Tommy."

Agnes had just enough rows of trees to run a final row along the east wall, and Josephine had moved to the other side of the freshly finished wall.

Before the boys could ask a thing about how many boulders they tossed, Fiddle's voice came over the headsets.

"As soon as Josephine and Agnes finish that row, let Bombi and me know. We've got a surprise for you." Fiddle and Bombi, who were both huge, were jumping up and down, pounding their gigantic fists, turning rocks, trees, and layers of earth into a pile of dirty rubble that was becoming a mountain.

Tommy and Billy were back with Ralph and Gypsum in no time. Agnes made the final drop to Josephine and headed back to the group. Josephine quickly and precisely laid in the last two bunches of trees so that there was now a stretch of wood piles, like those used to hold up Boston, that ran between two great rock walls. She quickly returned to the group and everyone hugged one another.

"That's beautiful," Gypsum said. Josephine and Agnes whipped their heads around to look at Gypsum.

Ralph held up a hand and said, "I'll explain later." He turned toward Gypsum and spoke into his headset: "Ready for you guys."

Instantly a large glowing ring appeared above their heads, perpendicular to the ground.

"Ready," Fiddle called to Bombi as Fiddle stood to the rear of the mountain they had created. Bombi began to shovel massive handfuls of the pile into the air, where it would be captured in the folds of space, which Fiddle was now channeling into his Tosser. Acres of dirt spewed forth from the Tosser like a well-directed fire hose, filling in the space between the walls, paving the wood pile bridge. Fiddle's aim was perfect, filling right to the edge of the receding glacier's ice shelf. Bombi was like a machine, keeping a constant flow of dirt funneling through Fiddle's enormous Tosser. The bridge filled up fast. Fiddle's Tosser slowly moved back toward Fiddle as he adjusted the direction of the stream, until...

"Stop!" Ralph cried out as the Tosser filled in, right up to the edge of the bank.

Bombi stopped throwing dirt, and Fiddle broke the connection with the Tosser, which instantly disappeared. The group walked over toward what used to be the edge of the bluff. Bombi and Fiddle arrived just as they all reached the transition between the new bridge and the old bluff.

"It's a little rough," Fiddle said as he looked at Bombi. "Shall we?" The two giants walked to the joining edge and began patting down the area, smoothing it with their massive feet.

"Hey, I want in on this," Josephine said as she grew to join them. Within minutes the transition was perfect: even the tiniest of creatures would be able to cross. Josephine returned to her normal size and Tommy gave her a big high five and then a hug.

"We're going to run across and get the other side," Fiddle said as he and Bombi trounced their way across the bridge, testing its strength as they did. Josephine didn't even hear what Fiddle was saying as she sunk more deeply into Tommy's hug.

"Agnes and Billy, it's time to move into phase two," Fiddle said through the headsets. Neither of them wasted any time.

Agnes changed into a bird and flew into a cluster of caribou, closest to the bridge. As she hit the ground, she transformed into a magnificent caribou buck and began running toward the bridge. The caribou closest to her were startled at first but watched her run. As they began to recognize that the big buck was running for open ground, they began to follow her. Soon the entire herd was in motion.

Billy ran like a streak through acres of wooded land, dropping little pellets of food and dusting the air with a powdered mixture that Fiddle had labeled "animal magic." He didn't even bother figuring out how to dispense the stuff; he just stuck a hole in each bag and ran so fast that it got spread around pretty evenly by the time he returned, leaving a final trail to the bridge. He ran out about halfway across the bridge and found himself in the center of a herd of caribou. Billy quickly made his way to the wall and ran all the way to the glacier side before Fiddle and Bombi could actually finish tamping it down.

"Hello, Billy," Bombi said as he tamped.

"Hello, Bombi," Billy replied. "Aren't you guys done yet?" Billy laughed and then ran over to the side of the edge on which Fiddle was working. "Almost done?" he asked as Fiddle patted the last rough spots down with his enormous foot and then slowly shrank to his usual size.

"What can I do for you, Billy?" Fiddle asked as he realized that Billy had something on his mind. Billy did have something on his mind, something that had been bugging him for a while.

"Do you remember when you showed all of us how you could do all of the stuff that we can do?" Billy had another question even as Fiddle nodded in recognition. "Well, I was just curious. Who's faster, you or me?"

Fiddle looked at Billy and then up at Bombi. "Does it matter, Billy?" Fiddle asked as he tried to make a point. "Who was just bigger, me or Bombi?"

"Bombi," Billy said quickly.

Fiddle replied equally quickly, "But it didn't matter; we were both helping and giving it our all."

Billy started to look a little disappointed and even humiliated as he said, "I get what you're saying, Mr. Fiddle, I really do. I just kinda wanted to know, y'know, for fun."

Fiddle knew that every opportunity for a lesson could also be an opportunity for understanding. "Well, Billy," he said, "There's really only one way to find out. We're going to have to race." Billy was so excited he ran around in tiny circles until Fiddle said, "You'd better save some of that energy. I'm pretty fast." Billy stopped running and looked at Fiddle, who said, "I'll race you back; pick your wall.

Billy looked at the east wall and then the west wall, which he was standing next to. "I'll take this one," he said, pointing to the west wall.

"All right, I'll go to the east wall, and Bombi will start us." Fiddle spoke into the headset, "Billy and I are racing back along the east and west walls, Ralph; please monitor who wins. Bombi is going to start us."

Agnes spoke into her headset, "Hey, I gotta see this; can you guys wait?"

Fiddle responded, "The herd is moving well on its own now, Agnes; you know how to get yourself out of there."

With that Agnes left the herd as an arctic tern and flew above the bridge, where she transformed once again into a snowy owl, her eyes zeroing in on the starting point. "Thanks, Fiddle, I'm in position," she said as she glided over the scene.

"Racers, to your positions," Bombi said as the herd of caribou continued north, off of the bridge and toward their frosty home. By this time a swarm of smaller arctic life had begun to follow the bait left by Billy and had worked their way to the bridge. "Ready," Bombi started. "Set, *go!*" Fiddle and Billy were gone instantly from their starting points and were moving so fast that even Agnes was having trouble spotting them.

Billy looked through the antlers of the remaining caribou and saw Fiddle on the east wall. He was keeping up.

Billy was carefully hitting each boulder at its flattest point although the wall was quite uneven.

He looked over to see how Fiddle was handling the wall, but there was no one there. He looked back to see if he had gained an edge, and then forward, but there was still no sign of Fiddle. Then Billy looked down at the water. It was smooth, flat as anything.

"That's it; he's on the water," he said accidentally into his headset as he ran down the side of the wall, pushing himself even faster as he hit the icy water. He was moving so fast that a plume of steam rose from his feet as he ran. Now he was running even faster.

"Pretty cool down here on the water, isn't it, Billy?" Fiddle said with a laugh.

"I don't know about you, old man, but I'm making this water boil, "Billy said as he turned it up faster than he was sure he could handle, and suddenly he was back. The earth beneath his feet was scorched as he came to a sudden stop just past the group assembled around Gypsum. Before they could see Billy through the cloud of dust, another cloud burned the earth on the other side of Gypsum. It was Fiddle. The dust settled, and Billy and Fiddle were standing across from one another.

"That was amazing!" Tommy shouted as everyone ran to congratulate Billy, including Fiddle, who was panting a bit and smiling from ear to ear.

"I have got to say, that was great fun! I haven't run like that in at least twenty years." Fiddle laughed as he held out his hand to shake Billy's.

"You are fast!" Billy exclaimed as he shook his master's hand. "Thanks for the race!" Billy felt totally pumped up. "I never would have tried running on water if you hadn't pulled that disappearing act," he said to Fiddle as they continued to shake hands.

"And I pushed myself to the limit, Billy, because you inspired me to," Fiddle returned. "Great fun!"

Agnes flew down and joined the group.

She ran to Billy and gave him a hug and then a high five. "You were amazing. You were so fast I had trouble seeing you until you started boiling that water down there And you, Fiddle, you were almost as fast, and you're ancient!"

She quickly turned a shade of red from embarrassment, and everyone, including Fiddle, burst out laughing. Bombi arrived a moment later and returned to his normal giant size.

"Nice race, you two. Very impressive, Billy. I haven't seen anyone faster than Fiddle in a very long time." Bombi moved toward a group of small animals who seemed to have lost their way. "We have to round them up and help them get across," he said as he marched his group toward the bridge.

"We'll be right there," Billy said as he turned toward Ralph. "And while we're on the subject of races, Ralph, who threw more boulders?"

Ralph looked at Billy and said, "Sorry, man, I didn't really keep count. I was too busy writing code to create shields for you guys so you could do your work without being seen."

Tommy patted Billy on the shoulder and said, "Hey, man, what's it matter? We rocked!" The whole crew burst out laughing.

"Billy had two thousand two hundred and seventy-five boulders on the first wall. Tommy had two thousand one hundred and six.

"Tommy had two thousand six hundred and thirty-three boulders on the second to Billy's two thousand and four," Gypsum said from behind Ralph's back.

"So Billy had more on the first wall, but Tommy had more altogether, Gypsum concluded, adding, "Two winners; deal with it." Everyone laughed again, and Tommy and Billy gave one another a high five.

Lots of cute little animals were wandering from the path all around them, so everyone did their best to wrangle them toward the bridge.

"Agnes and I can head up into the woods to make sure we flushed them all out if you guys want to keep these little guys moving," Josephine said as Agnes changed into a bird and headed up toward the woods. The rest agreed, and the round-up continued. Josephine grew and followed Agnes's lead. A group of arctic foxes seemed to be stuck halfway up a hill that Agnes was circling.

"Try to get these little guys out of here," Agnes said to Josephine as she lofted higher.

"I think I see something farther up."

Josephine drew in close to the skulk, repositioned her hoodie, changed her size, and wrapped up the skulk of foxes within her hoodie. She quickly grew larger while holding her parcel of furry friends and was at the edge of the bridge in a few steps. She had the entire skulk in her bare hands at this point and laid them at the start of the bridge, where Tommy waved to her as he urged the pack of assorted animals on in their trek across the bridge. Josephine turned back toward the hills.

"Ralph, you should take a look at this," Gypsum said privately through his headset. He ran back to Gypsum. "A drilling operation roughly thirty miles northwest of us just had a major explosion," Gypsum said as she indicated its location. "It is not yet clear whether or not the water has been disrupted enough to affect the bridge."

Ralph spoke to everyone on the headsets. "We have a situation, and we need to hurry; our bridge may become compromised." He waved his gloves over Gypsum, and the entire area's water conditions were evaluated. "Josephine and Agnes, get as many of the animals as you can find down here now."

Fiddle said, "How's it going up there, Bombi?"

Bombi responded quickly, "Almost there, but I need to stay with these little guys, or I'm afraid they'll just turn back."

Fiddle became very large and moved back to the beginning of the bridge. "Tommy and Billy, wrangle those guys in front of me, and help Josephine and Agnes get the rest moving when you are able."

Agnes was high up in the hills when she called to Josephine, "Three more up here." She took another pass. Josephine spotted the group of arctic hares and snatched them up in a single try. She made it to the bridge in no time, and Billy doubled back to wrangle in the hares. Fiddle gave Josephine a big high five as she turned back toward the hills. He was moving slowly forward with his feet pointing out like duck's feet, urging every slow-moving straggler to cross the bridge, when Ralph said, "We have a wave. It's heading our way and may hit the west wall."

"Bombi, I need you in the water," Fiddle said through the headset. "We're just going to have to hope that the little critters stay headed in the right direction. Billy and Tommy, see what you can do to help with that."

Just then Agnes noticed a little fox, stuck in a tiny cave-like hole, high up in the hills. She let Josephine know its location but decided it would be best to get it herself. She quickly changed to a large snowy owl, swooped in, and picked it out of the hole with a fantastic display of flying acrobatics. "I got him," she said just as Josephine arrived. Agnes flew the fox to safety on the bridge and returned to her normal form.

"Incoming aircraft," Gypsum warned, and Ralph waved his hands over the area.

"The shields aren't working," he said. "I've been working on the code to cloak all of you close-range, but it isn't working."

Fiddle and Bombi were in the water. The wave was rushing their way. They had to stay there to block the wave and preserve the wall. Tommy, Billy, and Agnes were on the bridge along with hundreds of animals, and Josephine was behind him, a giant, high up in the hills.

Gypsum started a countdown. "The aircraft will have visibility in thirty, twenty-nine—"

"Stop it, Gypsum," Ralph snapped. "Why can't I do this?"

Gypsum responded calmly, "I don't know, Ralph; I'm not the one with the gloves. Twenty-two seconds to visual contact."

"That's it," Ralph said as he raised his hands and concentrated.

Billy was scooting around near the start of the bridge, ushering the animals forward. Ralph aimed the palm of his right glove at Billy, and Billy vanished, slowly; the animals around him began to disappear, and then Tommy vanished. The wave crashed into the bodies of Fiddle and Bombi, sending a giant spray of water into the air. Agnes quickly transformed into a snowy owl, her wingspan too vast to calculate as she beat her wings against the spray, forcing the water away from the bridge. The animals were safe.

"Five..." Gypsum counted down as Ralph made a swath with both hands, obscuring the entire bridge and everyone on it. "Three..." He turned one hand to Fiddle and Bombi and the other to Agnes, and they were gone, and as he drew his hands back in, he turned the truck, Gypsum, and himself invisible.

"Zero," Gypsum said.

"Josephine," Ralph said to himself as he quickly turned toward the hills, certain to see her massive form still high on the hillside but she was gone.

Josephine had heard the aircraft approaching and knew that she had to hide herself. She quickly became smaller and smaller until she was her regular size. She could tell that the airplane was low. There would be no reason for a girl her age to be standing on the side of a hill in the middle of the Arctic wearing jeans and a hoodie. She was standing in a fairly open area in about a foot of snow. She continued to shrink as the airplane cruised over the side of the hill.

As she became smaller, the snow enveloped her, and for a moment she became frightened of the cold. As she did, it began to affect her.

Josephine panicked and forgot how to turn off the switch. She began to freeze.

Josephine tried to speak into her headset, but the cold set in so quickly she could only make sounds like mumbled shivering.

The airplane passed over the area without incident.

"All clear," Gypsum announced, and the entire group cheered.

Ralph waved both hands over the entire area, returning all of the animals and the entire crew, as well as the truck, Gypsum, and even himself, back to visible. Fiddle returned to his normal size, as did Bombi. Agnes flew down and landed next to Billy in her human form, where they hugged one another. "We did it!" Fiddle cheered as he and Bombi joined Billy, Agnes, and Tommy on the bridge.

The animals were all scurrying in the direction of the glacier when Tommy said, "Where's Josephine? Ralph, did you turn her back?"

Ralph strained to answer, "I didn't even get a chance to make her invisible; there wasn't time."

Bombi grew quickly and scooped the entire group up, rushing them to Ralph and Gypsum.

"Find her, Ralph," Fiddle ordered as soon as he was dropped.

"Josephine," Ralph said into the headset. "I'd better try a private conversation. Josephine, can you hear me?" Ralph said as he raised his hand over Gypsum. "Bring me in to her last known coordinates." The view quickly changed to a spot in the hills. He moved his hands like he was swimming under water and cruised in closer. "Give me the last known readings on her headset," Ralph said as he encircled a radius of roughly one hundred feet with his hands. "She's here," Ralph said as he pointed. Tommy and Agnes moved in for a closer look. "There, in the center of that patch of snow."

Before he could turn for confirmation, Agnes was in the air with Tommy dangling from her claws. Billy's feet were leaving smoke for at least a mile, and Fiddle and Bombi were throwing each other up the hillside like a giant pair of circus performers. They all converged upon the spot to which Ralph had directed them simultaneously.

Tommy scooped his hands in gently around the spot where Josephine's tiny body must have melted itself into. "I feel something," he said as he searched with his hands.

Tommy brought his hands together and pulled them from the snow. He held them open, and the snow fell away from Josephine's body. Everyone was silent.

"Did you find her?" Ralph asked.

"Ralph," Gypsum said. "Look, I'm showing you a live feed from the satellite above us." Tommy was holding Josephine in his hands. She was a pale blue, and she was not moving. Tears began to well in the eyes of every one of the team as Tommy turned to Fiddle for hope.

Fiddle sadly shook his head and said, "It's just too cold."

Tommy stood up from the place he had found Josephine and, holding her in front of his lips, said, "But I'm not!" He looked directly into her still open eyes and said, "Feel my warmth."

Tommy breathed into his open palms, and steam rose into the air. "Wake up, Josephine," he said softly as he continued to breathe ever warmer air upon her. All of the snow around him began to melt as he whispered, "It's me, Tommy; please come back to me."

Josephine moved her legs and then her arms to lift her head up from Tommy's palm. "You saved me," she said. Then she kissed his palm and stood up.

Everyone cheered and wiped all of the tears from their faces.

Bombi wiped his nose on his sleeve, which was really his own fur.

Agnes and Billy had been hugging each other while staring at Josephine. When they realized she was alive, they took a step back from one another and smiled in embarrassment. Billy wiped a tear from Agnes's cheek with his thumb. She pulled her sleeve over her hand and wiped a tear from his, and they laughed out of sheer relief.

Josephine immediately turned off the cold, returned to her normal size, and hugged Tommy with all her might. He protected himself from the cold with a single thought and held her close.

Bombi hugged Fiddle.

Ralph said, "Come back here this instant; I need somebody to hug." Gypsum made a slight cooing sound.

Ralph looked over and smiled as Gypsum radiated light around her, wrapping Ralph from head to toe. As he twirled around to look at her lights swirling all around him, he felt a strange euphoria. He turned to face Gypsum and, using his gloves, wrapped her in the same swirling of lights. The tiny light within her center glowed brighter and brighter.

A moment later the rest of the team had gathered around Ralph and Gypsum, who quickly stopped their "hug."

"What was that?" Billy said as he watched the dazzling light show fade.

At the exact same time, Ralph and Gypsum said, "Maintenance."

Fiddle walked toward the truck, whistling "If I Only Had a Brain" from The Wizard of Oz.

"It's time to pack up," he said. "We only have a short window of time left to help anyone who may have been injured in that explosion."

Gypsum flashed an image of the region of the explosion and said, "There were no injuries; it was an intentional blast; it's all over the feed."

Fiddle kept walking toward the truck. "It isn't only the people I'm concerned about."

"Narwhal!" Bombi exclaimed as he ran toward the water. He ran down along the bluff until he was a safe distance from the bridge before he dove in. His splash was minimal considering his bulk. The Magnificents moved toward the water.

"Bombi has stopped swimming," Gypsum announced through the headset. "He's about one hundred feet out to the northwest."

They walked closer to the water while keeping their eyes fixed upon the spot. Slowly a long pointed horn arose from the water, attached to it was a large narwhal. The Magnificents looked at one another and then back at the narwhal.

Bombi's head popped up next to the narwhal. "It's all cool," he shouted as he wrapped a furry arm around the narwhal. "My friend here says that there are no reports of injuries to any of the species in the area."

A cheer went up from the Magnificents as Bombi swam his way back in.

"Okay, let's pack it up," Fiddle announced as Bombi reached land.

"Can everyone come over here?" Ralph asked through the headsets.

He looked at the gloves on his hands as the Magnificents all followed him over to Gypsum. He turned to the group and said, "Smile!" The whole team smiled at once, and their headsets fell from their faces and turned into rings. Ralph held the rings aloft with his gloves and guided them all back to his hands. He dropped his hands and flung them back up. His gloves had become rings. The rings flew off his hands, into the air, and united. A twirling pen fell toward him, and he caught it without looking.

He held the pen aloft. "Say good-bye to Gypsum, everyone," he said. Numerous forms of gratitude were expressed, from thanks to waves, and the group said good-bye to Gypsum. Ralph looked into Gypsum's glowing center and said, "See you soon."

Gypsum said, "Good-bye," and Ralph triple-clicked his pen. Gypsum collapsed into a single tube that he guided into the backpack.

Fiddle and Bombi walked away from the group.

"I don't care if that blast didn't hurt anybody; it's still wrong what they're doing. You keep sticking up for humans. You keep telling me not to get angry. I have a right to be angry. Humans are wasteful and self-absorbed." Fiddle let Bombi talk. "If you had it your way, I'd go back to sleep for fifty years, hoping that you and the Magnificents would set things right. Well, I am not gonna do that." They walked for a moment or two in silence.

Fiddle asked as he turned back toward the truck, "So what are you going to do?"

Bombi let out a low laugh. "Don't worry," he said. "I'm not going to do anything to the humans, at least not yet. No, I think I'll follow our little friends north, make sure they get where they're going. And then, then I'm going to keep my eye on things."

Fiddle nodded. "All right, Bombi; that sounds like a good plan. But if something does happen, you know how to contact me. Do not hesitate. I will round up the Magnificents, and we'll be here in no time."

"I know you will, Fiddle," Bombi said as they worked their way back to the rest of the group.

The Magnificents were all standing by the truck. Ralph had Fiddle's backpack on his shoulder and was holding out the pen. "Here you go, Fiddle," he said as he started to pull the backpack off his shoulder.

"No, Ralph; the pen is yours now, and so is the backpack." Fiddle smiled. "It's up to you to take care of Gypsum now."

Ralph easily hoisted the pack back onto his shoulder and put the pen behind his ear. "Cool with me," he said. "She's nice and light."

~ 231 ~

Bombi held his arms out wide and said in his big cuddly voice, "Bombi hug." The Magnificents and Fiddle all fell into his embrace. "Bombi like," Bombi said as he held them close. They stayed that way for a minute until Bombi opened up his mammoth arms and they all stepped back.

"Billy like," Billy said, doing his best Bombi imitation. Everyone stared at him.

"What?" he said. "It's growing on me!"

Everyone was still laughing as Bombi walked away backward, waving his big hand to say good-bye.

~ *Chapter 17: The Trip Back Home* ~

Fiddle asked if anyone was hungry. None of them had even been thinking about food. However, the moment he said it, they were hungry.

He walked toward the truck and said, "Great. I know about a place where we can get a fantastic hot dog and s'mores that'll make your mouth beg for more."

The Magnificents piled into the truck and headed for their seats. Ralph stopped at the closet behind the driver's seat and gently placed the backpack inside, and then he headed to his seat. This time he didn't go all the way to the back. He wanted to be closer to his friends. The seat belts hugged the Magnificents into their seats.

Fiddle said, "We're going camping."

Before anyone could respond, the truck lifted off the ground and shot straight up. When it stopped, the truck was parked in a rectangular dirt patch bordered on three sides by lengths of roughhewn wood. Fiddle sprang from the driver's seat and rushed to the closet, where he pulled a backpack and a cooler from inside.

"Bring the cooler, and meet me outside," he said as he bounded out the door.

The Magnificents followed him slowly. Billy grabbed the cooler and went out first.

Fiddle was sitting in a reclining foldout chair in front of a huge tent with little lanterns hanging on either side of the zippered doorway. "Who wants to search for firewood?" he said, looking at Josephine and Agnes. They turned and looked at the boys.

Billy put down the cooler and sat on it. Ralph and Tommy just looked down.

"I thought so," Fiddle said as he pulled a pen from his pocket, pointed it at the truck, clicked the pen, and a door on the side of the truck sprang open. A couple of logs tumbled out of the open compartment.

"Firewood," Tommy said as he hopped over to the truck. He tossed some logs at Billy, who caught them easily and tossed them into the pit.

Fiddle pointed his pen at the logs. An intense beam of light hit the wood and instantly caused it to catch fire. He did this in several places within the wood pile, and in no time the fire was roaring. Fiddle turned the pen to his backpack and flipped five tubes into the air. As they hit the ground, he clicked the pen. Each tube opened out into a canvas recliner, just like the one Fiddle was sitting on, one for each Magnificent.

Billy stood up and opened the cooler while the other Magnificents went for the chairs.

"Looks like we got water, orange juice, or lemonade," Billy called out as he inspected the cooler further. "Hold it," he said as he moved more ice around. "There's also root beer, ginger beer, and iced tea." He popped the top off a root beer with his bare thumb and took a swig. One by one the Magnificents gave him their drink orders, and he delivered them with a smile. "And now for the hot dogs," he said as he pulled a giant bag of natural-casing wieners from the cooler.

"Pass 'em around," Fiddle said as he gave a handful of tubes to Josephine. Tommy was sitting next to her, so she took one and gave the rest to him. Tommy took one and then passed them to Ralph, who took one and passed them on to Agnes, who held on to hers as well as the one for Billy.

"All right," Fiddle said. "Hold out your tubes like this." They all followed his instructions, and he clicked his pen. Each tube opened on one end, and a long fork slid out to a full length of a few feet. Billy walked around and put a hot dog on each one. Agnes was holding two; she smiled at Billy as he pierced the hot dogs with the forks. He stood there for a moment until Fiddle cleared his throat. Billy had forgotten to give him a hot dog, so he quickly put one on Fiddle's fork, returned the bag to the cooler, and sat down next to Agnes.

"Thank you, Billy," Fiddle said. "I am so proud of you." He looked around the campfire at each one of the Magnificents. "I am delighted with all of you. You have used your powers with great purpose, despite the fact that those powers are so new to you. But I must make an apology first."

Fiddle looked around and saw that everyone's dogs were still in the air. "Go ahead, people; put those dogs over the fire."

With that he held his fork out, pressed a button on the handle, and the fork stretched to the length required to reach the fire. He released the button. Suddenly the Magnificents pressed their buttons and watched their dogs race to the fire. It was a big fire, and there was plenty of room to cook all of the hot dogs.

"Tommy, and Josephine, in fact each and every one of you deserve my apology. I am sorry I acted as though nothing could be done for Josephine. We all know that changing time to save Josephine may have had effects beyond our control, so Tommy exercised great wisdom in that moment. Our entire mission could have been botched if he had chosen to jump back in time to save you, Josephine. However, I knew that Tommy possessed the power to warm you back to health. I knew that you had not died; I could still feel your life energy clinging to your human form. I could have saved you, and I would have if Tommy had failed."

The entire group looked at him a little harshly.

"You all have a right to be upset with me. I have asked great things of you without enough guidance, but that was because I knew that Bombi had to meet you and to see what you could do, to restore his faith, not only in me, but in humanity. And I have to say, you have done that better than I could have hoped for. So relax, enjoy the fire, the food, and each other's company. We have a beautiful night here, comfortable sleeping bags, and tomorrow we hit the beach. Cheers!" He held his ginger beer up high.

"Cheers!" the Magnificents responded as they all held their drinks up and clinked their bottles.

Josephine made just her arm grow and individually clinked her bottle with all of theirs, and great laughter ensued. "Thank you all," Josephine said as she looked around the campfire. "Thank you for coming to rescue me."

She had a tear in her eye as Tommy said, "That's what friends are for."

"To the Magnificents!" Fiddle toasted with a half-empty ginger beer.

"The Magnificents!" they all joined in.

"Whoa-ho-ho, my dog's on fire!" Billy exclaimed as his hot dog burst into flames, and everyone started laughing.

Ralph took the pen from behind his ear, pointed it at the burning hot dog, rubbed the side of the pen, and grinned as the pen produced a sudden burst of strong air that blew the fire out. "Thanks, man!" Billy said.

Ralph responded, "That's what friends are for." Everyone laughed.

The rest of the night was perfect. Billy ate the most hot dogs, while Fiddle was by far the biggest s'mores consumer. The stars were brilliant and beautiful overhead, so not a single one of them slept in the tent. They all fell asleep around the campfire and dreamed until morning, all except for Ralph.

He couldn't stop thinking about Gypsum. He kept telling himself that it was stupid to want to talk to a machine, and then he would immediately tell himself that she wasn't a machine. He lay awake trying to convince himself that it was a total waste of his time to think about having a conversation with Gypsum because she wasn't even a she until he changed her voice. Then he scolded himself for being so presumptuous to assume that Gypsum was male simply because she had a tin-like, masculine-sounding voice. He pressed on his head from both sides and told himself to let it go and just stop thinking of her, and then he saw his father. He was standing next to a tree about thirty feet away from the campfire.

Ralph said, "Dad?" and his father disappeared. He got up from his comfortable, folding canvas recliner and walked toward the spot where he had seen his dad. Nothing was there. Ralph pulled the pen from behind his ear and rolled it between his fingers in a clockwise motion. A strong flashlight beam emitted from the tip of the pen, clearly showing footprints in the dirt, precisely where Ralph was looking. He heard a snapping sound and turned the flashlight toward its source—still nothing. Then Ralph concentrated on a single thought. He considered what code he might use if he were working with Gypsum, how together they might be able to see all things invisible, and then he channeled that thought into the pen. The woods lit up like a searchlight. He was seeing every form of energy amplified a hundredfold. He rolled the pen counterclockwise, and the light disappeared, but the images remained. He could see all that was invisible, without the pen or Gypsum.

That was when he saw his father again. He was scurrying from tree to tree in an effort to remain hidden, but he could not hide from Ralph.

"Dad," Ralph called out again, and his father started to run. Ralph took a few running steps in his father's direction, and his dad ran faster. In a moment he was out of sight. Ralph heard the sound of a car engine starting far off in the woods, and then he saw the beams of a pair of headlights winding their way down a faraway road. He turned around, confused and lonely, even though he was surrounded by his friends. Ralph thought that it was no longer useful to see all that was invisible, and, in a flash, all of it was gone. He walked back to the campfire, lay back down, and stared at the stars. Exhaustion finally took its toll, and Ralph fell to sleep.

"Of course he wants us to wake him up," Ralph heard Billy say as he felt a tickle on the tip of his nose. Billy and Agnes were standing over him as Billy tickled his nose with a long blade of grass.

"I'm awake," Ralph said in a slightly grumpy tone.

"Ralph, you have got to see this beach," Billy said, paying absolutely no attention to Ralph's tone.

"Oh, yeah, the beach," Ralph said, dropping the grumpy like a sack of hammers. "Hey, is that bacon I smell?"

Billy laughed. "Oh yeah, we all ate already, but there's plenty left for you, man. Last one finished does the cleanup!" Billy scooped up Agnes, who looked totally different in a bathing suit, and ran her down to the beach.

The dust hadn't even settled when Fiddle emerged from the tent, saying, "That kid loves to mess around, doesn't he, Ralph?" Ralph nodded his head as Fiddle waved his hand toward the picnic table, inviting Ralph to a feast of bacon, bagels, assorted cream cheeses, strawberries, and a bowl full of apples, oranges, and bananas. "Go ahead, Ralph; eat what you want, and don't worry, I've got cleanup. There are swimsuits in the closet in the truck, in the compartment labeled 'Fun in the Sun.' Oh, also, I suggest putting the pen in a safe place. It's not very likely to stay in your ear while you swim."

Fiddle set a glass on the picnic table in front of him and asked, "Lemon water or juice?"

Ralph stared at the pitchers with a glazed look.

"Right; lemon water it is." Fiddle smiled a warm and open smile as he poured. "What's on your mind?"

There was quite a lot on Ralph's mind, but none of it made sense to him, so he had no idea how to respond. He decided to go with the thought that would probably sound less weird to Fiddle.

"I thought I saw my dad here last night," Ralph said. He drained the glass of lemon water.

"Well, we are in Minnesota now, Ralph, so I imagine it's possible," Fiddle offered.

"Okay, but he disappeared when I called out to him."

Fiddle scratched his chin, which had some fairly decent stubble on it, and guessed, "Maybe you were dreaming."

"No," Ralph said calmly in a faraway voice. "Because I got up and looked for him. There's tracks over there," he said, pointing to the area in which he had found his father's footprints. "I couldn't see him, but I knew he was there, so I thought about seeing all that was invisible, and I even used the pen. Everything was so bright, all the energy, all the animals and their spirits, and my dad. I saw him and he was invisible, but he ran away from me. I even heard him running away through the woods and saw a car driving away." Ralph hung his head.

"Was it your dad's car?" Fiddle asked patiently.

"I don't know. I couldn't see what kind it was; there was too much to look at, and it was far away."

Fiddle set a plate full of bacon strips, an everything bagel with chive cream cheese, and a pile of strawberries in front of Ralph and said, "Sometimes when I'm out in the woods at night, I think I see things. When I look at energies at the same time, it's very hard to tell what is what. It has taken me years to understand all that I am seeing. We will be back home tonight. Why don't you ask your father then? Maybe he has a reason for not wanting you to see him."

Ralph felt relieved that Fiddle didn't think he was going crazy. He was especially calmed by the fact that he had even acknowledged the possibility that he actually had seen his father.

Then the fog cleared from his head as his eyes came to rest on the bacon.

After he had consumed an entire plate of bacon, Ralph joined the rest of the Magnificents on the beach, where they were throwing a Frisbee back and forth over distances far too great for ordinary kids.

They could all do it and do it accurately.

He saw the disk flying in his direction and made a dramatic leap to catch it between his legs. He had always seen good disk players doing that but had never actually tried it himself.

Before his body made contact with the ground, he made the catch and completed a 180 while tossing the disk to Agnes, who was a good hundred yards away in the water.

She dove under the water and then shot out of it like a dolphin, catching the Frisbee with ease.

After she splashed down, she threw a perfect tomahawk throw to Tommy, who was walking on a fallen tree trunk.

He rolled the trunk with his feet a few feet forward, flipped into the air backward, caught the disk with the back of his knees, and retrieved it with his hand in time to land back on the tree trunk, where he proceeded to roll forward, gaining speed. Tommy began airbrushing the disk into the wind in a counterclockwise direction with his right hand and slapped it with his left, causing the disk to fly along the beach in an arcing motion, landing right where Josephine stood.

Josephine let the disk roll across the outstretched fingers of her right hand, down her arm, across her body, and out along the other arm and hand, grasping it at the last second between her fingertips and thumb.

"Bravo!" Fiddle cheered as he joined them on the beach, carrying his collapsed chair and umbrella, a book, and a water bottle. He planted himself in the middle of the group and began to read, filled with confidence and certainty that he would not be hit by an errant toss by some lousy Frisbee player.

He was right.

The Magnificents played for at least an hour without coming anywhere near him, until Billy could no longer resist the urge.

He threw a zinger right at Fiddle's head and gave no warning.

By the time everyone else realized that the disk was going to hit Fiddle directly in the nose, there was no time to warn him.

Then, suddenly, Fiddle leaned ever so slightly forward, tilted his head down, moved his left hand up behind his neck, eyes still on his book, and caught the disk, flat against the back of his head.

No one moved.

Fiddle read to the end of his page, stood up from his chair, placed his book on the seat, and popped a helicopter throw directly up into the air, only a foot or two over his head.

The Frisbee was spinning at an incredible speed as Fiddle nail delayed the disc, balancing it on the nail of his index finger. He slid the nail down to the rim, and worked the disc in a freestyle routine that started behind his back, then between his legs, around his neck, and across his body. He tapped the disc as it hit his fingertips, spun his body around in a 360 in the opposite direction, and caught the disc with a backhand on his way around.

"Awesome!" the Magnificents shouted as they all ran over to him.

"You have got to show us how to do that," Billy said with total hero worship.

Fiddle pulled his sunglasses down and peered over them at Billy, saying, "Why? Weren't you watching the first time?" The whole group burst out laughing, and Fiddle joined in the game.

The Magnificents played all afternoon until Fiddle announced, "It's time to go." They all acted like any kid would at that age, saying, "Aww," in unison.

"It's a bit of a drive, and I promised your parents I'd get you home before too late," Fiddle explained.

"Excuse me, Mr. Fiddle; why can't I just use a wormhole?" Tommy asked respectfully.

"You could, Tommy," Fiddle replied, "but I'd just rather that you didn't.

"I'd kinda like you guys to have some time to think about what you've been through before you get home and have to act like normal kids. The time you take to talk with each other and share your feelings about all of this is every bit as important as having the abilities. And one more thing," Fiddle said as he walked back toward the campground with the Magnificents on his heels. "I feel honored any time any one of you wants to talk to me. After all, I'm the one who got you into all of this."

Breaking camp was a breeze. All of Fiddle's gear worked so slickly it hardly seemed like work at all. The Magnificents filed into the truck and took their seats as Fiddle started it up.

"I forgot to mention earlier that those seats you are in back there can turn in any direction, which makes talking to each other a little easier on the long drive," Fiddle said as he headed for the road. "All you have to do is think about which way you want to face, and your seat will do the rest, keep you safe, adjust the airbags—nothing but the best for you guys!"

"Thank you, Mr. Fiddle," they all said in unison as they swerved their chairs around until they were in a neat little circle.

They talked first about Josephine dying, or, more fortunately, not dying. They all cried a bit more while they were talking about it and swore to never let their guard down and to remember above all that the Magnificents were a team and that they would always work as a team. They acknowledged that nobody was any better than anybody else on the team because every member of the team brought an essential element to their success.

"Even if somebody wins a race, it doesn't matter," Billy said. "It's just cool, right?" Billy was doing his best to let his competitive side drop within the Magnificents, but he was pretty sure he was going have some fun back at school. The rest of them could tell that Billy was as loyal as they came, so they delighted in the way that Billy wanted to shine, plus it was awesome to just be able to watch the stuff he could do.

"Billy, all the stuff you do is cool, man," Ralph said as he leaned into the center of the group.

"I got something weird to talk about," he continued. "So I guess I'm just gonna ask. Does anybody else miss Gypsum?"

Tommy nodded as he said, "And Bombi too."

"I miss both of them," Josephine said.

"It would be weird not to miss them, man," Billy said. "I mean Bombi is *the man*, or like whatever he is, and Gypsum saved Josephine's life, and like you did and, well, Tommy totally did, but, like you all did it, y'know?"

"Yeah, and we totally needed another girl just for balance," Agnes said. "It's too bad she can't hang with us. It's too bad Bombi can't hang with us. I sorta don't want to go home."

Ralph pulled his pen out from the armrest of his chair, the safe place he'd put it after Fiddle had recommended he do so. He held it up and said, "Do you know how much fun school would be if I could bring Gypsum along?"

"They wouldn't let you bring her in to class or tests or anything," Billy said, really wishing he could bring Gypsum to class *and* to take tests.

"Okay, you guys," Ralph said. "I've got one more weird thing. Last night, when all of you were asleep, I saw my dad. He was standing just outside our camp. I called out to him, and he ran. Oh, but first he became invisible. Plus I saw everything else that was invisible, and that's when he ran away for good and took off in his car."

"Hold on a second, Ralph," Josephine said. "Can you go through that again and sort of break it down bit by bit?"

Ralph agreed that he may have told the story in a confusing way, so he started over. He did a much better job of it the second time around, and everyone believed that he had, in fact, seen his dad. They came up with all sorts of theories as to why Ralph's dad would show up and how he would know where to find them, and everything came down to Fiddle.

"Hey Fiddle, in that letter to our parents, did you tell our parents where we were going for camping?" Tommy asked on behalf of the group.

"Nope," Fiddle responded.

They discussed it some more and came up with a theory that the campsite was very popular.

"Is that campsite really popular, Fiddle?" Ralph asked as it began to grow dark outside.

"Well, in a manner of speaking it is, but only with those who know of its existence. Why?" Fiddle responded.

"Can you figure out why Ralph's father showed up in our camp, and why he was invisible?" Tommy asked, again on behalf of the group.

"I already told Ralph that he should ask his dad. I don't go around making assumptions as to why people do a great many things. Doesn't pay," Fiddle said. "Maybe it's private and personal."

The Magnificents stopped talking about deep things and started a game that Agnes had learned in improv class, where one person would start a story and the next would have to say the next line of the story by beginning the first word of his or her sentence with the last letter of the last word from the previous sentence. Doing it turned out to be far easier than describing how to do it, particularly without a time limit, which proved to be a far more creative way to do it. They had great fun and came up with a fairly decent story that Agnes recorded on her smartphone.

"Okay, everybody; we're back, ' Fiddle said. "Dropping off in the same order I picked you up. Tommy, we're almost to your house."

Everyone said good-bye to Tommy as they pulled up in front of his house. Tommy stared at Josephine the whole time.

Billy said, "We'll see you tomorrow."

Tommy walked slowly backward and then hopped out of the truck and ran up to his house.

"Next stop, Josephine's house," Fiddle announced as they drove around the corner.

They all said their good-byes as they reached the house, and everyone said how glad they were that she wasn't dead.

Jim and Alice were sitting on the porch, waiting for Josephine. Jim started walking quickly to the curb as the truck arrived. Fiddle swung the door open, and Josephine got out, trying to block her father's view of the inside of the truck as she climbed down the steps. He stepped aside, let her get off the truck, and then jumped up onto the second step.

"What do you have these kids sitting on back there, cardboard boxes?" Jim Connors took a hard look at the back of the truck. "School bus seats?" Ralph, Billy, and Agnes were sitting in three separate rows of school bus seats. "There are school bus seats in here?" Mr. Connors shook his head. "What kind of mileage are you getting on this heap? Is that tax money they're using?"

Fiddle motioned toward the door and said, "School caught a deal on this one. Gotta get the other kids home now. Josephine's a great kid; they had a wonderful time. G'night now." He fluttered the doors, urging Mr. Connors to get off the steps. Josephine's dad turned and stepped down. Fiddle whipped the doors closed and drove off.

The interior of the truck returned to its normal awesomeness without disturbing Ralph, Agnes, or Billy.

"Can you imagine what would happen if he knew?" Agnes said as they left Jim Connors scratching his head and squinting at the truck as it drove away.

Fiddle made the truck belch a little fake smoke out of a nice fat tailpipe that bounced a little as the truck made its way down the street. Fiddle swung the truck around a couple corners.

"Billy, good-bye, and thanks," Fiddle said as he pulled up to Billy's house. The house was well lit, and there was the colorful glow of a large-screen TV reflected in the window.

Everyone said good-bye and Agnes gave Billy a slow wink and a smirk. Billy smiled his new happy hero smile and hopped out and ran up to his house. Actually he was running in slow motion, looking just as normal as he could.

He knocked on the door and his mother opened it and hugged him and kissed the top of his head. She waved to Fiddle and closed the door.

Agnes said, "I don't think my mom's going to open the door, hug me, and kiss my head, but I would take one of the three."

Fiddle turned the truck, glanced back at Agnes, and said, "I'll kiss your head before you leave this truck." He looked back at the road and said, "We all love you, Agnes."

Ralph quickly added, "Like a sister!"

Fiddle continued, "And I think your mother must love you too. Thank you for everything you did; it was amazing."

As they pulled up to her house, she jumped out of her seat and said, "Don't you mean magnificent? Bye, Ralph." She stepped quickly to the driver's seat and kissed Fiddle on the head and then promptly left the truck.

"Well, Ralph, I hope you find the answers you seek when we get you home, and thanks for all your great work. You were absolutely amazing with Gypsum and your mastery of the gloves, and you did it so quickly. One of the best pens I have ever given in the hands of one of the best I've ever seen.

Well, actually there have only been six since I have been alive, so it really isn't the greatest compliment if you overanalyze it, but the feeling is there!" Fiddle put his thumb high in the air, waving it so Ralph could see it clearly. "Thumbs up, Ralph; great work."

Ralph said, "Thanks. I was wondering what you were going to do with Gypsum while we're not on missions."

Fiddle responded, "I wasn't planning on doing anything with her ever again."

"*What?*" Ralph yelled.

"Settle down," Fiddle said as he moved a flattened palm slowly downward. "I don't think I said that right. Gypsum is not for me to do anything with, Ralph; she's yours now. She goes with the pen." Fiddle stopped the truck a moment later.

"She goes with the pen?" Ralph said. "Really?"

"Yes, really," Fiddle responded. "And so does the backpack. And there are more tubes in the backpack."

"No, there aren't, Mr. Fiddle. I checked before I packed her away."

"Check again," Fiddle said as he swung the door open and Ralph's father stepped into the truck.

"Hey, Fiddle," Ralph's dad said familiarly.

~ 247 ~

"Hey Peter," Fiddle replied. Ralph bumped his head on part of the closet above his backpack as he heard the greeting.

"Wait, you two know each other?" Ralph pulled the backpack with Gypsum inside out of the closet and hoisted it onto his back, smiling as he turned and looked at the back of the truck. It was still as decked out as ever.

"So you're seeing all of this, right, Dad," he said, pointing at the seats, the TVs, and the tech.

"Yeah, a little newer than when I drove it but still the same. Are you ready to go?" Peter asked his son.

"Hold on dad," Ralph challenged, "did you just say that you used to drive this truck?"

Peter put a hand on Ralph's shoulder, smiled and said, "I sure did!"

"Okay, I have another question" Ralph said. "Were you at our campsite in the woods last night?"

"I was," Peter admitted.

"Why didn't you let me know then?" Ralph asked.

"I felt stupid. I wanted to see what it was like again to hang out with Fiddle and to go camping in the old spot, but I didn't want to cut in on your thing, y'know? I shouldn't have run away, and I'm sorry. I knew when I was driving away that it was wrong, but I wasn't sure how you would handle it when you found out." Peter confessed.

"I love you, Dad," Ralph said as he hugged his dad. "Even if sometimes you are invisible."

They all laughed as Fiddle swung the door open.

"See ya," they all said in unison, and then they laughed again.

Peter and Ralph stepped off the truck and toward their house, and Fiddle swung the door shut.

He drove off in silence.

"So tell me about it, Ralph," Peter said. "I want to hear everything that happened, right from the beginning, because with Fiddle back around, this is certainly not the end.

~About the Author / Illustrator~

Barry McMahon holds extensive experience in the corporate and private sectors, a BFA from Bowling Green State University, and numerous credits as an author, software developer, and scenic painter. Among his previous creative achievements are the children's book *Happy Dumm-Dumms*; two musical albums; scenic design and storyboard artwork for major films, as well as acclaimed artists such as Prince and Carmen Electra.

But the accomplishments of which McMahon is proudest come not from his professional endeavors, but from his personal life and his relationship with his wife and children. Father to a blended family of five, he has shared countless special moments learning and growing with his children, who have inspired him to create rich stories replete with empowering messages that encourage imaginative thinking, problem-solving skills, and the development of talent.

For years, McMahon has enjoyed reading epic series with his family, and, now, with the release of *The Magnificents*, he offers the first installment in his own.

www.ingramcontent.com/pod-product-compliance
Lightning Source LLC
Chambersburg PA
CBHW072214170626
46813CB00003B/940